WITCH ACCUSED

KRISTA WALSH

RAVEN'S QUILL PRESS

OTTAWA, ON

Raven's Quill Press, 56A Mill St E Unit #683, Acton, ON, L7J 1H3
www.kristawalshauthor.com

Publisher's Note: This is a work of fiction. Names, characters, places, and incidents are a product of the author's imagination. Locales and public names are sometimes used for atmospheric purposes. Any resemblance to actual people, living or dead, or to businesses, companies, events, institutions, or locales is completely coincidental.

Cover Design: Deranged Doctor Design/2024

Witch Accused / WALSH -- 1st ed.
Paperback ISBN: 978-1-998398-15-7

For everyone who acknowledges their fear and
stands up to fight anyway

Chapter 1
Alyssa

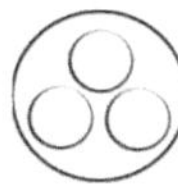

Thursday, 1:00 a.m.

I FILLED A pint glass at the tap and set it down in front of the sloth demon at the end of the bar.

"Last one for tonight, eh, Davis?" I said. "You still owe me for the last two."

"Yeah, yeah, Mooney. I'm good for it." He waved me away, and I rolled my eyes when he shifted on his stool to angle his back to me.

With anyone else, he would have disappeared from view, his ability to blend into his surroundings making him all but invisible. Years of familiarity with his low-key antics allowed me to see through the illusion, which made it easy to keep tabs on him.

"I'm telling you, Lys, you should have kicked that guy out years ago," Simon Fletcher grumbled as he passed me, his amber eyes shooting daggers in Davis's direction.

"He's harmless. And he's right—he's usually good for it. He might be a drug-dealing drunk, but he doesn't bring trouble to the pub, which puts him a step above a few people who come through here. He also single-handedly covers our bills."

My best friend-slash-business partner didn't return my teasing grin, his attention still pinned on Davis. "He's far from harmless, and if he hasn't brought trouble yet, it's because your good luck outweighs his bad. That protection will only last so long."

I frowned and slid my hand down Simon's arm, catching the tips of his fingers behind the bar, out of view of the patrons sitting around the bartop. "Hey, what's wrong?"

He dragged his gaze over to meet mine, and I caught the unease swimming within it before he blinked it away and pasted a smile on his handsome face.

"Nothing," he lied. "I just have a hate on for sloths."

"Mmhmm. I'd buy that more if Davis wasn't here every single night, and you've never—okay, fine—you don't always have an issue with him. What's going on?"

Simon sighed and bowed his head to set his lips close to my ear to keep our patrons from overhearing.

"When I went out to drop the trash, I noticed people

scoping out the alley. Three, maybe four, guys. They saw me and ran off. I don't know what they wanted, but I don't like it."

I frowned. "Magic?"

"All of them. Couldn't tell you what kind, though. Not demon."

"I'll check the wards in the back if you want to watch the bar. If the only way they can get in is through the front, then whatever they're after, we can handle it."

Simon nodded, and I crossed around him to the back door.

Magic was forbidden in the pub during business hours. There were a few protection spells around the doors and windows to make sure my patrons had a nice, relaxed time whenever they stopped by and some wards on the back door for added defence, but that was it. Not only because of my firm belief that magic and business did not mix, but also because Simon was a chaos demon. The slightest magic in the air had the potential to set off his power, and then all bets were off about what happened next. My supernatural customers knew the rule. They also knew that to break it meant a permanent ban, and as Mooney's Pub was one of the few supernatural-friendly establishments in Ottawa's Centretown, there weren't many who wanted to test how strictly I enforced it.

The only exception to the rule was the unofficial clinic in my back office. It didn't see much use these days with legit supernatural medical clinics opening around town and the

Peaview Supernatural Hospital just a few blocks away, but my regulars knew where to go in a pinch for minor healing spells.

Always to heal, never to harm—a leftover philosophy from my failed healing days.

So if some assholes were sneaking around looking to cause trouble, they were in for an unpleasant surprise.

The wards around the back door hadn't weakened much since I'd cast them a month ago, so I gave them a few touch-ups and let them be. A look out the window revealed a parking lot empty except for my and Simon's cars with no one moving around near the alley, and I crossed my fingers it stayed that way.

I didn't like trouble in my pub. Mooney's had been a staple on Somerset Street since my grandfather had opened its doors fifty-seven years ago, and I had done my best over the past six years to maintain its reputation as a safe place for supernaturals of all types. Over the years, it had become the preferred after-work hangout spot for the local public servants, which I loved. They rarely got drunk enough to be a pain in my ass, were decent tippers, and were usually gone long before last call. Weekends were a bit wilder as they let off steam, but there was an unspoken agreement that anything too crazy should be taken to The Afterlife, the supes-only nightclub a few blocks over. So far I'd never needed to flaunt my magical heritage to maintain the peace. The fact that the Mooneys were one of the oldest and most powerful witch families in the city was secondary, or even tertiary, to the fact that I offered a great stock of local craft beer and Simon, bartender extraordinaire, worked wonders with the cocktail menu.

With the back door secure, I popped into the office to double-check the windows, skirting around the large, black antique safe tucked into the corner. There was nothing to see from this vantage point either, so I tightened the wards and returned to the bar to relieve Simon from the floor.

The rest of the night went smoothly. At some point, the snow started, one of the first falls since the mid-January thaw, causing people to rush in with white flakes speckling their hair, collars turned up, hands clasped together to fend off the chill.

All the while, I kept my eye on the door and my pulse on the wards in the back, but nothing happened to make me jumpy.

Last call came around two-thirty in the morning, when only the supernaturals remained, the mundanes believing we'd closed at the legal hour. It was earlier than our usual four a.m. close, but only a half-dozen stragglers were still around and I wanted to get to bed. A few at a time, they filed out, Davis dragging his heels after everyone else.

"All right, bud, this is your last call too."

He grumbled and pulled on his coat when I turned off the mounted TV in the back nook. "See ya tomorrow, Mooney."

I waved him out the door with my rag, but seconds after he

stepped outside and disappeared into the darkness, a burst of green-tinged magic threw the door inward. It slammed so hard into the wall it cracked my lovely robin's egg blue plaster.

"What the crap!" I ducked behind the bar and summoned my magic into my palms until it swirled in a purple-hued ball.

The green spell lingering in the air screamed elemental magic. Witch. In *my* pub. What the ever-loving hockey puck?

"Lys, are you all right?" Simon asked as he ran out of the back office, his amber eyes glinting bronze.

"No, I'm not all right. Someone just busted up my wall! What even is that? Haven't they heard of knocking?"

I poked my head over the bar just in time to watch half a dozen men push their way in. These guys were dressed entirely in black with expressions nowhere near the friendly faces I was used to seeing from my public service post-work regulars.

One of the men stepped ahead of the others, staking his claim as their leader, and my upper lip curled with disdain. His thinning brown hair was slicked back, his goatee was neatly trimmed, and his black turtle neck hugged his wiry frame. He looked like a cross between Steve Jobs and a pretentious art professor.

Whoever these bastards were, they obviously had a flair for the dramatic and no fashion sense.

"Alyssa Mooney?" he demanded.

I shelved my magic but kept it close to the surface as I

stood up. I didn't want to have to use it. I was a healer, not a fighter. But damn if I was going to let a bunch of bullies push me around in my own pub.

"Only to my friends, my family, and my accountant. Everyone else leaves me alone. I'd love it if that included you."

The witch sneered, and green magic coated his hands before he threw a ball of it my way. I leapt into the open as Simon rushed to knock me out of its path. I rolled across the floor to the relative safety of a knocked-over table, and Simon doubled back to find cover behind the bar.

"Was it something I said?" I drew my magic once more into my hands. Simon's eyes flashed, and a bottle from behind the bar flew towards the group huddled in the doorway. It smashed into one of the men, and a scream rang out as glass shattered.

Three tumbler glasses followed the bottle, and I hoped Simon remembered we would need those when we opened for the day.

Before he emptied our entire stock of drinkware, I rose to my feet and launched a ball of atmospheric magic at Mr. Professor. He blocked it and tried to redirect it, and I grinned as my spell stuck to him like plastic wrap, preventing him from using his own.

He struggled to shake it off, throwing his body around as though it would make a smidge of difference, and I used his distraction to shift my attention to his lackeys. Three of them stood huddled near the door, all mini-mes of the professor, eyes wide, magic weak but at the ready, and it was the work of a moment to throw a purple web their way, catching them in my net to nullify their power. In a blink, their magic extinguished and they crouched lower, the man on the far left appearing almost relieved to be forced out of the fight.

I was so focused on them that I would have missed the bolt of silver magic sparking towards me from the left if Simon hadn't called my name. At the last second, I ducked and rolled, and the spell hit the wall over my head, sending my favourite painting to the ground and cracking the frame.

"You're going to pay for that," I shouted.

"You can send me the receipt from the Frostmines," a man called back, his voice rich, deep, and infuriatingly confident.

What the hell was he talking about?

The Frostmines were an extension of Moongrave Prison, the facility up north where supernatural criminals were shipped off to freeze their toes and stay out of trouble. Only the real pieces of work went that route, and only a special subsection of those were sent to the Frostmines, not mines at all but a subterranean set of cells reserved for the hyperpowerful.

"Okay, yeah, I think you might have blown up the wrong pub?" I called from behind my cover. "I'm Alyssa Mooney? Owner of the bar? Unless the CRA is cracking down hard on my missing a line or two on my taxes, I'm pretty sure there's been some mistake."

The air vibrated as another spell brewed somewhere near the door, but I didn't sneak a peek to see who or what it was.

"Keep talking, princess. You're making it real easy to pin you down."

I looked up and cursed as a silver bubble drifted over my head, ready to drop down and catch me under what I suspected was a sticky trap. What the hell was this magic?

Steering clear of the smashed pieces of picture frame, I crawled across the floor until I was within easy reach of the bar and threw myself behind it, landing next to Simon, who'd taken a defensive position next to the ice.

My pulse raced and adrenaline had sharpened my vision so I could take in every tiny detail on the shelves around me. I really needed to dust.

"Any ideas what this is about?" I asked between ragged breaths.

"I told you we shouldn't have painted the front door red. Some people have issue with ostentatiousness."

"Dammit, Simon. Maybe you're right, but yellow would have pissed off the shifters."

"Dodge." He shoved me out of the way as another silvery bubble dropped where we'd been sitting.

I popped up behind the bar and threw a blast of magic towards the source of the bubbles, a man who'd come through the front door behind the cowering mob of misfits.

A curse and a crash as the silver-spell-slinging witch darted out of its path, but I was ready with a follow-up spell even as Simon unleashed another round of chaos. The tables and chairs in the far corner rose in the air and spun in a wooden tornado towards our assailant.

Both chair and magic hit the man at the same time, the spell causing the wood to explode in a burst of splinters, and the witch dropped to the ground, his arms over his head to protect his face.

Simon and I came out from either side of the bar, ready to go on the offensive now that the playing field had been levelled, but before I had time to launch another spell at the downed witch, he was back on his feet, silver spell in hand, the brunt of it aimed at my chest just as mine was on his.

In the momentary standoff, I fought to catch my breath. My lungs ached with the unexpected exertion, and blood stained the sleeve of my favourite sweater. I was exhausted after the long shift, confused as all hell about this intrusion on my pub, and furious about the damage.

By the expression on the witch's face, he was equally unimpressed by the way his night was going.

Something about his magic and his face was irritatingly familiar, but although I took in the strong jaw, the strawberry-blond hair tied out of his face, and the wide breadth of his shoulders under his black peacoat and grey shirt, the recognition never landed. As I stared into the intensity of his violet eyes, I was almost compelled to apologize for the inconvenience. Then I remembered my painting and tightened my grip on my spell.

"Perhaps now would be a good time to explain why you're here?" I said.

He sneered, his full lips pulling back to reveal even white teeth that stood out against the scruff along his jawline. "This ignorant act won't work. How about you come with us and we'll let the big boss answer your questions."

I turned my attention from Purple Eyes to the man I'd assumed was the leader of the coven. He stood glowering at me, his magic still bound by mine. "You're not the big boss?"

"Regional manager," he growled.

I bit down on a smirk and nodded. "Mmhmm. Great title. Didn't realize the witches in this city had grown so corporate. My family must be stuck in the dark ages. So what? Do the professors work for you?" I asked Purple Eyes. "What exactly were you hoping to use them for? Comic relief?"

He shot them a dark look. "They claimed to be strong enough to help me take down a single witch, but it looks like it's down to me, princess. I suggest you make it easy on yourself."

I let go of my spell and propped my hands on my hips. "Listen, Silverware, the only princess I know lives six blocks away and is probably fast asleep or preparing for another day in the office. So you can either quit the patronizing nicknames, or you can politely explain that I have a long-lost grandparent with a title I never knew about. Either way, stop trashing my pub. Sound good?"

"You're not a princess," Regional Manager said. "Trace, just tell her the charges so we can get out of here."

Trace. The name settled against that screaming familiarity, and my stomach dropped. Trace Wyatt? Memories hit me of news broadcasts and TV interviews, of my sister fangirling on a night out—of a man tackling another man to the floor and binding his wrists with a ziptie. I reassessed the man in front of me. Aside from his renowned and rare telekinetic magic, he didn't look much like the bounty hunter I'd seen only once in the flesh. The stories my patrons whispered about him over their drinks described nothing less than a devil. Always caught his mark. Powerful witch. Relentless. Ruthless. This guy might rock a hard body and a striking set of eyes, but I'd nearly taken him in this fight.

More importantly, "Why the hell is a bounty hunter after my head?" I crossed my arms. "And by your smooth entrance into my place, I'm going to guess 'dead' is the preferred form of delivery?"

Simon stepped closer to me, sliding between me and the hunter as though ready to sacrifice himself to prevent Wyatt from getting his hands on me. I appreciated the gesture but hoped he was ready for me to blast him out of the way if it came to it. I wouldn't let my best friend take a hit meant for me.

"You're wanted for magic theft and the murder of the fae general Vivien McCree," Wyatt said.

I blinked.

Uh, what?

Chapter 2
Alyssa

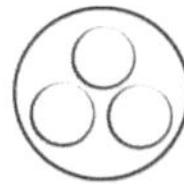

Thursday, 2:30 a.m.

EXCUSE ME VERY much?"

I had to have misheard. Magic theft? I rarely used the magic I'd been born with, let alone had interest in absorbing anyone else's. Did my magic feel fae to him? If so, Wyatt was very bad at his job. And as for the murder...

"The general's a regular," I said. "A very well-liked regular." A rock lodged in my throat as I pictured the tawny-skinned woman with starry eyes lined with deep crow's feet. "She told me to call her Vivi." I ground my teeth and locked gazes with the bounty hunter. "I haven't seen her in at least a month, and why the hell would I kill her?"

Wyatt's sneer deepened, so full of contempt I half-expected

him to scrape the soles of his boots to clear me off them. "I'm not expecting you to confess, Mooney. I was hired to do a job."

"By whom?"

"Confidential."

"Relevant. I'd like to know who my accuser is."

"Come with me, and you can meet them in person."

I snorted a laugh. "You'd give up your death bonus? That's very generous of you, Mr. Wyatt. Too generous. I doubt I'd make it to your car alive."

Simon snarled, his amber eyes taking on a sharp bronze glow, and across the room, the pool cues hanging on the wall rose into the air and launched at the witches still in the doorway. The three bound in the corner ducked in a huddle as a cue impaled itself in the freshly painted door. The other cue turned mere inches away from Wyatt's head and flew back the way it had come, smashing into the glasses above the bar.

Regional Manager succeeded in escaping my plastic wrap spell and threw it aside as he shouted "Enough!" but I gave him no time to engage. With a flick of my wrist, I launched another spell at him, this one sealing his mouth shut.

"The grown-ups are talking," I said as I closed the gap between me and Wyatt. "First, I didn't kill anyone, and I didn't steal their magic, which you should know by now." I summoned a purple orb into my palm. "That's all witch power, baby." I squeezed my hand shut, extinguishing the spell. "Second, I'm not going anywhere with you. Third, after Simon and I finish throwing you out of here, I'm going to find out who hired you, and I'm going to charge them for the damage to my pub, so not only will you *not* get paid for this job, but you'll owe me. Big bucks."

Was that a hint of respect I spotted in his eyes? It was gone so quickly I couldn't be sure, but I liked to think so.

It made his next words less irritating.

"First, I don't believe you." He summoned his silver magic into his palms. "Second, yes, you are."

He launched the spell at me, and although I threw myself out of the way, it caught me around the ankle and pinned me to the floor like a weighted anchor. Damn, the son of a bitch was fast.

"And third"—he stepped towards me—"the day one of my bounties gets the better of me is the day I retire."

He knelt down to grab my arm and haul me to my feet, but before he got a good grip, Simon's bronze-tinted chaos washed over us in a tidal wave.

I held my breath, always a good idea when trapped in a chaos bubble. You never knew if the air would turn to water or be sucked out of the atmosphere, or if the floor beneath you would vanish or turn into a pit of writhing snakes. The unpredictability was half the fun—and half the horror.

Today, it worked almost entirely in my favour. Wyatt's spell evaporated, Wyatt himself, along with his cronies, was shoved outside onto the patio, and my shirt disappeared. Two out of three wasn't bad.

I marched over to the front door, mustering whatever confidence I could in my ratty pink bra, and glared at the witches now lying in a tangled heap. Wyatt lay stretched on top, and I met his eye.

"First, I don't care. Second, no, I'm really not. Third"—I grinned—"I guess it's time to start planning the party."

Wearing my smuggest expression, I threw a purple net over my attackers to keep them in place until the spell faded, then grabbed hold of the door and slammed it shut.

As soon as they were out of sight, I summoned a protective spell and smeared it across the door to keep them out. Wyatt and his buddies were welcome to try to get through it, but by the time they did, Simon and I would be gone through the back door and any further mess they made of my pub would be added to their tab.

I turned around and took in the disaster awaiting me. My shoulders slumped and fatigue weighed me down. It had been a long, busy shift, and all I'd wanted to do was crawl into bed with a cup of tea and throw on an episode of *Bridgerton*, but instead I was left with this crap.

"I guess we're opening late today," I said, proud of myself for how well I was holding up, all things considered. I hadn't lost my cool. I'd kept pace with Wyatt's clever quips and badass magical moves. Not too shabby for a witch who'd missed most of her family's recent coven meetings, or for an Ottawa pub owner whose exposure to the chaotic was limited to her favourite business partner and the occasional drunk public servant.

But when I took a step forward, my legs gave out, and I slumped into a shivering mess on the floor. Tears rolled down my cheeks, and I couldn't get my hands to stop shaking.

"Hey, hey, hey." Simon rushed towards me, dropped to the floor, and bundled me against his chest. His sweater scratched against my cheek, my bare arms, my bare stomach, and in the middle of my adrenaline-fuelled hysteria, I realized I was sitting here in my bra. As if I needed the extra humiliation.

As though Simon realized it at the same time, he peeled off his sweater and pulled it over my head, wrapping me in the smell of him. Cedar and hops. A scent that travelled all the way into my heart and filled me with a warm comfort.

"You're okay," he murmured against my ear as he returned his arms around me. "You kicked their asses hard tonight, Lys. You done good."

A laugh escaped me, and I clung to him, needing my best friend's steadiness.

"If only Mom could see me now, eh?"

"She'd be proud."

I doubted it. My mother was many things, but a healer first

and foremost—just as she'd trained me to be. She'd just be happy I'd survived. Gramps, on the other hand, would give me the highest of fives.

Simon kissed my temple, and out of a habit I hadn't been able to shake I closed my eyes to savour the sensation. How long had I desired this demon? From the moment he'd walked through my door six years ago? From the first time I'd seen him toss a bottle in the air for a perfect catch-and-pour? We'd long ago accepted we were not meant to be, our magics too incompatible to let something as wild and uncontrolled as *passion* rise between us, but my love for him had deepened into something fiercer and more permanent. He was family, my rock, and I was so glad he'd been with me tonight.

Simon eased himself to his feet and offered his hand to help me to mine. "We'd better get you out of here before they escape that net."

I hugged my arms around my middle and waited by the back door while Simon collected my coat and purse from the office. I was still too shaken to make it that far on my own.

Now that I'd had a minute to run through the madness of the past half hour, a few facts rose up to grab me by the nose:

Vivi McCree was dead.

Her magic had been stolen.

Someone believed I was responsible.

Anyone with magic and the right spell could steal someone's power—the most heinous of crimes in the supernatural world—but how the holy hell anyone had connected my name with Vivi's boggled my mind. We'd only ever crossed paths here in the pub. I knew her friends better than I knew her. A garden fairy, Sasha, and a naiad, Ria. I'd known them for years, and even still, I mostly saw them here. Were they okay?

A heavy weight fell onto my shoulders, and I started, looking around to find Simon had draped my coat around me.

"The warmth will help with the shock. I closed the till and locked the office. You ready?"

My teeth were chattering. When had that started?

I nodded, and he briefly left my side to turn out the lights before taking my hand and escorting me across the parking lot.

Despite my fear, enough rationality remained for me to summon my magic into my hands to prepare to face off with anyone who came at me as we hurried towards our cars, but the night remained quiet. I doubted it would take long for Wyatt to break through the spell he was trapped under, but so far it seemed to have held them off.

"I'll give you a lift home," Simon said, directing me to his Jeep. "You're in no fit state to drive."

I looked to my Nissan. "But—"

"It'll be fine until later. I'll walk here before we open and drive it to you after shift. Because you're not coming in today, right?"

Below my shock, a spark of indignation lit within me at the idea that these witches would keep me away from work. I hadn't missed a day in six years.

But Simon had a point. I'd forced the issue tonight, but Trace "Never Lost a Mark" Wyatt wasn't about to give up because I'd shooed him out the door. He would try again, and next time he would know what to expect. I needed to call Gramps, the head of our coven and a member of the Ontario Witches' Council, and get him working on this with me.

Simon and I didn't talk as he drove us through Centretown towards my place.

It wasn't far, only a five-minute drive, and I hated that I couldn't walk to work. But the realities of the job—the hours, the errands I needed to run throughout the day—made driving necessary. It was why I'd switched to electric. One less gassy beast on the roads. Be the change, right?

We pulled into the driveway of my grey-blue two-storey duplex, and Simon turned off the car, dousing the night in silence. The house appeared still, my downstairs tenant no doubt still asleep given the hour. I hoped the silence meant none of Wyatt's team had made themselves comfortable on watch duty. If they were arrogant enough to think they could ambush me at the pub, they probably hadn't bothered trying to subvert my wards here. As long as I stayed inside, my defences would hold until the issue got sorted.

Goddess, I would need to make a lot of phone calls tomorrow.

I curled my hands in my lap, my fingers lost in the long sleeves of Simon's sweater.

"Thanks for the lift." I cleared my throat. "I don't suppose you want to come up? Have some coffee? Watch a crap movie?"

Keep me company? Take me to bed?

It was a horrible idea, but the thought of going upstairs alone created dark clouds in my head.

The look he gave me when I worked up the nerve to peer at him over the collar of my coat told me he heard as much of what I didn't say as what I did.

Pain. Regret.

"Lys…"

"No, I know. We've been there. Chaos demon and witch. No go. Explosion waiting to happen."

I returned my gaze to my hands as Simon's fingers came into view and rested over mine. He pumped the smallest amount of bronze power between us, and it wound between the purple spell I held queued up. A warm tingle drifted over my skin, warming my knuckles against the frostbitten evening, and immediately the hem of the sweater turned bright blue, clashing with the original maroon wool.

"Okay, but what if I think my bedroom is due some redecorating?" I asked, more for the joke than in earnest. I understood his point, and I liked my bedroom the way it was.

It still sucked.

He chuckled as he grabbed my hand and kissed the back of it. "I'll stay here until you're inside, and I'll call you in the morning so we can figure out what the hell we're going to do about Wyatt, all right?" He tightened his grip on my hand until I looked up at him. "Stay inside."

I rolled my eyes. "Yeah, Dad, whatever." When he still didn't let me go, I dropped the 'tude. "I promise. I'm going to line up a show to watch until this is over."

"Thank you. I can't have anything happen to you, Lys. I really can't."

My heart warmed with his concern, and I cursed the Fates that made any connection between us as volatile as bleach and ammonia.

I pulled my hand free and slid out of the Jeep, then slung my purse over my shoulder and speed-walked to the door on the side of the house. A last wave at Simon, a flash of his lights to tell me he saw me, and I was inside, door locked and warded.

Relief settled over me like a blanket as soon as I cast the spell, and exhaustion weighed down my eyelids as the last of my adrenaline washed away.

What a night.

I dragged myself up the stairs to my second-floor apartment, let myself in, and locked and warded that door too, just to be safe.

A bone-deep shiver ran from the base of my neck down to my toes, and I stripped off my coat, kicked off my boots, and went directly into the kitchen to start the kettle for a cup of tea. This time of night, decaf was everything, but I needed warmth.

The sound of the kettle elements warming up started the process of easing my tension, and by the time I changed into a pair of thick grey socks, my favourite blue-and-green plaid flannel pyjama bottoms, and a graphic tee with a bunny witch on it, I could almost have forgotten my nightmare of an evening.

Before I returned to the kitchen, I pulled Simon's sweater back on. The baseboard heaters kept the apartment comfortable, but what I needed right now was a hug, and if I couldn't have the real thing, the sweater would have to suffice.

My emotional support sweater.

I pulled the collar up over my nose and let it sit there as I poured my tea. I added milk, let it steep, then threw the teabag onto a plate on the counter. Many a person had called my tea preferences blasphemous, but those people soon found themselves newt shaped.

Don't worry, they got better.

I took my cup into the living room, sank into the deep cushions of my old blue couch, and turned on the television.

Three sips into my tea, five minutes into my show, I fell asleep.

Then woke up an hour later with a cotton mouth, a different episode of my show playing, and cold tea.

"Great. Just the way I hate it," I grumbled, and took my mug back into the kitchen.

After a quick debate about whether I wanted to warm up my drink or dump it, I opted for more sleep and poured the tea down the drain. The discarded teabag glared at me from its plate, daring me to leave it there, and I picked it up and threw it in the compost bin.

Or, perhaps more accurately, at the compost bin. Then I watched it slide down the pile of refuse to land on the counter.

If ever I'd needed a sign that I'd overbooked my hours in the pub this week, it was staring me in the face. And offending my nose.

I peered through the window to the shed by the side door where my tenant and I kept our garbage and recycling bins. Five steps away from the door, near the back of the house.

The *warded* house.

At three-thirty in the morning.

I spotted no cars on the street, no figures lurking in the shadows. If there was ever a time to dart outside so I wasn't confined with the reek of rotting food until Gramps helped me solve this problem, this was it. With a simple cloaking spell to hide me from any prying eyes, I'd be there and back in no time.

I pulled my boots back on, grabbed the green bin, and

plodded down the stairs. My brain was hazy with shrugged-off sleep, but I wasn't so far gone as to have lost all judgement. As soon as I stepped beyond the wards, I'd be vulnerable, and what I wanted now was sleep, not another showdown.

With my free hand, I drew on my magic and wrapped it around me in a soft blanket, manipulating the atmosphere to create a blind that would allow me to remain unseen. The spell didn't work well in the middle of the day, but in the darkness, draped in shadow, I'd managed to scare the crap out of Simon a time or two, so I was confident it would work well enough for the thirty seconds I'd be outside.

I opened the door and hurried to the shed. Not out of fear, but because it was frickin' freezing. My foot slipped on a patch of ice, and I wheeled my free hand in the air to catch my balance. Not even an eggshell spilled. Gold.

I dropped the compost in the larger green bin, closed the door, and hustled my icy butt back to the door.

Easy peasy.

A noise from the front of the house caught my ear. My downstairs tenant? Bit late for Ann to be coming home, but I wasn't her mother.

I opened the door, enjoyed the hit of warm air wafting down from the stairwell, and had a second to recognize a stream of silver magic wrapping around me before the lights went out.

Chapter 3
Alyssa

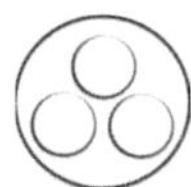

Thursday, 4:00 a.m.

I CAME TO in the dark.

Memories of my night rushed through me: the crunch of gravel as someone stepped through the darkness, the unfamiliar scent in the air of bergamot and coffee, and the feeling of a lasso jerking me around the chest as someone yanked me backwards and hoisted me off my feet.

My terror spiked, and I tried to twist around to take in my surroundings, but the space was too cramped for me to budge more than a few inches. The material under my cheek and hand was soft, and the smell was distinctly car.

I was in a goddess-damned trunk.

A streak of anger rose through the fear, and I latched on to it as a far more useful emotion.

Fucking Wyatt.

I searched for my magic, and although it was sluggish, bound under the bounty hunter's silver weave of power, it responded enough for me to direct the smallest glow towards the end of my finger. Enough to see by.

A quick scan of my surroundings showed he'd at least had the decency to empty the trunk before he stowed me in it, but that didn't remove the insult of being carted around like luggage.

At least he hadn't killed me.

No, I would not give him any leeway. The son of a bitch had come to my home and staked the place out. Had he watched me make tea? Had he witnessed my ever-so-graceful slip-and-catch on my way to the green bin? How had he seen through my cloaking spell? From here on out, I would make a point of flipping off windows in case anyone else thought spying on me was a fun way to spend their night.

I forced my attention away from future revenge and back to the trunk. It looked to be a newer vehicle, which meant it was more spacious than it might have been, thank the goddess, and more importantly, that there had to be an interior latch. Specifically to help people in my situation from being stuck here.

The light from my finger wasn't enough to brighten more

than an inch or two around the glow, so I held my hand close to the fabric and slid it slowly in one direction, then the other, searching for the catch.

The car went over a bump, and I was thrown against the ceiling, cracking my head on a piece of curved plastic. I bit down on a curse, though it nearly slipped out when I heard a muffled "Sorry!" from the front seat.

Yeah, well, he would be sorry. Sorry when he reached his destination, got ready to make his grand reveal to whoever had hired him, and found me gone. Ha ha, fucker.

My left eye now half-closed thanks to my altercation with the car, I returned to my search.

There. Finally. A little plastic latch tucked on the inside of the locking mechanism. If I'd let my eyes adjust to the darkness, I would have spotted the glow-in-the-dark strip along the back of it.

I hooked my finger underneath it and pulled. It stuck.

Son of a…

A closer look at the locking mechanism showed a hint of silver seeping through the crack. Not too strong, not designed to keep me in—some kind of soundproofing, if I had to guess—but enough to block my escape attempt and make my next step more of a challenge.

I kept the latch under my hand so I wouldn't lose it and directed the glowing spell on my fingertip into the mechanism.

I hoped my idea worked, because the rest of my magic was trapped until I had enough time and focus to undo Wyatt's binding spell. Which I would do. He might think he was Mr. Great and Powerful Bounty Hunter, but he had no idea who he was messing with.

A witch who hadn't made much use of her power in six years, sure, but one who came from Ottawa's strongest witch family and who'd spent most of her teenage years training to be the best.

With a "So, there" sitting on the tip of my tongue as a shield of confidence, I sent out my tiny spell and sagged in relief when the silver tendril unravelled, followed by the thunk of the lock. Good. I hoped I busted his trunk and doing groceries would be a pain in his ass forever.

I tried the latch again, and this time it clicked. The trunk swung open—not the subtle crack I'd hoped for, but a full lift—and I rolled out, keeping my head tucked into my arms to protect my face and skull from the landing.

He'd been speeding pretty quickly on the empty road, but thanks to the snow, the worst I suffered was the shock of impact and the scrape of my elbow against the slush-covered asphalt. Simon's poor sweater. If I'd ripped it, Wyatt owed me double the cost of the damage he'd done to Mooney's.

It took me all of three seconds to recognize where we were, an empty stretch of road close to the middle of nowhere in one direction and pockets of civilization in the other. Including a few recent housing developments. If I made it to someone's front door, I could call Simon to come get me.

Using my cloaking spell hadn't worked, so I had to hope I was a faster runner than Wyatt.

Come on, high school track and field, don't fail me now!

I tore along the side of the road without looking behind me. That was how people tripped and fell on their faces and got nabbed by the people chasing them. I'd seen the movies. I knew how this worked.

Then why'd you leave the house, dumbass?

Later, I would have a serious conversation with myself about negative self-talk, but right now I couldn't help but agree with the critical voice in my head. I'd made a bad judgement call, and now I was running for my life.

Blood rushed in my ears and my lungs burned, but I pushed my legs faster when I heard the skid of tires on the side of the road. A door slammed. I ran faster. A turn appeared up ahead, along with the dark stare of house windows. Almost there.

I flew off my feet and landed on my stomach in the dirt, the air bursting from my lungs, my ribs and the palms of my hands screaming.

A glance at my ankle showed a loop of silver magic. With a curse, I tried to summon a spell to get rid of it, but my power was still bound under Wyatt's suppression magic. I cast a look over my shoulder to find him walking towards me. Not running, just striding quickly, confidently. The arrogant bastard.

A pulse of fury sent my magic wild, and it tore through the binding and the snare around my ankle. In a breath, I was on my feet and running again.

"Goddammit," I heard him say, and I mentally waved my middle finger at him.

Footsteps pounded the pavement behind me as he sped up, and I filled my palms with magic, ready to unleash it at the first opportunity. Extra space between us would give me more time to get help. I was almost within screaming range, and he'd better believe I would do it. I'd been blessed with a solid set of lungs.

I hit the street corner, the front door of the closest house came into view, and a heavy weight slammed into my back, sending me again face-first onto the ground. Strong arms wrapped around me, and although I bucked him off, I couldn't wriggle my way free. My magic surged between us, throwing him back a few inches, and I lurched forward, but he circled his fingers around my wrist and hauled me towards him. A moment later, I lay on my back. Wyatt lay on top of me, and our magic went to war, purple straining against silver, the two colours so evenly matched I would have called the effect of their battle beautiful if I wasn't so seething mad.

"Get. Off. Me," I said through clenched teeth.

"And let you run again?" he asked, his breath fogging in the cold. "That'll be a hard no."

I directed a pulse of atmospheric energy towards his sensitives but found my assault blocked by a warding spell he'd already wrapped around his nethers in anticipation of my move.

His eyebrow quirked, and his smugness made me double down on my attempts to escape. The ground was freezing, snow was soaking into my back, and every time I gained an iota of leverage, the slick surface gave way beneath me. When my elbow slipped and the back of my head slammed against the icy asphalt, I squeezed my eyes shut against the flashing stars.

"Are you done?" His weight hadn't shifted on top of me, his mass of toned muscle and black peacoat working with the elements to hold me down without any effort on his part.

I was onto him now. He was the type to work smart instead of hard. How many bounties had he caught by sheer luck?

"I'm done when I'm home, warm, and never have to see your face again."

"I can give you two out of three."

I groaned. "Fine, you can have the couch. But only for tonight."

He chuckled, and his magic slinked around me, skirting mine, outmanoeuvring my defences. I watched, too stunned to prevent it. How had he learned the nature of my power so quickly that he was able to get ahead of it?

I took back what I'd thought. This guy was good.

My shock wore off as the silver wrapped around the purple and squeezed, my magic compressing against me, once more on the verge of being bound, and I pushed back. The battle of wills began in earnest as we lay there in the snow, neither of us moving a limb, until both of us were out of breath with the exertion of our silent struggle.

"I have to admit," he panted, "you are nothing like I expected."

I sneered. "You, on the other hand, are everything I imagined you'd be."

His eyes twinkled over that damn cheeky grin. "You've imagined me before? I'm flattered. I'd love to hear what direction your… imaginings took, but maybe we should move somewhere warmer."

A growl of frustration escaped the back of my throat, and I struggled against him again. My arm slipped free, and I smacked him over the ear. He grunted, reached for the side of his head, and I bucked my hips to roll him off me. I pushed myself to my feet and made it all of three steps before he was behind me, his hand closing around my arm. When I jerked away, I earned nothing except to drag him towards me.

He stood an easy six-two to my five-eight, but if he thought his height would intimidate me, he hadn't done enough homework. My brothers were both six-four, and they'd hardened me to any guy's looming.

"Why can't you say you didn't find me?" I asked, putting my whole weight on my arm to try to slide free. His grip held fast.

"Do you know how many people have tried that line on me?"

"Did any of those people kick your ass and outsmart you twice?"

"No," he conceded with a hint of a smile, and I wanted to smack it off him. Why wasn't he frazzled? Annoyed, at the very least? Why did he act like everything I did amused him?

"Exactly," I said, as though he weren't infuriating the piss out of me. "And if you drag me back to that car, I'll do it again. Why not save yourself the headache?"

Finally, his smile vanished. The lines around his eyes and mouth tightened, revealing a very different man from the one I'd dealt with so far tonight. Suddenly, the height difference seemed much more significant, and I forced my spine to remain straight when he closed the gap between us.

"Because I never walk away from a job, princess. Not for bribes, not for begging, and not for skipping out on a challenge. You're accused of murder and magic theft. If you have issue with that, take it up with the person accusing you, not with me."

The snow that had soaked through Simon's sweater seemed to seep through my skin into my blood. In the heat of our skirmish, I'd forgotten my problem wasn't with him but with the person who'd accused me. A much bigger problem, and so much worse.

"I didn't do it."

He shrugged. "Not the first time I've heard that one, either. But that has nothing to do with me."

With his fingers still tight around my arm, he started hauling me back to the SUV. I fought him every step of the way, but the ground was slippery, and he was stronger. My magic fizzled when I tried to summon it, exhausted by the earlier stalemate.

"Why not just kill me, then?" I demanded, digging my heels into the ground to jerk him to a stop. Anything to gain a bit more time to come up with a plan.

"What?" He turned towards me, annoyance now flashing in his eyes.

"At the pub, you seemed ready enough to end me and collect your money like a good little hunter. Why not finish the job?"

His magic surged, as strong as it had been since I'd first met him, and wrapped around my throat. I froze, held my breath, heard my heartbeat pound in my ears.

"You make it tempting," he growled, the low rumble of his voice vibrating through me to rattle against my racing heart. Just as quickly, he dropped his spell, stepped away, and continued his determined plod towards the vehicle with me in tow.

"But the kill is no fun if I lose the element of surprise. You're my client's problem now." He pulled us to a sharp stop beside the car. "Get in the trunk."

I looked from the cramped space to him and snorted a laugh. "Not a chance."

He jerked me closer, scooped me into his arms and tried to drop me in, but I channelled my inner cat and thrashed and writhed until he dropped me into the snow, still holding my wrist.

"Aren't you curious?" His tone had changed again, cajoling now. "Don't you want to meet the person who accused you? Don't you want to try to convince them you're innocent? Because I could let you go, and you could run home, but if it's not me, it'll be someone else tearing your pub apart. This murder needs to be solved, and your face is stamped on it. You want to fix that? Get in the trunk."

He'd almost convinced me. "I'm not getting in the trunk."

"They expect you to be in the trunk."

"And I expected to be curled up in bed. Tough tits."

He choked on what sounded like a surprised laugh, but his pull on my arm eased.

"Fine. But they will expect you to be bound."

I hesitated. What the hell was I doing, considering going with him? I should keep fighting. If he was open to negotiating, it had to mean he was tired, right? I could escape him. Go home. Call Gramps.

But Wyatt was right. If I didn't face my accuser, this would never be over. My family might be able to get me out of it, but what if they couldn't? Farewell, pub. Goodbye, regulars. So long, Simon. I was innocent, dammit. What did I have to run from?

My mouth went dry, and I dropped my chin in a tentative nod. It was possible that wherever Wyatt took me, I would never walk out, but at least it would be on my terms, not hunted like an animal.

My heart was in my throat, my pulse racing, my legs longing to fight or flee, but I stood still as he took my other hand and tightened a rope of silver magic around both wrists, trapping them together. Tears pricked my eyes as his net draped over me and my magic dampened. Caught. Caged.

I swallowed hard and met his gaze, which was devoid of sympathy though far from cold.

Stiffening my shoulders to show courage I didn't feel, I added iron to my voice and said, "I call shotgun."

Chapter 4
Alyssa

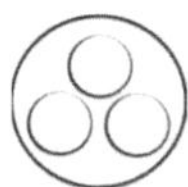

Thursday, 4:30 a.m.

ALTHOUGH MY NERVES didn't settle the rest of the trip up that dark, empty stretch of Prince of Wales Drive, the heat blasting through the vents was glorious, and I huddled as close to them as possible with my hands cuffed as they were in front of me.

The drive wasn't nearly long enough. Barely five minutes later, Wyatt swung a left and pulled into the parking lot of a swanky inn. He stopped the car but left the engine running, and we sat in silence, waiting.

What were we waiting for? Was he hoping my heart gave out from adrenaline and terror before he had to hear what might come out of my mouth in front of his client? Because I did not intend to go easy on any of them.

"Are you warm enough?" he asked after a few minutes had passed.

I looked at him in surprise. "Do you care?"

He averted his gaze and shrugged, but I'd caught his expression before he turned away. Call me crazy, but I'd swear it was concern.

"My clothes are soaked. I'm in a sweater and pyjama pants and unlaced boots. I will never be warm enough without twenty minutes in a steaming shower and a cup of tea in my belly." I hmphed and sagged back in my seat, tempted to leave it at that. But my damned social politeness, ingrained in me by my mother, nudged me to respond to his show of consideration, and despite my bitterness, I added, "But I'm warm*er*, thank you."

"Good. Then let's go in before they send out the hounds."

He got out of the car, and although I'd opted to come here somewhat voluntarily, I couldn't bring myself to join him. My legs grew heavy, my mouth dry, my breath quick. Panic pushed my heart into a gallop.

What the hell had I been thinking, agreeing to this? The person waiting inside the inn had put a bounty on me—with a preference for my death over my capture. They didn't want to hear denials about a crime they claimed I'd committed. They wanted to pin it on me, sweep it under the rug, and move on. I had agreed to walk into my final hour.

Anxiety wrapped around me, sloshed in my stomach, sent chills chasing after hot flashes, and I swore I was going to throw up all over Wyatt's nice, clean front seat.

Good.

My door opened, and the bounty hunter stood there, one hand extended to help me out, but I didn't move.

"You really can't let me go?" I was ashamed by how small my voice sounded but impressed that any sound had made it through my rapidly closing throat.

"Afraid not."

Simon's face flashed before my eyes. My pub. My house. My friends. My family. No one would know what had happened to me. I didn't have a will. Simon was a partner in the pub so management would stay in good hands, which was a relief, but everything else was up in the air. Unfinished.

Tears stung my eyes, and my panic edged towards hysteria. What would happen if I broke down and started shrieking? If I curled into a ball on Wyatt's front seat and refused to leave and made such a scene I caught the attention of the mundanes in the inn?

The thought tempted me, and as I imagined it, a thread of courage spun around me. I had options. They were slight and would probably fail, but my life wasn't over yet. I wouldn't stop fighting until I breathed my last.

Resolved, I raised my cuffed hands for Wyatt to lift me out

of the car, and he kept his hold around my upper arm as we crossed the parking lot and climbed the exterior stairs to the second floor. He knocked on the fourth door down, a voice called for us to come in, and he ushered me inside a warm, cozy, single room. A double bed sat in the centre, an end table on either side, both lights on, and a television mounted across from it, currently set to a rerun of *Game of Thrones.*

A man sat on the bed with his legs stretched out, hands behind his head. The vision of holiday relaxation. Except for the suit, the tie, and the service weapon in its holster on the bedside table.

Considering it was only a little past four-thirty in the morning, I didn't envy the guy his job.

Any thoughts I had that this was the person who'd hired Wyatt, however, faded when my eye fell on the woman sitting at the desk.

The first thing I noticed was her perfect posture. A finishing school's wet dream. The sleek line from the base of her skull down past her shoulder blades was an even plane I could have balanced a teacup on without spilling, displayed to advantage by a blue angora sweater that sat high on the throat and swept low in the back. Her hair was cut into a severe black bob to reveal the subtle points of her ears, and her lethal sharp nails were painted a soft pink.

From her figure, the ears, and those nails, I knew what I

would see when she turned to face us: eyes swirling with stars. This woman was fae. Had to be. A human with posture that stiff would have snapped in half ages ago.

The man on the bed turned down the volume on the TV but didn't turn it off, didn't say hi, and didn't acknowledge me. To Wyatt, he gave a deep-furrowed frown before he returned his attention to the Khaleesi and her badass dragons. What I wouldn't give for one of those right now.

I waited for someone to make introductions, for Wyatt to announce our presence, but instead we stood there for a full minute, two, three, while the woman at the desk finished whatever she was writing.

She set down her pen and set to work folding the paper, her long, tapered fingers not wasting a single motion, and over her shoulder, she said, "Mr. Wyatt. I was informed you had no issue weighing your conscience against the promise of a hefty bonus cheque, yet your quarry stands here alive."

My courage flagged under her cold tone, and Wyatt's grip on my arm turned supportive, holding me steady so my legs didn't take me crashing to the ground.

"I put taking the path of least resistance over the extra cash," he replied, his flat voice matching hers, with none of the warmth or humanity he'd shown in the car. Even our banter while we'd duked it out on the side of the road had held more emotion. "In this case, that meant leaving her to your justice."

The woman sniffed, which I could only guess was supposed to be a mirthless laugh, set down her envelope, and turned to face us.

My thoughts shrivelled in my head as I took in her appearance. The depths of her dark eyes shining with swirls of light suggested her age was far greater than Vivi's had been, and the general had celebrated her ninetieth birthday last year. I was even more struck by her beauty: sharp cheekbones, a pointed chin, full lips, a broad nose, and a confidence in the way she held her head that made me feel about two inches tall.

I had no idea who she was—she'd never come into the pub— but from her attitude alone, I knew she was someone important.

Someone important who wanted me dead.

Beneath my abject terror was the urge to give someone a high five. Look at me, the subject of some VIP's loathing.

I wanted to throw up.

She barely spared me a glance, but I felt that glance like a string of barbed wire slicing me from head to toe.

"Very well. Leave her. Peter will see you get paid."

My lungs constricted, and I looked to Wyatt. I'd fought so hard to get away from him, but now he was the only familiar sight in the room. He couldn't walk out. If he did, no one would ever see me alive again.

"I didn't do it," I spat out, realizing belatedly how pointless it was to use the same line on them as I had on Wyatt. This woman was no more likely to believe me. Summoning the only certainty I had, that of my complete lack of involvement in this crime, I squared my shoulders and, in a stronger voice, said, "I did not murder Vivi McCree, and I did not steal her magic. She was my friend, and I would never have harmed her. If there is evidence to suggest I did, I demand to see it so I can refute it or explain it."

All those nights watching *Law & Order* had finally come in handy.

The woman's stare bored into me, filled with so much contempt, disdain, even disgust, that I half-expected her to gag at the sight of me. I didn't care. She could think me no better than a smear of dog shit on her Jimmy Choos as long as she agreed to hear me out.

"You were seen leaving Viviane's house around three in the morning. Your freckled human face was caught on camera. Unmistakably. Down to your… ponytail." She flicked her fingers at it as though my hair choices had offended her on a deep, personal level.

Whatever. I was too stunned for my feelings to be hurt.

"That's not… I was at home. I never went out."

But of course I had no way of proving it. I would have just come home from work, which meant I'd been alone in my apartment tearing through reruns of *Friends* and passing out on my couch.

This was why a social life was important.

Instead of an alibi, I had four walls rapidly closing in on me, and if I didn't think of a way to convince this woman I hadn't killed Vivi, they would squeeze the life right out of me.

Desperate, I turned to Wyatt and met his emotionless stare. "I swear. I never went out. At the very least, you can see I didn't steal her magic, can't you? You bound me, we fought. Did you see any fae magic?"

His gaze flicked towards the woman at the desk before it landed on me with a faint swirl of remorse. "I can't see your magic, so I don't know. You're a stronger witch than I expected, but is that all your own power or is part of it stolen? I can't swear to anything."

It sounded like it pained him to crush my last hope. That was nice.

I returned my attention to the woman. "Please, give me a chance to clear my name. I want to find out what happened to Vivi as much as you do. I can help. My family has influence in this city and can help me get answers. I have friends in the government who can look into it, I—"

"Enough," the woman said. She flicked her fingers again, and with a golden glitter of fae magic, my lips clamped shut. "Mr. Wyatt, you've done your duty. You may leave."

He dropped his chin in a nod and started to turn towards the door, then stopped, turned back. "Pardon my insolence, but aren't you curious to know if Miss Mooney is telling the truth?"

"No."

He barked an incredulous laugh. "But—"

"We have her on camera, Mr. Wyatt. What more proof would you like?"

"But if she says she wasn't there…"

"Are you this gullible with all your marks, or only the ones with large breasts?"

I blinked and held back from looking down to check out my girls. Sure, they looked good in the sweater, and since I'd changed into my PJs, I was braless, but I'd hardly call them impressive. Involuntarily, my gaze strayed to the chest of the woman in front of me, and I supposed, in comparison, mine was larger.

I gave myself a mental slap. Was this really the time?

She started it.

I told myself to shut it and waited for Wyatt's reply, but the woman continued without giving him a chance. "Regardless of your weaknesses, Mr. Wyatt, your job is to fetch, not to pronounce judgement. Peter will finish what you failed to do."

The next few seconds happened so quickly I barely had time to process it.

As Peter slid off the bed to come towards me, Wyatt threw out his hand and a wave of silver magic sent the man sprawling back onto the bedspread. With his other hand, he threw a spell at the woman, and a moment later, she slammed into a translucent silver wall that had risen across the room.

The stars in her eyes burned. "Mr. Wyatt!"

"If I can't prove anything, you'll have her back in twenty-four hours."

Barely a breath later, the binding around my wrists was gone, my magic was free, and my hand was wrapped in Wyatt's as he tore out the door, dragging me behind him.

"Get to the car," he said as he threw a spell back at the inn door. It slammed shut, and I heard a click as his magic turned the lock.

I didn't question him. My frozen legs needed a moment to get with the program, but as soon as they did, I sped past him down the stairs, tore across the parking lot, and threw myself into the passenger seat. The engine purred to life before Wyatt had closed himself into the driver's side, and in another moment, he was speeding out of the parking lot back onto Prince of Wales, driving in the opposite direction of downtown.

"What the hell was that?" I asked, unable to think of anything else to say.

His jaw flexed as he cast me a dark look, and he shook his head. "Goddess help me, I have no idea. But you better be telling the truth, princess. Because if you're not, and if we don't find Viviane McCree's real killer, then I just signed my death warrant with a fae duchess."

Chapter 5
Alyssa

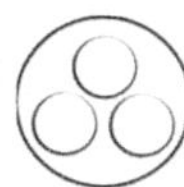

Thursday, 4:45 a.m.

IT TOOK A moment for Wyatt's words to register, and I stared at him in horror, throwing a look over my shoulder back the way we'd come. "That was Dara Josef-Levesque?"

"In the flesh."

"You just trapped Dara Josef-Levesque and her personal bodyguard behind an invisible wall? Wyatt, they'll kill you!"

"Trace."

"What?"

"Only marks call me Wyatt." His violet eyes flicked towards me. "You don't quite qualify. Though after this, you do owe me."

My expression turned bland. "I won't charge you for trashing my pub, how's that?"

"It's a start."

He turned onto Fallowfield and sped down the stretch of road.

"Where are we going?" I asked as we narrowly missed a delivery truck turning left.

"Buddy of mine has a place in Stittsville. Off the radar, warded against magical tracking. If we're going to hunt down a magic thief, it's the best place to go until we have a plan. It'll keep Dara off our heels for a few hours, anyway." He cast me a sideways glance. "Were you serious when you talked about government connections who could help you?"

Heat filled my cheeks. "I mean, I have government connections, and they might know someone who can help me. My family's probably the better bet."

"You're looking to clear your name. Dara won't believe anything you bring her if it comes from family. If you trust your fed friends not to rat you out to anyone in Meril's court, call them."

I snorted. "Yeah, that's not a problem."

He reached into his coat pocket and handed me his phone. I accepted it, swiped past the lock screen—*Great security, Mr. Bounty Hunter*—and opened the phone app… only to remember these weren't my contacts.

"What is it?" he asked.

I shot him a look. "How many phone numbers do you have

memorized these days?"

"All of them?"

"Show off," I grumbled, and opened his browser to go to the department's website.

Supernatural, Magical and Occult Affairs Canada—or SMOAC to those of us who referred to them regularly—wasn't difficult to find for those who knew it existed, but its design was horribly out of date, as most government sites were, so it took a while to navigate before I found the number I was searching for.

Madison Prince, minister's chief of staff, great-something granddaughter of Meril, queen of the supernatural realm beyond the unseen wall. She was my best chance for clearing my name, not only because she was my friend, but also because she was as eager to stay off Meril's radar as I was.

Her voicemail clicked in after the fifth ring, and I cleared my throat twice, wincing at my awkwardness.

"Madi, hey, it's Alyssa Mooney. It's almost five in the morning, and I just met with Dara Josef-Levesque, who—funny story—wants me dead because of a false accusation of murder and magic theft. Goddess, I wish I was joking. I got away from her for now, but if you know anyone who could help me not die over this, I would really appreciate it."

Wyatt—Trace—gave me his number, and I repeated it for Madison to call me back when she could.

By the time I hung up, I was shaking all over, and Trace cranked the heat, directing all the vents my way and flipping on the heated seat.

"Th-thanks." I wrapped my arms around my middle and burrowed into the leather seat.

Snowflakes hit the windshield with increasing speed, and by the time my shivering stopped, I could barely see outside. Exhaustion swept over me, goosebumps made my skin tingle, and what I longed for more than anything was my bed.

Instead, I was stuck in a car with a man who'd first tried to kill me, then kidnapped me, then saved me, on the run for my life to the home of an unknown alleged ally, waiting until regular business hours for a callback from my possible ticket to freedom.

Ugh.

In an effort to keep my eyes open, I shifted towards Trace, taking in the sweep of his strawberry-blond hair. If it were loose, it would have reached his chin, or maybe his bottom lip, but pulled back as it was, it tickled the nape of his neck. After the encounter with Dara, a few loose strands hung around his eyes. The stubble along his jawline caught the glow as we passed beneath the streetlights, reflecting sparks of golden fire.

"Why are you helping me?" I asked. "You could have taken your paycheque and left me there. Wouldn't have made any difference to you. Just another job."

After a slight hesitation, he shrugged. "Call me a sucker, but I like to know I'm bringing in the right person when I collar someone. Most of the time, their history tells me everything I need to know about what they offer society. Your record was clear. Pub owner the past six years. The middle child of a respectable magical family. No criminal record—not even an unpaid parking ticket. To go from that to magic theft, let alone murder… It doesn't smell right. Also your alibi sucks. Home alone watching TV? A guilty person would have come up with something better."

I didn't know how I felt about his implication that my life was boring. It wasn't. Quiet, sure. Predictable, often. But boring?

Yeah, all right, fine. To someone whose life involved travelling the country searching for wanted criminals, my life was boring. And, it turned out, inconvenient, because I had no one to vouch for me in the middle of the night.

"Can I ask you a question now?" he asked.

"Mmm," I replied, too tired to create unnecessary words.

The corner of his mouth curled into a smile. "At the pub, while we were fighting, you called me Silverware. What was that about? Is this some new insult the kids are slinging these days, or do pub owners reserve their curses for familiar items? What should I expect next? Pint glass? Dirty rag?"

"Maybe all those things." I wrinkled my nose. "No, it's just the best I could come up with at the time to describe it."

"Describe what?"

The pestering nudged me further from sleep, and I wanted to order him to hush. But seeing as this was his vehicle and my life currently rested in his hands, I summoned the energy to say "Your magic. Obviously."

His eyebrows rose. "Is that what you meant at the hotel? You see magic as colours?"

This question startled me right awake, and I sat up straighter in my seat. "How do you see it?"

"I don't. I sense it more than anything. A vibration, or a ripple in the air. What do the colours mean? Different for every person? Every type?"

I blinked at him, surprised by his interest. Most people didn't care about my family's genetic quirk of differentiating magical strains.

"Mostly type," I said. "Sometimes the texture changes depending on the spell, but different magics have different colour signatures. Fae is sort of a golden glitter. Necromancy is black. Demonic ranges from red to bronze. Elemental magics are green. My family line is mostly atmospheric energy, which looks sort of purple." I drew my magic into my hand and watched it dance around my palm before shooting Trace a pointed look. "Untouched by golden glitter."

He nodded. "That's why you hoped I could back you up

with Dara."

I dropped my hand into the warmth of my lap. "My cousins, siblings, and I used to challenge each other to spot as many different signatures as we could when we went downtown. Loser treated everyone to ice cream."

"Bloodline gift," he said, as though explaining it to himself. "So my magic is silver?"

I nodded. "I've never seen silver aside from yours. Telekinetic, isn't it? That's what's swirling around the gossip channels about you, anyway."

He nodded. "Mostly. I've never heard of anyone seeing it as a colour before. Sorry I wasn't able to help you."

"I forget sometimes that it's a limited ability." I thought of the summers and holidays filled with family get-togethers. The Mooneys were a large clan, and most of them shared my ability. As for my adult years… well, I rarely had an opportunity to use my power these days, so the only exposure I had to the supernatural was Simon. "My partner is a chaos demon. We tend to minimize the amount of magic he comes into contact with during work hours. And most of my life is work hours."

I stared intently at the warp-drive effect of the snow coming at the windshield, pointedly ignoring the curious look I'd earned.

"I thought I recognized his magic," he said. "Never met a chaos demon in person before. Must make family dinners challenging."

Was that a hairline crack in the glass, or only a trick of the light?

"Simon and I don't enjoy family-dinner status. Friends-to-dinner, of course. Coworkers. Occasional barfight partners."

Why was I telling him this? I should have lied and said, "Yes, every day is an unpredictable circle of whether our magic will play nice with each other or set the house on fire. It keeps the passion strong." Even if just to make the daydreams of the past few years real for one goddess-blessed minute.

But also, it was none of this guy's business.

As though he realized it, Trace let the subject drop and said, "So if you can see magic, you should be able to identify anyone who possesses magic they shouldn't, right?"

I tore my gaze away from the hypnotic pattern outside. "In theory. The two signatures would have to be pretty different." My eyebrows rose as a thought occurred to me. "If it was another fae, I might not see it. Why are we assuming it was a witch?"

He flexed his jaw. "Because murder is bad enough. A family feud would mean the whole city is in for a bad time."

I sat with that cheerful thought for the rest of the drive. The storm worsened, forcing Trace to hyperfocus on the road, and I didn't mind having the mental space to myself.

Somewhere out there, a murderer had pinned a crime on me, and I had no idea who or why. A fae duchess wanted me dead, and the man who was supposed to kill me had sided with me over her, effectively adding the target on my head to his own. My resources were slim. Trace's were unknown but more extensive than mine, which meant my options were to leave him, go home, and do my best to sort this mess out by myself, or trust him to help us both.

Neither option whispered to me of rainbows and kittens.

In fact, both screamed at me of fire, volcanoes, and sharp pointed sticks jabbing me in the back.

I wished I'd kept Trace's phone to call Simon. I didn't want to get him involved, but I wouldn't have minded letting him know I was all right and getting his two cents about what the hell I was supposed to do next.

Not that I needed to speak with him to know what he would say. *Get the fuck out of that car and away from Wyatt. He's a bounty hunter who tried to kill you. What the fuck are you thinking?*

And he would be one hundred per cent correct.

But Trace had also barricaded a fae duchess and her bodyguard in a hotel room and removed the binding around my magic, and it seemed rude, somehow, to tell him to peace out.

Besides, I had to face facts: of the two of us, who was more likely to have the skills to track down Vivi's real murderer?

Hint: it wasn't me.

My family had influence and I had connections within SMOAC, but how far would that get me if Dara didn't believe my family or if Madison's contacts didn't believe me? Or if they didn't have the capacity to do me any unofficial favours? The last thing I wanted was any of this investigation to be on record. That would be asking for an ass-kicking down the road. Investigated for murder? Goodbye, liquor licence.

So, sorry, Simon. Good advice aside, I was going to have to ignore it for the time being. But at least I'd have his sweater to keep me warm. He'd have to be satisfied that I wouldn't die of hypothermia before the day was out.

Not long after, we pulled into a quiet residential neigh-bourhood lined with cookie-cutter modular homes. Each one with light-hued vinyl, a small, white-painted porch, and large windows staring down from the second floor. Cozy. Idyllic. The last place I would have expected Trace to take us.

"Who is this person?" I asked, peering through the passenger window at a well-kept house as he pulled into the unshovelled driveway.

"He's a demon, I think? Part demon, anyway. His name's Chip. No, it's not his real name, just like Trace isn't mine. No, I don't know what his real name is. No, I won't tell you what mine is. And please, please, do not ask him too many questions or he will boot us out of here so quick we won't have time to stylize our landing."

"Noted." This guy sounded fun.

When Trace turned off the engine, the doors unlocked, and I eased my way into the snow, which came up to mid-calf and tumbled into my open boots.

"I hope Chip has a pair of extra socks I can borrow until these dry off," I mumbled under my breath, but Trace had come around the front of the car and heard me.

"He won't. He'd be horrified if you asked. If he notices you need them, he might give you a pair, but if you try to give them back, he'll set them on fire. To reduce any chances of being tracked."

I nodded. "Right. Yeah. Of course."

We trudged up the walkway, and Trace pressed his thumb over a scanner where the doorbell would have been. A light above the door blinked once, twice, and then a voice called out, "Who the fuck is she?"

Chapter 6
Trace

Thursday, 5:30 a.m.

I BOWED MY head with a groan. I should have left the witch in the car until I'd walked Chip through the mess I'd piled on myself. It would have been better for everyone.

Now I'd have to explain the incredibly stupid thing I'd done while freezing my ass off instead of sitting somewhere warm and comfortable, because there was no way in hell my buddy would let us in before he'd looked up every last member of Alyssa's family to see if she could be trusted.

Despite knowing the answer, I stared into the hidden camera and said, "Come on, man, it's fucking freezing out here. Can we make the introductions inside?"

"And have this strange sweater woman tell all and sundry

what I get up to in here? I don't think so."

"She's with me. Doesn't that get her through the vetting process?"

A scoff pierced the speakers. "You could be here under duress."

I looked at the strange sweater woman in question. At this moment, she appeared anything but threatening with her high-lighted brown hair half out of its ponytail, her eyes bruised with exhaustion, and her arms wrapped around her middle to fend off the chill. Her plaid pyjama bottoms and unlaced boots sold the image of a vulnerable, docile twenty-eight-year-old female.

But it had only taken thirty seconds of trading spells with her to appreciate just how strong a witch lay under that quiet facade.

Maybe Chip had a point.

"All right, Sweater Woman, tell him who you are." I dipped my lips to her ear, catching the whiff of sweet aloe vera where it wafted off her skin, and turned my face from the camera so Chip couldn't read the words as I added, "Don't lie, but don't add details. He'll know the truth before you finish talking anyway, but too much backstory will make his head explode."

She nodded, her eyes wild and the corner of her lip twitching upwards as though she were caught between amused and stunned. I understood all too well. Even after knowing him so many years, it was my usual state of being when dealing with the most paranoid man in the city.

"Um…" Alyssa began, and I cringed. I should have warned her about speech fillers. Chip tended to distrust them, seeing them as stalling tactics for people making up the answer they thought he wanted to hear. "My name is Alyssa Mooney, owner of Mooney's Pub on Somerset?"

"Parents?" came the brusque reply.

"Henry and Mary Mooney?"

"Current address?"

She blinked. "Mine, or…?"

I pressed my lips together and did my best not to laugh. The poor woman. I wished we were here under better circumstances so I didn't feel bad about laughing at her expense.

"Theirs, obviously," Chip said.

"Obviously. Right. Ashton, Ontario? They live with my mom's dad?" She cast me a desperate look, and I nodded my encouragement. We'd get inside a lot faster if she indulged Chip's eccentricities.

"Hmm." Chip sounded unimpressed, which I took as a good sign. If he'd found anything concerning, he would have stopped talking altogether. "Says here you work with a chaos demon. Suggests a person prone to taking risks and not thinking long-term. I'm not sure if you—"

"Excuse me very much," she cut him off, her hands propped on her hips. "What the hell do you think you know about Simon? He's the best partner I could have asked for, and a damn good bartender. On time, innovative, clean. A hell of a lot better at his job than you would be, all hidden behind your cameras and speakers."

I raised an eyebrow and gave the camera a pointed look. Interesting. That was the second time mention of the chaos demon had hit a nerve with her, and this time she'd lashed out at the only person who could offer her a warm meal and safe haven for the morning. Based on that, Chip's character study didn't seem far off.

Were she and this Simon guy sleeping together? Somehow I doubted it. She didn't strike me as that reckless. Sure, I'd known her for all of three hours, but the research I did into my contracts was thorough. I hated leaving anything to chance.

Which was why I'd barricaded a fae duchess in a hotel room and sped across Ottawa in the small hours of the morning to give Alyssa Mooney an opportunity to defend herself.

What the hell was I thinking?

"Right," Chip said. "Off you fuck, then."

Alyssa's eyes widened. "Excuse me? Listen, buster, I have no idea who you are, but if you think you can make snap judgements about people standing on your porch in the snow at five-thirty in the morning based on a few weird questions and a camera, then I'm probably better off without you anyway. Trace, drive me home. I'll take my chances with the duchess."

Still hugging herself against the cold, she turned on her heel and marched through the snow towards the SUV.

Shit. Well done, Chip.

We were off to a great start. Without Chip, we were left with a blessed few options to keep us out of sight until we came up with a game plan.

I didn't have time to shoot the camera a dark glower before Chip called out, "What is this about the duchess?"

Alyssa stopped, turned, looked at me. I shrugged and half turned to the door.

"Dara wants Miss Mooney dead for magic theft and the murder of her general. Miss Mooney denies her involvement. We now have less than a day to prove her innocence before I've dared Dara to find us and get rid of us both."

"For fuck's sake, Wyatt, why didn't you lead with that? You know I live to make life difficult for those fae assholes. Come inside, coffee's on."

The lock on the door clicked, the red light by the camera went out, and I rolled my eyes. He was such a bastard.

Alyssa blinked and staggered forward. "What's the catch?"

I met her gaze. Under the yellow glow of the streetlight, specks of brighter emerald green glinted in her irises, and I had a hard time looking away. "The catch is now we're stuck working with him. I hope you're ready for a whole lot of what the hell."

Chapter 7
Alyssa

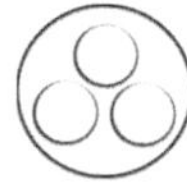

Thursday, 5:40 a.m.

"WHAT THE HELL?"

I stared around what I guessed was once intended as a living room and had been converted into… a command centre? A battle station? The ultimate gaming hub?

Already, from the little I'd learned of Chip standing on his front porch, I doubted the latter, but it was by far the least terrifying option. He looked like he could take over the world from this room.

A wide, curved desk sat in the middle of the beige carpet, with three ultra-wide monitors taking up a chunk of the space. Along the left-hand wall was a series of metal shelving units, each one filled with various technical accoutrements. I wasn't about to try to guess exactly what they were. On the shelves farthest from me, I swore I spotted some serious weaponry tucked among the cables and accessories and made a note to steer clear.

Blackout curtains were drawn tight across the large picture window, even at this hour, and the extra layer of darkness was stifling. My blood screamed for space and light and air, but I shushed it and clung tighter to myself. Our time here was temporary. As my mom always said, I could do anything for a few hours.

Even if they were my last hours before oblivion.

Would oblivion be better than this suffocating room?

Maybe.

The owner of the house sitting in the fancy-pants chair at the desk turned to face me. Thick stubble rolled across his cheeks and under his jawline, disappearing under the collar of his red graphic tee that peered out from a high-collared black zip-up. The T-shirt appeared to have an old-school advertisement for a CB radio printed on it. Sharp brown eyes assessed me from behind a pair of thick black frames perched on a long nose, and I did my best not to cower under that stare.

What was there to be afraid of? I could take this guy. I was choosing not to.

I curled my socked toes into the carpet in what I swore was a subtle attempt to self-soothe and not a gesture of absolute terror.

"So," he said. "Witch."

I blinked. "Yes?"

What was it about this guy's unpleasantness that made me doubt what I knew to be true? I cleared my throat and, with more certainty said, "Long line."

"You could go back to Caligula and I wouldn't care. You try any spells on me, you'll regret it, capisce?"

I opened my mouth to put him in his place with his assumptions about my personality, but a look from Trace made me bite my tongue and offer a nod instead. This whole eggshell-walking thing was going to get real old real fast. I much preferred openness. Honesty. Telling someone to fuck off in the politest, most diplomatic way while wearing a bright smile.

"Right," Chip said, as though the exchange had cleared everything up. "So. Kitchen. What is the situation?"

I wasn't sure at first what to make of the "kitchen" addition until he led us out of the living room into the hi-tech room beside it. Seriously, the Jetsons would have been impressed by this place.

Trace peeled off his peacoat and draped it over a high-backed black dining chair, then headed straight for a black-and-chrome contraption sitting on the counter that, by the delicious aroma emanating from it, contained the coffee Chip had tempted us with.

Much as my mouth watered at the idea of a hot, caffeinated beverage, my brain was just as drawn by the bounty hunter walking in front of me. He wore a dark grey T-shirt over a long-sleeved light grey shirt, and the style choice hugged his muscular frame in ways that made my thoughts short-circuit.

When he pushed his sleeves up to his elbows, revealing a pair of corded forearms, I forced myself to tear my eyes away and focus instead on the coffee maker. How did the machine even work? It looked like some kind of weird space pod.

Trace poured a cup, turned to hand it to me… then pulled it back with a shake of his head.

Excuse-me-what-the-fuck?

I might have said it out loud.

"You don't need caffeine," he said, setting the mug on the counter.

"I most certainly do. Have you seen me?"

"You're about to fall over."

"Exactly my point."

What was he not getting here?

"You need to sleep. How long have you been awake?"

I crossed my arms and hit him with my best glare. "About twenty hours. I was about to go to bed when some asshole abducted me while I was putting out the garbage."

Chip raised an eyebrow in Trace's direction. "Dude."

Trace rolled his eyes and pointed back to the living room.

"There's a couch and a blanket in the back corner. I've slept there myself a few times. It's comfy enough. Use it."

I didn't move and didn't relax my stance. We'd known each other for three hours, most of which he'd spent destroying my life, and he thought he could tell me what to do? More than that, he thought I was going to leave him to tell this stranger all the details of my predicament without my direct oversight? He might have helped me out with Dara, but that didn't mean I trusted him to be on my side.

As though he read my mind, he said, "If we're going to solve this murder, you need to be rested. Even if it's only a few hours. I promise to be objective in whatever we talk about."

Why did he have to be so logical? With a huff, I dropped my arms. "Fine. But be sure to mention how you trashed my pub."

Chip shook his head as I marched out of the kitchen. "Dude."

Alone in the living room, I sought out the aforementioned couch and dropped onto it. It was indeed comfy, and up close it looked clean enough. Bonus.

I pressed my back against the cushions, not so trusting as to turn away from the room, and reached for my magic to drape over me in a basic ward. But as soon as I made contact with my power, a sharp zap jolted me out of my dozy comfort.

What the hell was that?

I reached for it again, slower this time, and as I got closer, I picked up the telltale signs of a counter ward. The son of a bitch had anti-magic spells on his house.

When he said I'd regret casting on him, he wasn't joking. If just summoning my magic had given me a shock, using it in an assault burst would have done me some serious damage.

Which meant I was stuck here, vulnerable to any physical attack by these two strange men in the other room.

Yup. Really conducive to a good night's rest.

I'd just resigned myself to staying awake when sleep slapped me upside the head and dragged me under.

Chapter 8
Trace

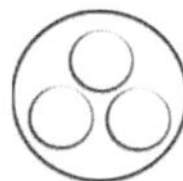

Thursday, 5:45 a.m.

I KEPT MY eyes on my coffee as Alyssa stomped out of the room, trying not to smile at her offended display and avoiding Chip's pointed look.

Damn that man could stare. For someone who interacted in person maybe three times a year, he'd perfected his soul-stripping glower that made you feel like your insides were exposed. I found it wasn't nearly as effective if I didn't look back. It flayed me only to the muscle instead of to the bone.

"So?" Chip demanded when enough time had passed and I hadn't offered anything except to compliment his coffee selection.

I glanced towards the living room, but Alyssa was out of

sight on the couch. Not that it mattered. She was welcome to hear anything I said. I'd promised to be objective, and I'd meant it.

"Dara says she has video evidence of Alyssa killing a fae general."

Chip waved his hand in the air as though shooing away a bad smell. "I don't care about any of that shit. What I want to know is why you got involved."

I held up my hand to shut him up. It was one thing for Alyssa to hear her own issues talked about, but mine were a whole other story. To be sure we wouldn't be overheard, I poked my head around the corner and found Alyssa already dead asleep, her brow smooth, her breathing even, her hands curled between her thighs as though she were trying to warm them. Keeping my steps light, I crossed the room, grabbed the throw blanket from the back of the couch and draped it over her.

Chip would no doubt judge the hell out of me for the simple gesture, but after the night that woman had suffered, most of it by my hand, I couldn't help myself. She deserved that small comfort at least.

Confident now that anything I said would be for Chip's ears alone, I returned to the kitchen to discover his stare had deepened. Now I felt it straight to my marrow. Judgy fucker.

"She says she didn't do it," I said, answering his question.

"So has every other mark you've ever picked up. You're not the type to be distracted by a nice rack, so what the fuck, man?"

What was it with people thinking I'd lost my senses over breasts?

Sure, the image of Alyssa Mooney standing confidently in the doorway of her pub clad only in jeans and a tattered pink bra had been seared into my memory, but that was irrelevant. I had my options if I wanted to fondle someone, and my heart had been a no-go zone for over a decade. My reasons were personal and had nothing to do with her.

"She says she didn't do it." As though the repetition would satisfy the nosiest man I knew.

Yet the way I said it must have set something off in his brain because a dawning awareness filled his eyes. "Ah. All right, so you know why you're helping her. Does she?"

"Does she know I spent three years of my life trying to prove my innocence against accusations of spirit theft? No, I neglected to mention that part of my history."

"So what you're telling me is you're totally biased and running head first into a potential hurricane of awful."

"Yeah. Pretty much."

Chip let out an exaggerated sigh and bowed his head. I downed the rest of my coffee.

What did it matter? What was done was done. I'd drawn my line in the sand with Dara, and now we had less than twenty-four hours to prove my gut right or figure out how to extricate myself from a shared death sentence.

Cool.

That was fine.

Chapter 9
Alyssa

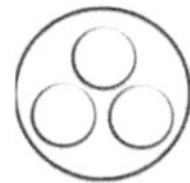

Thursday, 6:30 a.m.

VOICES WOKE ME up.

I would have sworn I'd only gone down for a few minutes, but the first hint of dawn trickled into the room around the blackout curtains, splashing the walls with the sort of cold purple light that made you want to hunker down under the blankets and appreciate how warm your toes were.

Except the blanket draped over me—the blanket I didn't remember draping—was a microfibre throw instead of my cotton duvet, and instead of my memory foam mattress under my cheek, there was a soft couch that had nearly swallowed me under the cushions.

As the details of my day from hell came back to me, I

homed in on the conversation happening in the other room.

"…never gone up against someone with power like hers. Not the strongest witch I've faced, but she's subtle. Graceful. Like one of those Olympic gymnasts with the ribbon."

"The Olympics are a scam."

"Don't care, not my point. I just mean she's interesting."

My brain tickled as sleepiness fell away, and my attention hooked more firmly on what they were saying.

"Don't do it."

"Do what?"

"Get attached. You've already taken a step towards Crazy Town by throwing Dara off, and now you're sniffing around after an unknown witch? The Trace I know and love has more sense."

I hoped so.

"I'm not sniffing. She's a mark, that's all, and I find it good practice to understand my enemy."

His enemy? So much for being in this together.

"I threw Dara off for her own sake. She was making a mistake, and if she killed off Mooney only for it to turn out someone else did it—"

"She wouldn't bat an eyelash. She's fae royalty. The life of some human witch would not make her quake in her designer boots."

"Fine, maybe not, but it would bother me. Especially if the

general's death isn't a one-off. A murder being personal and a one-time thing, I might believe, but magic theft? How often do you hear of anyone being satisfied with a single steal?"

"And you're sure Cheers over there isn't your guy?"

I was all ears, my body tense, frozen, ready to run depending on Trace's answer. Which was longer in coming than I would have liked.

"I don't know for sure—"

"Trace," Chip groaned. "Man, what are you doing to me?"

"I don't know for sure," he repeated more forcefully, "but her magic doesn't feel fae."

"Oh, well, if it doesn't *feel* fae."

"Why steal it only to hide it? If she even could. Viviane was strong."

"You'd better hope you're right, because I'm not saving your ass if you get into trouble again."

"Yes, you will. Of course you will. You said it yourself—you love me."

"Yeah, yeah, yeah. So what's the plan?"

Since this seemed like a good time to get up and join the conversation, I fought my desire to remain a heap of fatigue and warmth on the couch and sat up.

My head felt battered by the conversation I'd overheard—the price of eavesdropping, I suppose—and I found myself dawdling over the blanket, double-checking the evenness of my corners and the alignment of my fancy diagonal drape over the back of the couch.

Nothing Trace said had come as a surprise, but it certainly motivated me to find answers. The sooner we found Vivi's killer, however we were going to do that, the sooner I could get back to my pub, my bartender, and my life.

When I was satisfied with the blanket, I went into the kitchen. The two men looked my way and went quiet.

"Can I have that coffee now?" I asked.

Chip, ever the hospitable host, said nothing, but Trace gestured to the coffee machine in an invitation for me to help myself. I crossed the room to the snazzy coffee maker, praying there was still caffeine lurking at the bottom. My anxiety was likely to spin off the rails with a single sip, but I needed to be awake for whatever came next. Luck was with me for half a cup, which I poured into a black mug sitting with two others next to the machine. The brew was cold, but I didn't care.

"So?" I asked after I took a sip, hiding a cringe at the bitter strength. "What'd I miss?"

"We were just talking next steps." Trace pushed a bowl of fruit my way, and I grabbed a banana of appropriate ripeness to take the edge off my sudden hunger. "Dara mentioned a video, so Chip will help us track it down."

I almost made the silly mistake of asking "How?" before I remembered the setup in the other room. Trace had brought us here for a reason, and that reason obviously wasn't coddling and reassurance. Chip didn't seem like he had it in him to be anything other than surly or sarcastic.

Instead of asking questions, I settled on "Cool. A good start until Madi gets back to me."

"Madi?" Chip asked.

Trace didn't raise his gaze from the apple he plucked from the bowl. "Mooney's contact in SMOAC."

Chip snorted. "Fucking Smokers. Anything they can do for you, I can do without the government oversight. You think they want to help you out, but as soon as you bring them into this, you're on record, and once you're on it, they never lose track of you. So if you expect one of them—"

He carried on with his rant as Trace met my eye over a bite of his apple. Amusement glinted in his violet gaze, and I hid my face behind the giant mug of coffee. If Chip was this bad now, how much worse would he get when Madison returned my call?

"We all know you out-resource the government in every important way," Trace interrupted him, "so why don't we start now? With luck, we won't need the feds to poke their noses in."

Chip grunted. "I'll get set up."

"We'll be there in a second. I'm going to start another pot of coffee. Want a cup?"

"Do you even have to ask?"

Chip left, and I crossed the kitchen to pour my sludge

down the sink. If fresh coffee was on the menu, I wasn't going to torture myself.

"Bit of a caffeine addict, is he?" I asked.

"Man lives off coffee and fresh fruit. It's a weird combination, I know, but he seems to get by. You want a top-up?"

"I'll take anything that won't skim the lining off my stomach."

As he poked around the coffee contraption, I snuck a look in the fridge and was relieved to find a variety of foodstuffs within. Trace had been joking. I didn't know why that made me feel less uncomfortable.

Heat filled my cheeks when I closed the door and caught him grinning at me.

"Checking for milk," I mumbled.

As soon as the coffee was ready, we brought our mugs into the living room. Trace set Chip's on the desk and had barely stepped away when Chip let out a triumphant "Ha!"

He leaned back in his chair and crossed his arms, making space around his monitor for Trace and me to step closer.

"First off, someone needs to tell Dara's people their security sucks. When I crack a system, I prefer it to be a challenge. Second… well, I guess we know why she's after you, don't we, Cheers?"

He could have kept talking for an hour, and I still wouldn't have known what to say. I sensed Trace's eyes on me and felt

Chip's suspicion like a poking stick in my side. In the moment, I even doubted myself.

On the monitor, in black and white, a woman was leaving Vivi's house. The time stamp matched the time of the murder, and the face was one hundred per cent mine.

Chapter 10
Alyssa

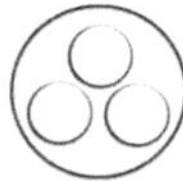

Thursday, 6:45 a.m.

HEAT POURED FROM the top of my head, followed by a chill that left me shivering. I closed in, folding my arms around myself, wishing Simon were here to reassure me, wishing I had some explanation, wishing I were a million miles away from this video, these people, this disaster.

"I-I don't understand," I said, and Trace caught my arm as my legs wobbled, steadying me. "I wasn't there. I swear I wasn't there. But that-that's me, right? How can that be me?"

"Mooney."

I pressed my empty hand against my forehead. "Oh goddess, is this, like, some body snatcher thing? Was I possessed? Mind controlled? Did I kill my friend and have no idea I did it and now they're going to execute me for it?"

"Can you take out her batteries or something?" Chip asked Trace.

"That's my face," I said. "You watch yourself walk away from a murder and see how well you take it."

I was shaking so badly now that my coffee sloshed over my fingers and dripped onto the floor, and Trace plucked the mug from my hand.

"First let's put this out of reach of the computers, or Chip will steal my mark out from under me and earn the bonus."

"Fuckin' A."

Trace set the mug on the side table by the couch, then came back and rested his warm, solid hands on my shoulders. "Next we're going to breathe."

He sucked in a breath and let it out slowly, meeting my gaze to get me to mirror him, and out of habit, I did. Air filled my oxygen-deprived cells, and as my panic quelled, I found myself staring into his striking pair of eyes. They weren't as wholly violet as I'd originally thought in the dim light of the pub. Streaks of his silver magic cut through the iris, creating a swirl of colour that stole my breath even as I worked to reclaim it.

"There. You with us?"

It took a moment for his words to worm their way through my distraction, but once they did, I managed a nod.

He let go of my arms, and although my breathing and heart

rate were back to normal, I reeled when he broke eye contact, having fallen so deeply into his stare.

I blinked a few times and turned back to my face on the monitor. Panic nudged me again, but I took another breath to shove it aside and stepped closer to see over Chip's shoulder. He shot me a nasty look when my elbow deigned to brush his arm, so I created more space between us but didn't take my eyes off the screen. He huffed and returned his attention to the video.

"Now that you've finished freaking out, let's take a closer look at what we're dealing with."

He clicked a bunch of things on the screen, hit some buttons on the keyboard, zoomed in, zoomed out, brought up some code, created a wormhole, launched a space shuttle, and solved a game of Solitaire as far as I could tell, but in the end, a few minutes later, the top half of my face took up most of the screen and he sat back with another satisfied "Ha."

Trace rested his hand on the desk and leaned forward, and I marvelled at his courage in touching The Setup. His questioning expression morphed into something sterner. Angrier. The silver in his eyes danced with the violet, and he clenched his hand into a fist.

"What am I missing?" I asked, squinting to get a better look.

As Chip had centred the image around my eyes, I started

there, specifically at the reflected light in the pupil that made them appear to be glowing. Too much so to have been caused by anything natural.

"What is that? I look like something out of a bad horror movie."

"That's because it's not you," Trace said. "It's a shapeshifter, and I can guess who it is."

"Yup." Chip crossed his arms. "Only one son of a bitch is twisted enough to take on a job like that." He threw me a sideways glance. "Someone must have gotten hold of your DNA, Cheers. I thought you witches knew better than to leave stuff like hair and fingernails lying around."

I grimaced. "My apartment wards haven't been broken, so they must have grabbed something from the pub. I'm too all over the place to think about scrubbing every used glass. That changes as of now." I smacked my palm on the desk. "Son of a bitch."

"Hey, hey, hey!"

I stuffed my hands in my sleeves with a huff. "Sorry, but fuck. You're telling me this shapeshifter stole my spit and wore my face to kill Vivi?"

"I doubt they did the actual killing," Trace said. "Not their style. But confusing the issue by throwing suspicion on someone else? Absolutely. They'll cause any kind of mischief for a hefty payday."

I shoved my finger towards the screen. "This is more than throwing suspicion or causing mischief. They pinned a target to my back."

Trace nodded. "That's why we're going to talk to them."

I started. "We're what?"

"Someone hired them to be there, at that time, with your face. That means they would have stolen your DNA ahead of time, which means this crime and the killer's escape route— you—were planned well in advance."

My mouth went dry and my vision swam again, but I grabbed the edge of the desk to hold myself up. "But... shouldn't we wait for my contact to get back to me? Shouldn't we take this to the authorities?"

Chip snorted. "That is your face on camera. You might luck out that they believe someone else is wearing it, but if Dara puts the pressure on and insists it's you, the Smokers won't waste resources to prove otherwise. Someone put effort into pinning this murder on you. Not by chance, not on a whim. You have enemies. Powerful ones. Who do you think the government will side with?"

I wanted to ignore his warning. Madison would believe me, and she would know what to do. But it was seven o'clock in the morning. She wouldn't get my message for at least another hour, and every second that passed brought me closer to Dara tracking us down.

So either I put some extra faith in Trace's ability to see our way out, or I waited and prayed.

I shuddered.

"Fine," I said. "Let's go talk to the shapeshifter."

Chapter 11
Alyssa

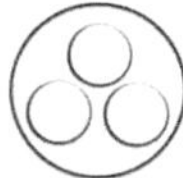

Thursday, 7:00 a.m.

As I PULLED on my boots, actually taking time to tie up my laces now that my socks were in a relative state of dryness, Chip asked for my phone number.

"So I can prep communication for you," he explained before I could worry his brusqueness had been some kind of twisted flirtation.

I gave it to him, and he turned his back on me as though I'd blinked out of existence.

"I've texted you their last known address," he said to Trace, who was pulling on his coat. "They've been moving around a lot lately, which isn't suspicious at all."

"Thanks, as always. I'll keep you posted." Trace flipped up

his collar and flicked his hair out of his eyes. "Ready, Mooney?"

I looked down at myself and wished I had something other than pyjama pants to wear. If I was about to interrogate the person who'd been hired to set me up, I'd feel a lot more intimidating without the flannel. But having met Chip, there was no way in hell I'd ask if he had any women's jeans lying around, so I shrugged and started for the door.

As soon as we stepped onto the porch, the security system beeped and the ker-thunk of a heavy lock rattled behind us, the whole process as welcoming as when we'd arrived.

The snow had stopped, and the frozen light of morning touched the sky, hardly enough to brighten the drifts of snow that had swept across the driveway over the past few hours.

We trudged to Trace's SUV, and I slunk into the passenger seat, already bummed by the cold, the snow, and my barely slaked exhaustion.

Trace blasted the heat and gave the engine a minute to warm up while he climbed out and, using brush and magic, cleared the snow off the car. Once the SUV was road-worthy and the interior was as toasty as a perfect summer's day, he backed away from the house and navigated through the residential streets towards the highway.

Sleep tugged at my eyelids as the warm air washed over me. I gave myself a shake and asked, "Exactly what kind of shapeshifter are we dealing with here?"

"They're a facestealer."

I blanched. "That sounds friendly."

His white teeth flashed in a smile. "Their kind propagated in Germany in the 1600s and helped drive the witch hunts over there. German hunters called them mirror demons, able to take on the face and form of any creature, but if they are demons, they're low on the hierarchy. They don't actually steal, obviously. And like all creatures, they're not all nasty little bastards, either. Most only shift to blend into mundane society. Shiny, though… they're a greedy son of a bitch."

I snorted. "Shiny?"

He smirked. "They never gave me a name, so it's what I call them. Mostly to piss them off. It's the eyes. They creep me the fuck out. You'll see."

"So you've had dealings with this shapeshifter before?"

"Once or twice." His jaw flexed. "Never on a murder case, and never—unfortunately—as a mark. I wish I had. Then maybe you wouldn't be in this mess."

My insides warmed, and I was about to thank him for the sentiment until he crushed it by adding, "Unless whoever hired them found another way to drag you into it, which seems likely considering the trouble they've gone through."

I leaned my head back and stared out the window at the snowbanks lining the on-ramp as we merged onto the 417. Who would hate me this much? My life was pretty insular. I had my family and my pub. The occasional night out with friends, but those were usually tame. Yet for whatever reason, someone wanted me dead.

The sun was peering over the horizon now, giving a cheerful "Good morning!" as it peeked out from under the layers of heavy grey cloud, soon, no doubt, to be hidden for the rest of the day. Because of course it couldn't be nice out. I was on the run for my life in my PJs without a coat in the middle of February with a series of snowstorms on my ass.

What god did I kick in the balls without realizing it?

We drove across the city, past the exit that would have taken me either home or to work, and exited off Montreal Road. Traffic was picking up as the early risers headed to the office, but the sidewalks were empty except for a few snowploughs taking their first stab at the waist-high drifts.

A few minutes later, Trace pulled into the visitor parking of a high-rise apartment building and turned off the engine. I heaved a sigh at the idea of stepping back into the cold when I had just warmed up, but the unpleasantness was tempered by the thought of staring down the shapeshifter who had impersonated me. They knew why I was in trouble. They knew who wanted me dead. My need to get that information was motivation enough to keep me warm against the stiffest wind.

Trace stuffed his hands in his pockets as we crossed the parking lot towards the front door, but my only option was to shove my hands under my armpits like the classy dame I was.

"When we get in there," he said as he held the door to the vestibule open for me, "I want you to summon your magic. Make as big a show as you can. Hold it steady but flaunt your power. Shiny doesn't have much magic of their own, so they're not likely to take the offensive, but don't be fooled by the submissiveness. One slip, and they'll tear your throat out."

My heart stuttered and, despite the chill, my palms grew sweaty. "I thought you said you'd never heard of them murdering anyone."

"Not in cold blood, no. Self-defence is a whole other story."

I swallowed the ball in my throat. "Great."

He waved his hand over the locked interior door as we entered the building, and his silver magic crept through the cracks until the mechanism clicked. We crossed the lobby, got into the elevator, and rode in silence to the tenth floor. Trace led the way down the hallway and stopped in front of number 1006.

It looked the same as any other door along the way, but the hair on the back of my neck stood on end, and my stomach coiled in on itself. Looking closer, I caught a hint of grey, oozy magic sliding across the surface. This facestealer might not have a lot of power, but the magic they did have did not sit well with mine. I suspected they didn't get many surprise visitors, their wards more than enough to keep most unwanted folks away. Including door-to-door salespeople and nosy neighbours. I made a note to reassess my own wards when I got home. If I got home.

Trace waved for me to stand out of view, and I leaned my shoulder against the wall beside the door. He rapped politely, returned his hands to his pockets as though he were a casual passerby, and waited for someone to answer.

Which, to my surprise, they did less than a minute later.

"Trace Wyatt, what an unexpected pleasure," a slippery voice greeted. Their tone slid through my ears, down my neck, and settled uncomfortably at the base of my spine, urging me to run or fight or, at the very least, scream and pee my pants. Fortunately, I avoided doing the latter as the lack of pants to change into would have made the next few hours very awkward.

"How goes, Shiny?"

A faint hiss in response. "Nothing to complain about now that you're here. Won't you come in? To what do I owe the joy of your company? A new case you need my help with?"

"Got it in one," Trace said as he stepped forward to push Shiny further inside. "I believe you know my friend Miss Mooney? She has a few questions for you."

I took my cue and stepped into the doorway. As Trace had recommended, I summoned my magic and swept it around me, making it rise and loom over my head like a hooded cobra, ready to strike should this creature make a single wrong move.

Sensing it, Shiny's bright eyes widened, and they stumbled backwards into their cluttered living room. "I see."

"Do you?" Trace asked, following them. I trailed close behind him and shut the door, closing the three of us into the dark space.

Were they allergic to the sun? They could have given Chip a run for his money with the effort they'd put into blocking every last ray of natural light with what looked like strips of black electrical tape stuck to every single window across the living room. Unlike Chip's place, there were no table lamps to cut through the dimness, so all we had to work with was the smidge of light that snuck through the spots where the tape had begun to curl.

Given the way the shapeshifter's eyes reacted to the camera in that video, I guessed their light sensitivity was up there with the vampires'. Would they burn the same way? Shrivel up? A not-small part of me wanted to dash to the window, tear off the tape, and find out, but until we learned whether they were willing to play ball with us and answer some questions, I didn't want to be a bad house guest and risk getting ejected before Trace had a chance to begin.

From what I could make out of the rest of the place, every available surface was covered in cardboard boxes and plastic bins, each one marked with black marker, though I couldn't make out what the labels said.

More impressive than the apartment was the shapeshifter. They stood almost as tall as Trace, their build slim and wiry, their limbs slightly too long to pass for human. Other than the bright eyes, which even off camera carried an unnatural green sheen, their nose, cheeks, and chin were as stretched as the rest of them. Their skin, the tone unclear in the shadows, glimmered with a faint glossiness, as though they'd stepped out of the shower and hadn't had time to dry off, and I wondered if they'd be slimy to the touch. Unlike the sunlight question, I had no desire to find out.

"You recognize Alyssa, I'm sure," Trace said when Shiny didn't add anything to their initial response.

"I… um… can't say I've ever…"

Trace pulled a sheet of paper out of his pocket and slammed it on the crowded kitchen table. It was a print-out of the video still. "You can see this all right, can't you? Looks like her, but that's you."

Shiny blinked, the glow in their eyes vanishing and reappearing in a way that sent unease slithering through my insides.

"I'm flattered you think—"

Trace closed the distance between him and Shiny, and I realized I'd been mistaken about their heights. He had at least two inches on Shiny, and he loomed in a way that took advantage of every centimetre. I helped him out by feeding into my magic, making it grow a little taller and wrap around me more tightly, ready to be unleashed.

Shiny's nervous gaze darted my way, then leapt back to meet Trace's, looking for all the world as though they were about to burst into tears if pushed any harder.

I didn't need Trace's warning to be on my guard. I'd watched enough abusive drunks try to get past me for another drink or their confiscated keys not to see through the facestealer's act. Shiny was in full control of their reaction, cowering because they thought it would make us leave faster. Too bad for them I had no intention of walking out of here without a name.

"Who paid the bill, Shiny?"

"I'm afraid you're mistaken, Mr. Wyatt. This isn't me. Perhaps you should ask your friend where she got her contacts. They're good quality."

"Who gave you her DNA?" Trace asked, ignoring the commentary.

"No one. I have no DNA for Miss Mooney."

"Bullshit. Either you tell me who, or I'm going to place a call to SMOAC and get you hauled in for hoarding body parts. Is that what you want, Shiny? For our truce to end like this?"

They looked at me again, and I dropped my arms into a more relaxed position. Let them believe I was ready to listen and open to negotiation. We were here on a mission of good faith. If they gave us what we wanted, they could return to their strange little life of gathering... body parts? Had I heard that correctly?

The boxes and bins took on a more sinister vibe, and I did not want to know about that chemical smell.

Apparently, however, my shift in position had the opposite effect, because instead of standing down and graciously telling us what we wanted to know, they bolted. That sickly grey magic thrust Trace into the table beside him, and then Shiny was on me, their fingers brushing my hand as they shoved me out of the way to get to the door.

For the record: their skin was just as slimy as it appeared and nothing I ever wanted to come into contact with again.

Before they could grab the handle, I threw out my waiting magic and wrapped it around them, forcing them back into the room as they screamed and scrabbled at the air in a vain attempt to escape.

Trace recovered from his stumble, closed the distance between them, and slammed Shiny against the wall, his large hand splayed across the shapeshifter's chest. His silver magic wound through my purple to tighten the bindings around them, and I watched in fascination at the way our two powers played with each other, weaving tightly together, leaving no space for anything to get through.

I pulled my attention back to Shiny and crossed my arms again. Negotiating Alyssa was done.

"Talk," Trace said, ignoring Shiny's wriggling.

"You know I can't give you a name. It goes against the confidentiality agreement I sign with every client."

"You put this woman up for a murder she didn't commit. Do you want me to call the duchess and tell her you were the one who killed her general?"

Shiny's eyes widened, and their attempts to get free of Trace's hold doubled. I felt the pressure of their magic against ours, watched the panic in their eyes when they realized they'd been blocked, and this time I picked up a hint of genuine fear in their gaze. The fight seemed to seep out of them as they sagged against the wall, but Trace was smart enough not to loosen his grip. "I'd rather you didn't. I had nothing to do with the murder. I was told to show up at that hour in that body, go up the stairs, pretend to come out of that house and come back down, making sure I was visible to the cameras. I never went inside."

"Good story. I'll believe it more if you tell me who sent you there."

"You'll put me out of business."

"Your business is garbage. I'm surprised you haven't had your ass hauled in ages ago. I can only assume you have some big names in your pocket for all the work you do, but I have evidence against you. You know I do. Evidence you can't brush off like you could this video. So either work with me, or it's so long freedom."

Their fear vanished under a grotesque scowl that made me tighten my hold on my magic. "Very well, but the information I have won't make you happy. Let me go, and I'll get you what you want."

Trace narrowed his eyes, then released them. I stepped away to avoid the possibility of any physical contact and slowly drew my magic back as Shiny stomped into the kitchen.

"They gave no names," they said. "It was a demon. Strong. Persuasive. He gave me this card and told me to call him if I wanted the job. As it happened, I accepted on the spot so never needed to use the phone number. But if you want to see where it takes you, be my guest."

Trace took the card and passed it to me without taking his eyes off the shapeshifter. I stared at the number and the black-and-white logo in the corner of a crescent moon surrounded by raindrops, but neither rang any bells.

"Thanks for your time," he said. "Now, I strongly recommend you ditch whatever DNA of hers you have left over. And if this person calls you again, you tell them your schedule is full. If I have to come back here for the same reason, you won't be chatting with my good side."

His eyes took on a silver glow that rivalled Shiny's, and the facestealer nodded in understanding.

Trace backed away, stretching out his arm to include me in our exodus, and didn't turn his back until we were close to the door.

"Mr. Wyatt?" Shiny called as I stepped into the hallway. Still deep enough in shadow that most of their features were obscured, the shapeshifter's strange face widened with a grin that sent frozen tendrils snaking through my veins. "Tread carefully. The owner of that card is not a person you want to mess with. If you try to get in his way, prepare for severe retaliation. I say this out of friendship."

The door slammed behind us as though a sharp wind had blown through the apartment, and we were left in the hallway with Shiny's warning ringing in our ears.

Chapter 12
Trace

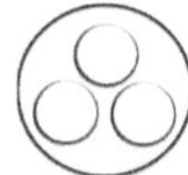

Thursday, 7:45 a.m.

I STARTED BACK to the car, not bothering to check if Alyssa followed me. My thoughts were buzzing too loudly with everything Shiny had said—and more with what they hadn't said. They were afraid. Afraid of having outed the person who'd hired them. Afraid the retaliation they mentioned would turn around and bite them in the ass.

Who the hell were we dealing with?

"Can I see the card?" I asked once we got into the car.

Alyssa handed it over, and I ran my thumb over the logo in the corner. It was familiar, though for the life of me, I couldn't place it. "Chip should be able to track this down." I snapped a photo with my phone and texted it over. "Whoever this person is, they were naive enough to leave a business card, so they shouldn't be that difficult to find."

"Naive or confident," Alyssa said with a shiver. "Maybe they don't care if we identify them."

I shifted in my seat to look at her and, without thinking about it, rested my hand over hers. Her fingers were frozen, but her magic tingled against my palm. Mine responded, lacing through hers, twining together, the same way they had in Shiny's apartment. The sensation was unnerving, out of my control. It made my heart rate kick up a notch and my breath catch in my lungs. I wanted to lean into it, lose myself for a moment, but that would be a bad idea. I pulled away from her touch. She slid her hand into her lap, and I turned up the heat, as though that was why I'd let her go.

"We'll figure this out, and they won't get away with it," I said.

I knew I shouldn't care so much. I didn't know this woman beyond what I'd dug up about her during my research, which, given her quiet life, wasn't much. She'd started a healing practice in her late teens that had been gaining traction until, for whatever reason, she'd given it up and taken over Mooney's Pub, though rumour suggested she maintained an off-the-books clinic from her office. The pub was doing well, and the one time I'd gone there for a pint, I'd been impressed by the quality of the craft beer, the friendliness of the staff, and the smile of the owner. From what I'd learned of her in the past few hours, she was the sort of woman who combined strength with grace, wit with caution, sass with compassion.

For all I knew, beneath that business-focused mind and doe-eyed facade lurked a monster, but despite that, I couldn't drop this until I knew for sure.

Flashes of my own brush with false accusations swept over me. Three years running from SMOAC and the Alberta Witches' Council, doing everything I could to prove I wasn't the one who'd stolen that magic, those souls. No one had believed me, just like Alyssa had few people who believed her. Not the people who mattered, anyway. The people who could end this chase long enough to find out the truth.

I thought of how vulnerable she'd looked sleeping on Chip's couch. How I hadn't been able to help pulling the blanket over her even though she was a grown woman who could have done it herself.

Ever since I'd launched myself into her life, I couldn't stop feeling guilty that if not for me, she'd probably be at home asleep right now—which was ridiculous because if Dara hadn't hired me, she would have hired someone else. Someone who might not have cared that everything about Alyssa Mooney screamed honest. Innocent.

With anyone else, she might already be dead, and the thought dropped a rock in my gut.

"So," she said, leaning back in her seat. "Where to next? Are we just going to sit here until Chip gets back to us?"

I looked around the parking lot. Although she was joking, it wasn't a horrible plan. We were out in the open, yes, but no one would be able to sneak up on us here. We had heat, comfortable seats… and no leg room, no coffee, and no distraction from each other's company.

It turned out waiting was a non-issue. I'd barely had time to think of alternatives before my phone rang. The screen read *Private Number*, but there was only one person it could be given the timing.

"I'm going to guess you recognize the logo?" I greeted Chip.

"I do, and you should too. Remember a few months back, you had the mark who was wanted for assaulting those women outside the club."

My head swam as the blood rushed out of it and suddenly the car felt too warm. Not wanting Alyssa to get uncomfortable if I turned off the heat—or have her get curious about that job, which had been a nasty business with a rogue vampire—I stepped out of the car and paced back and forth alongside it.

"You're saying the card is from the club?"

"Club Crescent," Chip confirmed. "Ottawa's darkest secret."

I scrubbed my hand across my jaw and did another lap

back and forth. Memories of my few visits to that dungeon-esque social scene, which I'd long believed I'd buried for good, rose from the pits in my mind. Bass thumping, lights strobing, drinks flowing. Crescent was the go-to place for suckers of the blood and soul variety, their willing victims eagerly awaiting them in the dim light of the underground space. It was a realm of decadence, desire, and—often—death.

As in all things, the vampires governed their own kind with strict adherence to their rules, but the incubi, succubi, and other demons who frequented the club were less finicky about guidelines, no matter how closely SMOAC monitored them.

Someone who worked there was after Alyssa?

"Any connection between Mooney and the club?" I asked, knowing Chip would have already looked it up. "Who's running that place now? Still Delvin Swain?"

I caught sight of Alyssa through the windshield, curled up on the passenger seat in her sweater and plaid pyjamas, her power so intense it buzzed over my tongue like strong coffee. I couldn't picture her in that hedonistic lair.

But what did I know? I'd met her five hours ago.

"The one and only son of a bitch, but nah, nothing I found," Chip said, and I ignored the relief that slid down my spine. "Not with her directly, anyway. Seems like Delvin's been poking around her pub, though. She has some prime real estate. Think he's looking to expand?"

Was that the motivation? If so, it seemed easy enough to find out.

But what did the demon's reasons matter when Delvin had more money than Croesus and the contacts to brush off whatever trouble he found himself in?

"There's something else," Chip said, and I stilled at the uncertainty in his voice. "Can she hear me?"

To be sure, I walked to the back of the car and leaned against it, propping my boot on the curb. "No."

A deep breath, a sharp exhale. "There's been another murder. Another fae. Another magic theft. A car was caught leaving the scene."

I knew what was coming, but I still cringed when Chip added, "The car is licenced to one Alyssa Mooney. The Smokers are after her now, man. But, hey, at least you know for sure she didn't do it." He paused to let that sink in. "I hope you find what you're looking for fast, or else I don't think she'll find her way out of this."

Chapter 13
Alyssa

Thursday, 8:00 a.m.

I JERKED OUT of my doze when Trace climbed back into the car. He sagged in his seat as though the weight of the world had dropped onto his shoulders and closed the door with a hefty tug.

"Everything good, then?" I asked, needing him to tell me the bad news first, assuming there was any good to be shared.

"Yeah, not so much." He put the car in drive and pulled out of the parking spot.

I looked at the melting snow on my boots, at the plough turning into the lot, at the light reflecting off the windows of the apartment building. Anything to distract myself from the rising apprehension filling the car, squeezing my lungs and making any speech impossible until the bubble popped.

"There's been another murder," he said.

Pop.

It was like a punch to the kidney. With very sharp, pointy knuckles that pierced my flesh and nailed me right in the innards.

I rolled down my window so I wouldn't vomit all over the car.

"Who?"

"Chip is looking into it. So far we know it's another fae, and that your car was involved."

Motherfu— "Goddammit!" I slammed my fist on the windowsill and buried my head in my hands. "What the actual fuck? I own a fucking pub, Trace. I serve people alcohol. Everyone should love me."

"And I'm sure they do." He sounded so infuriatingly in control of himself that I would have smacked him if he wasn't steering the vehicle. "But out there, somewhere, someone has it in for you. Fortunately, we're one step closer to finding out who it is."

My eyes widened. "Wha—The card. Chip recognized the logo?"

Trace nodded. "Have you ever heard of Club Crescent?"

Goosebumps bubbled on my arms. "Only rumour. Dark, twisted rumour."

He couldn't be suggesting what it sounded like.

"It's real."

He was. Wonderful.

"We're talking vampires and demons and weird sex stuff?" I asked.

Trace bit down on the inside of his cheek, and I swore he was trying to hide a smile. Whatever. He could think this was funny if he wanted, but I didn't want my name mixed up with anything so nasty. People were entitled to do whatever they chose with their lives—or unlives—but they could leave me out of it.

"Chip's theory is that the owner has their eye on Mooney's as prime real estate. Has anyone approached you lately about buying you out?"

"Of course. The pub's doing really well, so at least once a month we get someone nosing around, making offers. Only one or two regulars, and they haven't been pushy about it. You'd think if they were interested enough to jump to framing me for murder, they would have come off a bit more aggressive in person, don't you?"

"Maybe. I guess it depends on who we're dealing with. Any other associations you can think of?"

"Until two minutes ago, I didn't know the place actually existed, so no."

"Maybe you'll get a better idea once you see it in action."

My brain short-circuited. "You mean… go? To the club?"

The corner of his mouth curled upwards, but although a touch of amusement reached his eyes, it was mixed with grim determination. "Yes, that's what I'm suggesting."

"But—" I didn't want to go to some underground demonic sex club first thing in the morning. Hell, I didn't want to go last thing in the evening either. Not so much because I was afraid of what would happen to me. No, I was more terrified my brain would see things it would never be able to unsee.

Or worse, I'd wind up enthralled.

Consent was a critical aspect of sucker-human relations; acting without it meant being thrown to the SMOAC courts, and if the club had been around as long as the rumours suggested, they wouldn't want to risk their standing. But while consent was essential, under the intensity of an incubus's stare, giving it could often come as a surprise to the consenter. Or so I'd heard.

"Isn't it a bit… late?" I asked, gesturing to the clock, grasping at any excuse to skip this particular aspect of our investigation. If we could call it that. So far it had been more "random stumbling around in the dark that led to more questions than answers."

"The vampires will be gone, sure, but there are other demons who like to stay around a bit longer. Besides, I don't think we're looking for customers or staff. We're looking for management. Someone will be there."

A lump lodged in my throat. This really wasn't what I'd had in mind when Trace had whisked me out of Dara's hotel room. I'd imagined computer work. Phone calls. The odd knock at the door. The encounter with Shiny was far more in line with my expectations.

Demon sex club?

Not so much.

Trace was right, though. If the person who'd hired Shiny worked at the club, it made sense to go and find out who it was. Maybe I'd recognize their face when I saw them. Maybe the missing pieces of the puzzle of who had it out for me would fall into place.

So, fine. I would suck it up and roll with it.

Who knew? Maybe it would give me some ideas for the pub. A new aesthetic for Theme Night: Whips and Chains.

I looked down at myself and tugged on the sleeves of Simon's sweater. "Think they'll let me through the door in my pyjamas?"

Trace's mouth opened, then shut, and his jaw flexed.

"I don't suppose I could go home and change…"

He shot me a look that suggested I'd left my brains somewhere along the 417, but that only succeeded in pissing me off.

"Hey, listen, Mr. Bounty Hunter with all the connections—I've just got me, okay? I have an apartment in a house

I own, which is where I keep my stuff, and the pub. That's it. So don't look at me like I'm supposed to pull a closet out of my ass with all the accessories I need to fit in at a fetish bar, all right?"

"Mooney—"

"And stop fucking calling me Mooney, *Wyatt*. I have a name. It's Alyssa. Use it. If you have some great idea of where we can go to get me dressed, great. No doubt you have some Kinky Barbie buddy of yours we can turn to in a pinch, or—"

His ringing cellphone interrupted my raving. He pulled it out of his pocket, glanced at the screen, and tossed it to me. I caught it and let out a deep sigh of relief when I read Madison Prince's name.

"Madi, thank the goddess," I answered. "Please tell me you can help me."

"Before I say anything, can we back things up a step or fifteen? What do you mean Dara is after you? You're talking about Viviane, right?"

"Yes. I knew her from the pub. The duchess has me on video coming out of her place around the time of her murder. Except it wasn't me. It was a shapeshifter. A facestealer. Someone hired them to set me up. We think the person who hired them works at or owns Club Crescent, so now we're going there, but I'm in my pyjamas, so I can't get in."

My voice choked, and I wiped my tears away with the heel

of my palm. I didn't know at what point I'd started to cry, but it was such a relief to talk with someone who was good under pressure. Trace had held up well, but Madison was my friend and a professional problem solver. She would know how to fix this. She had to.

A slow exhale sounded down the line. "Okay, let's see if we can break this down. I'm so glad I called in for my messages before I left home. This is going to take another pot of tea. First off, this shapeshifter you mentioned—tall, thin, looks kind of like a sweaty hotdog with glowing eyes?"

I sniffled. "That's them."

"Then I look forward to passing your info along to our security office, because that shifter has been a thorn in my side for years, and I'd love to scare the crap out of them even if nothing sticks. Second, Club Crescent is not somewhere you want to go on your own, especially in pyjamas."

I didn't wonder that Madison knew it was a real place. She probably read citizen complaints about them on the regular.

"I wouldn't be by myself. I have Trace Wyatt with me." I glanced his way, but he was politely keeping his eyes on the road.

"*The* Trace Wyatt?" Madison's shocked tone filled the car, and I rolled my eyes at Trace's smug smile.

"The one and only," I replied flatly, hoping every nuance of my meaning made it down the line. Then I remembered I was supposed to be grateful for the arrogant bastard's help and added, "He's the reason we got the lead on both the shape-shifter and the club. He's gone out on a limb for me. But I don't know if he's going to be enough. I know it would put you in a difficult spot with the department, but please tell me you can help."

"If the security office is after you, there's not much I—"

I heard the apology in her tone, so I didn't let her finish that sentence. "At least tell me you have something I can wear to the club. I could do curbside pickup. You could say you never saw me if anyone asks."

"I don't, unfortunately. But you know who might."

I closed my eyes. "I would really rather not."

"What other options do you have?"

"She'll never let me hear the end of it."

"I'll make some phone calls about what angle security is taking on this case and meet you at her place in half an hour. Hopefully I'll have some good news for you by then."

Chapter 14
Alyssa

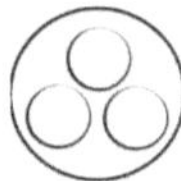

Thursday, 8:15 a.m.

FIFTEEN MINUTES LATER, Trace parked his SUV on a side street in Centretown and followed me into an old four-storey apartment building. I hit the intercom marked *OFF, F*, which earned a low chuckle from Trace, and waited for someone to answer.

"Yep?"

"Jet? It's Alyssa."

The door buzzed, and I crossed into the dingy lobby. The linoleum tiles were scuffed and curled, and the air reeked of stale cigarette smoke and food, but there was a welcoming vibe that wrapped around me and ushered me towards the slow-moving elevator.

"Who is this person?" Trace asked as he followed me into the rickety metal cage.

"Captain Bridget Dawson, SMOAC task force."

He blinked at me. "This is a horrible idea."

I groaned. "I know."

"The security office is out looking for you. You don't think they'll bring in the task force if they believe you're a big enough threat? I had reservations about calling the paper-pusher, but isn't this asking to get arrested?"

"Madi wouldn't have told me to come here if she thought Jet would turn me in, which tells me the task force isn't involved. Yet. If we get out of here soon enough—and goddess, I hope we do—they can claim ignorance. Though I am hoping Jet won't mind giving me a few tips on how to evade security's notice."

He frowned. "Then why do you think it's horrible we're here?"

"Because she undoubtedly knows everything there is to know about this club. Heck, she's probably raided it a time or two. And now she knows I'm going there. She's going to make so much fun of me."

Trace bit down on a smile, and I turned my back on him. Let him laugh. He didn't know Jet.

We got off the elevator, and I marched to her door. Confidence. Certainty. That was what I needed here. Jet understood a woman on a mission. She'd made a career of being exactly that. I had a legitimate reason to be going to a dark, vice-ridden cesspool, so she couldn't judge me.

I knocked, and a moment later, Jet answered. She was dressed in her training kit, with heavy boots, black pants, and a tucked-in white T-shirt. Her brown hair was pulled into a short ponytail, and she stood with her hand propped on her hip. "Club Crescent, Alyssa? Really? I thought your tastes ran a bit more vanilla."

I bowed my head as she chuckled and opened the door wider to let us in.

"Thanks for helping us out," I said, ignoring the commentary. "I hope you don't get in trouble for it."

"Only a risk if anyone finds out, and I don't intend to tell them. Technically, I'm never off the clock, but if you really killed those fae, then my grandmother is a vampire—and she spends too much time in the sun for that to be true. So believe me, if security comes asking about you, I'll do my best to steer them in a different direction." She frowned. "Do you want me to take things from here? I could go to Crescent for you, bully some answers out of the owner. It'd keep your face off his radar."

The idea tempted me more than I wanted to admit, but I made myself shake my head. "Whoever's after me is working hard to keep me in the mud, and I don't want you to get stuck there with me. Bad enough Trace is."

Jet shot him a glance, and he shrugged. "For the best you stay out of it," he said. "I've worked for years getting my network in place, and if anyone hears I'm working with the feds, I can kiss most of my contacts goodbye, and there goes my business."

Her frown deepened. "I don't like it, but I get it. Just know I'm only a phone call away if you change your mind. But I don't know why Madi thinks I'm the person to help you with wardrobe." She led the way through her living room towards her bedroom. "Yes, I have a leather jacket. That does not mean my closet is full of club-appropriate clothing. Does she know the last time I went to a club for any kind of social reason?"

"Eleven years ago," another voice spoke up behind us. I turned around as Madison came into the apartment. Her dark brown hair hung loose and smooth over her shoulders, high-lighting her glowing tan skin. Her hazel eyes sparkled with mirth, and she slung her purse off her shoulder onto Jet's kitchen island. "It was before we met. New Years. You got booted within half an hour because some guy grabbed your ass and you punched him through a wall."

Jet grinned. "Yeah. That was a great night. You seriously think I still have clothes from that era?"

"Yes," Madison replied blandly. She leaned towards me. "This woman hasn't cleaned out or updated her closet more than twice in the past decade."

"Sue me," Jet called from her bedroom. "I don't give a shit about clothes."

While she rummaged through her closet, Madison turned to Trace and crossed her arms. "So you're the notorious bounty hunter who's been keeping our streets clean in the most inconvenient way possible."

"Guilty," he said, touching his fingers to his brow.

"And your interest in this is…?"

"He believed me when I said I didn't kill Vivi, threw up a ward to get me away from Dara, and gave himself a twenty-four-hour deadline to clear my name or have his career ruined," I answered for him.

Madison stared, then nodded. "I see. Well, in that case, I guess I can rely on you to take care of my friend. You stand to lose a lot." She cocked her head as she continued to assess him, then her gaze flicked between the two of us and a faint twinkle filled her eyes, though she did her best to hide it by turning away. "Yeah, I don't think I need to worry."

I grimaced and ignored her, not giving her the satisfaction of asking. Madison was an empath, one of the strongest I knew, and by her expression, she'd picked up something from either Trace or me, and I didn't care to know what it was.

"All right," Jet said, coming out of her room. "I've narrowed it down to two options. Nothing flashy, but a lot better than plaid pyjama pants. Seriously, Alyssa, what the hell were you thinking? Trying to start a new fashion trend?"

"Trying to put out my garbage. Got thrown in the trunk of a car."

Her eyes widened. "What the fuck?" She looked to Trace. "You rescued her?"

He had the decency to look embarrassed. "I'm the one who threw her in the trunk."

I left him to explain, not needing to hear the whole story again, and closed myself in the bedroom. With a pinch of regret, I pulled off Simon's sweater, folded it, and left it neatly on the bed before adding my T-shirt and plaid flannels to the pile.

Unable to put it off any longer, I turned my attention to the outfits.

Jet was right, they were simple, which made me feel much better about what I was facing. Sequins at eight-thirty in the morning would have been too much. Even as it was, I felt like a sham. The black jeans hugged my hips and my thighs, and— admittedly—made my ass look fantastic. The dove-grey top, if I could call it a top, was more of a question mark. I'd quickly ruled out the dark green strapless thing with slashes across the front and back, but the grey option had straps all over the place, three thin strips at each shoulder, criss-crossing down the open back, and a plunging draped neckline.

If my nana could see me now.

I navigated my way through the straps, after the third attempt to get everything sitting correctly, and turned my attention to my face and hair.

There was only so far I was willing to go to fit in. While I didn't want to be thrown out or dismissed, I also wasn't a customer. So I refreshed my ponytail and dug through Jet's bathroom cabinets until I found an old tube of mascara.

Lessons from teenagehood rose to haunt me to never share eye makeup—especially old, dodgy eye makeup—but it was the best I could do under the circumstances. While the "dark circles under the eyes, tired but look like death" look might suit a demon or the undead, it wasn't my style.

Looking more presentable, I gave myself a last assessment in the mirror, then screwed up my courage to return to the others.

The stilted conversation I walked in on fell silent, and although I registered Jet's appraising stare and Madison's approval, it was Trace's reaction that held me bound.

He stood leaning back against Jet's wooden-top island, arms crossed, one foot over the other, looking completely at home, as though he and Jet went way back. But his mouth had fallen open, and his eyes had grown wide, pupils dilated and the visible iris fully violet.

My cheeks grew warm under his stare, my heart fluttered,

my fingertips tingled, and I told myself to simmer down. These weren't my clothes, and this wasn't me. It was a costume, and it was selling the role I intended to play. Perfect.

Yet his gaze felt like a gentle caress down my bare arms, and goosebumps bubbled over my skin.

As though he noticed, or maybe because he caught himself staring and wanted to hide it, he pushed away from the island, pulled off his coat, and tossed it to me. "No way you'll survive the trip to the club without a coat, let alone make it inside."

I dropped my eyes to the scratchy wool and pulled the lined sleeves over my arms. It was at least two sizes too big for me but warmed me instantly. Wafts of bergamot, musk, and shampoo tickled my nose, and I pulled the collar tighter around my neck.

"Right," Madison said, clapping her hands together. "Now that you're in character, what's your plan?"

I shoved my hands into the pockets of the coat, remembered the coat wasn't mine, removed my hands, and let them fall awkwardly by my sides. "Go in there, ask for the boss, and find out who wants me dead?"

Jet smirked. "Great way to speed up the process."

"Look, I don't do this whole investigating thing for a living, all right? I pour drinks. I bring food. I do accounting and housekeeping and inventory. This is all over my head."

"Don't sell yourself short," Trace said. "I've seen the way

you wield your magic. That's not the work of someone who's never trained with it."

He'd resumed his lean against Jet's island, and I found myself scanning the length of his lean, muscular body. His shirt sleeves were pushed up to the elbows, showcasing those damned forearms, and in this light, the grey of his shirt brought out the rich reds and golds in his hair. And still those violet eyes flashed.

I cleared my throat. "Yes, I can defend myself, but I'm hoping that particular skill won't be necessary where we're going."

Why was his only response to press his lips together and look away? Why wouldn't Madison make eye contact with me? Why was Jet wearing a grin I suspected was one hundred per cent at my expense? I was missing something, and none of it made me feel better about what my morning would entail.

"What?" I asked. "Am I walking into a cage fight or something?"

Jet chuckled. "Nothing like that. You'll be fine. But if you're looking for pointers, go in looking like you already have all the answers and just need confirmation. Statements over questions. Confidence is key." She held up her hands. "I know I'm the muscle of the supernatural security world and investigations are not my area of expertise, but I've watched our officers often enough to have absorbed the basics. You want to talk to the top dogs because anyone under them won't know anything and likely won't give you the time of day."

Madison nodded. "So far no one from security has answered my calls, but while you're gone, I'll keep trying. I can request a debrief on the case and see what sort of evidence is stacked against you. It's possible whoever killed these fae made a mistake they're not aware of and our office is only looking to rule you out as a suspect."

I hoped I was that lucky, but even if the official channels weren't looking my way, I was still at the top of Dara's hit list unless we dumped the real culprit at her feet.

"If you find who you're looking for and need me to put a bit of professional pressure on them, I'm happy to do it," Jet added. "Especially if it turns out to be the owner of Crescent. That bastard spends a lot of money and effort evading SMOAC's oversight, so I make a point to loom over him now and again to remind him he can only go so far."

Tears pricked the corners of my eyes and the back of my throat burned, but I managed to snuff out the sappier aspects of my gratitude to say thank you.

"Of course," Jet said as she threw her arm around my shoulders. "If this guy"—she jerked her chin towards Trace—"has to bump you off tonight to satisfy some fae duchess's need for vengeance, where am I going to grab a drink after work, eh? It benefits me to help you."

The idea of Trace *bumping* me in any way created an uncomfortable sensation throughout my body. I shrugged her off with a laugh and looked at Trace, who was smiling openly now, though his cheer faded when he glanced at the clock on the wall. He met my eye, and I nodded, all bodily discomfort gone. Procrasti-changing was over. Jet and Madison were firmly in my corner, which was a much-needed comfort, and now it was back to me and my unexpected ally to find out who wanted me out of the way.

Time to walk into the demon sex den and pray I came out unscathed.

Chapter 15
Alyssa

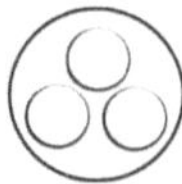

Thursday, 9:00 a.m.

NOT LONG AFTER, Trace and I stood on Sparks Street in front of an empty storefront.

"Oh no, they're closed," I moaned in exaggerated disappointment. "That's too bad. Let's go grab breakfast and figure out our options."

I started to walk away, but Trace grabbed my upper arm and tugged me back towards the storefront, guiding us away from the front doors and towards a narrow side door I would have walked right past. No doubt most people did. And to most mundanes, the door probably wasn't there at all, just some sketchy graffiti-covered access panel or whatever the perception filter created to protect their minds from reality.

In that moment, I wished I had a perception filter to hide behind. Unfortunately, I made out every single detail of the crescent moon surrounded by raindrops painted on the door. Someone had even livened up the logo by making the raindrops a deep crimson. Because that made me feel so much more positive about it.

Trace rested his hand on the door handle to pull it open, but I tugged my arm out of his grip and stepped back. He did me the courtesy of joining me, giving me a moment to brace myself.

"Before we go in there, what the hell was that back at Jet's apartment?"

He canted his head and looked me over, and again I watched his pupils dilate as his tongue skirted his lower lip. Was that a blush on those high cheekbones? "Which part?"

"Everyone else knows what to expect down there except me. Will there be fighting? Do I need to be ready to die if I pass through that door?"

I swore I spotted a flash of relief flicker across his face before he smiled, but I didn't put too much thought into it, more interested in his answer.

"Highly unlikely. But…" He rolled his neck and cupped the back of it, looking up at me from under his long eyelashes as he carried on some internal debate. Finally, he stood up straight, dropped his hand, and said, "The vibe of this place is different from what you'll experience anywhere else. The owner likes to keep the energy chill. Very, very chill."

"Like cold?"

He rolled his eyes as though I'd said something incredibly stupid, but I was done playing games. Either he told me what I was walking into, or I was leaving.

"Like laid back," he said. "Relaxed. But not in a spa kind of way. More in a drugged-up, out-of-it kind of way. The lowered inhibitions kind of way. So the air is pumped with pheromones, and they can make a person act a little… outside the norm."

I gave him my family-famous stony glare. "You're telling me I am about to breathe in a demon aphrodisiac and I'm expected to keep my wits to ask a very powerful being a bunch of very serious questions?"

"That about sums it up, yeah." He took hold of my arm again and this time didn't let go as he opened the door and steered me towards the steps leading into the darkness below. "Try not to get too handsy."

I gulped and followed him down the dimly lit set of stairs but stopped again in front of a second door, this one heavy, studded black metal with the logo etched into the centre.

"Magic leashed or unleashed?" I asked.

His voice was as grim as his expression as he replied, "Leashed. As tight as you can."

I nodded my understanding, and he pushed the door open.

The inside of the club was, in some ways, exactly what I expected. In other ways, nothing like.

Maybe it was the time of day, everyone gone except a few hungover-looking humans lolling in the booths along the wall or slumped over the bar and a few lingering demons finishing their drinks, but it looked… like a bar. A fancy, somewhat gaudy, bar. The bartop, made of sleek obsidian granite, matched the few tables in the room, and a full display of expensive liquor stretched across the back wall. Dimmed pot lights lit the bar area, with black-and-red-swirled chandeliers spilling a soft yellow glow over each centre table, while the booths along the sides remained shrouded in shadow.

The floor was black tile polished to a high shine, and the walls were painted a deep, rich red.

Everything about the place screamed decadence, and I imagined that for the right crowd it would be easy to lose yourself to the particular temporary oblivion on tap.

Beyond the mundane appearance, however, I saw the magic in the air. It brushed against my skin in swaths of shimmering pink. The hair on my arms rose to dance with it, and a shiver ran down my spine.

As we stepped farther into the room, a woman came out to greet us, and I had to force my mouth shut. She was easily the most beautiful woman I'd ever seen. Not only because of her flawless features with the ever-so-slightly pointed ears, her tawny skin perfectly made up to highlight its earthy undertones, or the way her black dress clung to every smooth hourglass curve, but also the way her star-filled eyes took me in, as though I were a glass of cold water after a long, hot shift.

"I'm sorry, we're closed for the day." Her voice reminded me of a well-aged Scotch, rich and smooth and intoxicating. Her attention landed on Trace, and a spark of recognition burned in her eyes. It didn't make me jealous at all. "Trace Wyatt? What are you doing here?"

"Good morning, Lady Reverie."

Lady Reverie? In the back of my mind, I snorted a laugh, but my amusement was washed out by the thought of how perfectly the name suited her. She was a walking dream.

"We're not staying," Trace continued, and I wondered how he could be so abrupt when all I wanted was to keep her talking. "Management in? We'd like to have a word."

The corner of Lady Reverie's perfect lips curled upwards. "The service not to your liking?"

The double entendre made me press my lips together, both to suppress a giggle and to hide the effects of the tingle that now spread through my blood, warming me, loosening my muscles. After so many hours of tension and stress, it felt good to let go of it, if only for a few moments.

"Personal matter," Trace said. "If you wouldn't mind."

I wanted to give him shit for his rudeness, but the woman

didn't look offended. She inclined her head and gestured to an empty place at the bar.

"Not at all. Why not have a drink while you wait? Can I take your coat?" she asked me, and even as Trace said no, I slid it off my shoulders and handed it over, enjoying the cool air on the back of my neck. I hadn't realized how warm I'd gotten.

Trace hooked his fingers under my arm, his cold hand against my heated skin creating a pleasant contrast, and directed me across the room. My legs had grown wooden and my head foggy while we'd stood in the entrance, and I was grateful to sit down on the black leather-topped stool. The bartop was cool and smooth under my fingertips, and I traced patterns along its surface. Trace stood beside me, closer than absolutely necessary, radiating warmth that soaked into me through the flimsy, strappy shirt.

Was I imagining the way he stared at me? We were supposed to be here in a professional capacity, but right now he was looking at me as though he wanted to eat me up. As though he wanted to devour my lips in a kiss that would set fire to the building. In my mind, I saw him leaning in, trapping me against the bar as his long fingers trailed up my hips and snuck under the sides of my top. His mouth was hungry, his tongue eager, and the length of his body was pressed against mine, leaving me no space to escape him. My fingers twisted through his hair, pulling him closer, and I hooked my leg around his hip to hold him in place, his hardening length against my aching core, the fullness of his desire close to the wetness of mine.

I remembered the way our powers played together, twining and coiling around each other in a way that, either fighting or working as one, so intimate and unexpected.

I shook off the fantasy, relieved to find I hadn't closed the gap between us in the passion of my daydream, and blushed at the vividness of it.

Although I was relieved he couldn't read my mind and witness the scene I'd just played out, I longed to experience the sensation of my magic twisting with his again. I summoned my power and sent it towards him. His responded immediately, swirling around mine, aiming to dominate. I pushed back, not willing to submit so easily. He sent out another blast, this one more forceful, and a gasp caught in my lungs. I returned the assault, wanting to wrap him up as he'd wrapped me. He rested his hand on my cheek, rough fingers now warm against my bare skin, and I leaned into him. Another surge of his power enveloped me as his magic tightened. Squeezed.

A moment later, I was fully bound, and the chill of my emptiness was almost as great as my confusion.

It was only when I looked around that I realized three other beings had turned to stare at me, lust written in their red-tinted eyes.

Trace had told me to keep my magic leashed. This was why.

My power had drawn all the suckers in the bar. Trace hadn't been responding to my magic in play, he'd been warning me, reminding me to tamp it down.

Ice water poured down my spine.

The pheromones in the air.

He'd told me, but I hadn't realized they would hit so quickly. Heat filled my cheeks, and I turned on my stool to face the shelves of alcohol, needing a minute to compose myself and not wanting to see his expression.

Nothing was more sobering than the mortification of misreading the room, and soon, all too soon, my head cleared, and my desire of a moment ago morphed into a pulsing fury that I had succumbed so easily to the trap of this place.

When Lady Reverie returned a few minutes later, I saw her for what she was, and my anger homed in on her as an acceptable outlet.

Not only fae, though the eyes and ears had fooled me. Succubus.

She'd no doubt had a great laugh at my expense. The witch with no self-control.

Fuck her, fuck Trace for bringing me here, and fuck the owner of this place for making it necessary.

The fae-demon scanned me over again and must have noted the change in my state of mind, because amusement danced in her eyes as she said, "The master will see you now."

Master. Gag.

With a grimace, I gestured for her to lead the way and followed close behind, letting Trace bring up the rear. Anything to prevent me from seeing his face.

We passed through the staff-only door, and immediately the vibe changed from Vice-Ridden Lust Palace to Corporate Chic. The black tiles continued from the club, but the walls were painted a neutral grey, and the art pieces on the walls were abstracts of familiar landmarks around the city. A few doors lined each side—regular office doors, not the metal behemoth of the entryway—and a wooden, windowed door waited at the far end. For the bigwig, no doubt.

I had no idea who ran this place, and although I was about to find out, I really, really, didn't care. I intended to have nothing more to do with Club Crescent after today. I would go back to believing it didn't exist.

My stance on that solidified when Reverie opened the door to usher us inside and I came face to face with said bigwig.

And in that moment, taking in the man who'd ruined my life not once but twice, I appreciated just how screwed I was.

Chapter 16
Alyssa

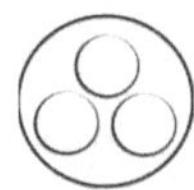

Thursday, 9:15 a.m.

THE OWNER OF Club Crescent sat behind a large mahogany desk, his suit-clad frame reclined comfortably in a large leather chair. He embodied the role of Club Owner, with his carefully styled hair, manicured nails, and cutthroat expression.

An expression that haunted my dreams even though I hadn't seen it in person in over eight years.

"Delvin?" I asked, not quite believing my eyes.

My brain, on the other hand, was screaming at me, telling me to run as quickly as possible and not look back.

I'd never had my past come up and bite me so thoroughly in the ass before. It was not a pleasant experience.

Memories swept over me of a beautiful woman with fire-red hair and sapphire eyes wasting away with a late-stage cancer she'd hidden from all her healers. An angry voice shouting at me to do more, threatening me when the woman's life expired.

I'd given up my healing career after that and taken over Mooney's, settling for backroom touch-ups for anyone in need. It hadn't been the woman's death that had scared me away—it was the reaction of the surviving family member that made the idea of continuing down that path less than palatable. Much easier to pour drinks and bring happiness to people's lives.

"Alyssa Mooney," Delvin greeted with the warmth of a northern blizzard. "I suppose I should have expected you, but I didn't think you had the intelligence to work out my involvement." His red-tinted gaze flicked to Trace. "I suppose she has you to thank for that, Mr. Wyatt."

Trace said nothing, his expression blank, though I caught the hint of surprise in his eyes.

Yeah, well, he wasn't the only one. I should have asked Trace beforehand what the owner's name was, but never in a million years would I have guessed I'd recognize it. And if I'd known who sat at the helm of this place, I would have flat-out refused to walk through the door. Fine, let me go on the run for the rest of my life, it was better than reliving one of the worst moments of my youth.

Though the fact that Delvin was associated with my situation cleared up a lot.

"You set me up." I swallowed hard. "You killed Vivi? And that other fae?"

He crossed his hands over his stomach and cocked his head to stare at me. Under his glare, I felt every ounce of his hatred. The animosity wasn't unexpected, but to go so far as to murder someone to get back at me?

I guessed it wasn't so much of a stretch that a demon would consider a life for a life fair trade.

The fury that had sparked in the club grew until it swept over me from head to toe and left me shaking. I clenched my hands at my sides and did my best to keep my magic in check when what I really wanted to do was launch it at him, pummel him into his stupid expensive chair and ruin his stupid expensive suit.

"I didn't murder anyone, no," he said. "Rumour has it you did."

His smugness told me everything I needed to know about his involvement.

The back of my throat burned, and if I could have breathed fire, I would have. Seeing him a charred chunk of demon would have been all too satisfying.

"I won't bother asking why you helped drag my name through the dirt. I guess my real question is why after all this time?"

His arrogant face shifted into a fanged expression of rage

as he lunged out of his chair and slammed his hands on his desk. "What is time to me?" The question came out as a cross between a growl and a hiss, and my magic rose in defence, wrapping around me and creating a barrier between us. "You think a few years would be enough to erase the love and grief of losing my mate? You know nothing, you incompetent bitch."

I breathed through the fear that sluiced through my guts and tried to hang on to my anger. It would serve me better. "She was dying, Delvin. She knew it. If she'd been honest about her symptoms, maybe I would have been able to help, but—"

"I don't want to fucking hear it!" he shouted, and with his hands tucked under his desk, he threw the entire heavy unit to the side. It slammed through the wall, pierced paint and Sheetrock, and lodged halfway between the ceiling and floor.

Reverie gasped behind me, and Trace's magic rose to match mine, his fingers splayed, ready to act, but he stayed quiet, watching the scene without stepping in. Smart man.

"I've heard your excuses," Delvin spat. "I've heard them in my dreams every single fucking night since Bianca's soul slipped from her body as she lay in my arms. All they do is make your destruction that much sweeter. I know about the bounty on your head. I know there are people looking to kill you and make bank on it, and I'm just disappointed that my current position as a respectful business owner prevents me from doing the honours myself."

My mouth prickled as though I'd sucked on a cotton ball.

He meant every word of it, and nothing I said would make him change his mind. At this point, it wouldn't matter if he did. The damage had been done. I had to remember that he wasn't the cause of all my problems—but he was one step closer to it.

"Who asked you to frame me?"

His rage evaporated so quickly the room dropped a few degrees, and his fangs elongated in a nasty grin. "Even if I told you—which I have no intention of doing—it wouldn't make a difference. You can't touch him. He'd kill you if you tried. No matter what you do, you're not getting out of this." In a blink, he closed the distance between us until he loomed over me. Black, leathery wings burst out from the back of his suit to stretch the width of his office, and his handsome features slid into a horrible mask of bumps and lava-red fissures. "And once you're gone, I will dance on your grave."

I didn't have time to scream before Trace's magic cut between us and threw Delvin against the wall beside his desk, pinning him in place. I turned to look at Trace and was struck by the silver fire burning in his eyes.

"That's not playing nice, Delvinorath," he said, and I barely recognized his voice. Magic layered his words, winding spells into every syllable, and Delvin thrashed beneath it.

Beside me, Reverie stood braced to run, but whether she intended to leave or rescue her boss was unclear. I opted not to give her the choice and threw a spell at her, shoving her into the hallway. As soon as she passed the threshold, I slammed the door shut and locked it, all without moving from my place, too shaken to take a step.

Trace stalked towards Delvin, his hands raised, magic swirling, and closed his fingers around the demon's throat.

"I don't take it well when scum like you threatens innocent people."

Delvin spat in Trace's face with a bitter laugh. "There are no innocent people in this room, bounty hunter. If our dear, sweet-faced Alyssa hasn't revealed her true nature to you yet, don't worry, she will. It's only a matter of time before she betrays you and destroys the people you care about."

Frustration filled me, and my magic responded, lashing out to add my binding to Trace's, but I had no opportunity to threaten him with severe bodily harm before Trace held up his hand and slashed himself across the palm with a knife that seemed to come out of nowhere.

"You will cooperate with us, Delvinorath, even if I have to drag the truth out through the remains of your teeth. I compel you to tell us the name of the person who ordered the move against Alyssa."

Delvin hissed, spraying us with droplets of acidic saliva that burned my skin where it landed. But the longer he resisted the command, the more he squirmed against the wall.

I'd never witnessed demon manipulation before, never met anyone who had tried to do it, so for me this was a new and horrific experience. I almost felt sorry for the bastard. After all he'd been through, I didn't blame him for his anger. That he was projecting that anger onto me and trying to throw me under the bus to satisfy an eight-year-long desire for revenge made me a little less sympathetic, but I still hated to see him endure such obvious agony.

"Do you really hate me so much that you would rather suffer than give me a name?" I asked.

"Yessss." The snake-like sibilance added extra menace to his reply, and with it went the rest of my compassion.

"Then Bianca is better off without you. She was a wonderful woman who cared for other people. She would be ashamed of you."

Would she? I didn't really know. I'd only met the witch a few times, and the last time she'd been on her deathbed begging me to end her suffering. I'd been too young, unable to go through with it, though I'd done my best to ease her pain. In the end, she'd thanked me. At no point had she accused me of failing or cursed me to a future of endless penance, so I had to believe she wouldn't have wanted her lover to ruin my life almost a decade later.

"You dare?" Delvin demanded, his twisted face turning a deeper shade of red. I wasn't sure if it was related to his fury or the increased pain of holding back from Trace's compulsion spell.

"I do," I said, crossing my arms. "I don't know what's there to greet us supes in the afterlife, but if she's waiting for you, I imagine she's ready to kick your ass right now. You've done your job. You've made my life hell. You've kept me awake all night, made me run through Ottawa in my pyjamas and cross the threshold into your club. Isn't that enough payback?"

He released a bellow that echoed through the room and, I was sure, reached the club proper. "Clyde Corrick, you fucking bitch."

As soon as the name was out of his mouth, the spell evaporated, and he collapsed to his knees.

"Thank you very much for your help," I said, and walked towards the door, not wanting to spend another second in his presence.

"Nothing you do will change what you've done," he growled after me. "Until my last breath, I will curse your name."

As Trace passed into the hallway, I paused in the doorway and half turned towards Delvin. "That's unfortunate, but more for you than for me. I'd hate to live my life running on grudges. Bianca would be sad for you."

On that note, I closed the door after me, leaving him to his hatred and grief.

Chapter 17
Alyssa

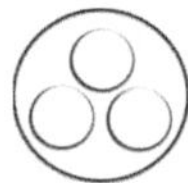

Thursday, 9:45 a.m.

I COULDN'T GET out of that underground cesspit fast enough.

I rushed through the club, pushing past Trace to reach the stupid reinforced door, ran up the stairs, and burst into the freezing February morning. Only once I'd taken a few deep breaths did I realize I'd forgotten Trace's coat with Ms. Perfection and was standing in the snow basically topless.

Fortunately, Trace wasn't as frazzled as I was, and he exited the stairway a few moments later carrying the coat.

He draped it around my shoulders and tugged it close around my neck. "That was… interesting."

I bowed my head, willing my heartbeat to slow, and slid my arms into the sleeves. "Thanks for being tactful."

"Want to talk about it?"

If curiosity had driven his question, I would have told him to fuck off, but there was only concern in his voice. "You heard most of it. His mate was terminally ill. There was nothing anyone could have done. But he took his anger out on a nineteen-year-old apprentice because it gave him power when he felt powerless. I was so much of a kid I took it all to heart. It killed my passion for the job, and I gave up my dream."

"I'm sorry." He sounded like he meant it. "But I can think of thousands of people who are glad you moved on to a new one. Mooney's wouldn't be the same without you."

He was standing so close I could see the rapid pulse in his neck, and his breath fanned my cheek. I cleared my throat to will away the heat pulsing in every corner of my body and held out my hand, still not able to make eye contact with him after what had happened inside. "I haven't lost all my skills, though. Want me to take a look at your cut?"

He set his larger hand in mine so the back rested against my palm, revealing the nasty slice that crossed diagonally from the heel to the base of his index finger. I rested the fingertips of my other hand over it, taking in the calluses and scars, the small freckle just below his middle finger, and summoned a gentle purple glow that slipped from me into him. The warmth of the magic offset the bite of the wind—though maybe it was more than the magic. My cheeks flamed, and other parts of me grew equally toasty. Enough to distract me, and the spell wobbled until I renewed my concentration. Once the magic was firmly in place, the cut began to close, sealing the edges first and moving towards the centre until all that remained was a pink line that would likely add one more scar to the mix.

"Incredible," he murmured, and my faced warmed even more under the quiet praise.

My mouth was dry, my heart raced, and I knew the smartest thing I could do was walk away from this man, but I didn't move.

Neither did he, and under the intensity of his gaze, as the adrenaline from our encounter with Delvin subsided, a different thrill ran through me. Trace's fingers curled around mine, and his body heat radiated off him to battle the cold draft coming down the air tunnel of Sparks Street. His breath stirred my hair, and his magic hummed.

He raised his other hand to my face, his fingertip caressing my jawline, and his touch was electric, as delicious as it had been in my pheromone-induced fantasy. Despite the heavy coat, goosebumps rippled over my skin, and I leaned into him to absorb his warmth, finally raising my chin to stare into his violet eyes. Only, in the morning sunlight, the violet was more of a soft blue, and most of that was taken up by a spreading blackness of his pupils. His breath hitched as he inched closer.

Then he blinked, shook his head as though to clear it,

and stepped back. "Sorry. The effects of the club air must be lingering. Thanks for the hand job." His eyes widened and he took another step away. "I mean, for healing my hand. That's... yeah."

My face flushed as I realized I'd once again been duped by a bunch of synthetic hormones. At least this time it hadn't just been me.

"Right, yeah. I think I can safely say my visit to Crescent was a one-and-done deal. That whole being overwhelmed by someone's pheromones thing? Gross. No thanks. If I want someone, it better be on my terms."

Trace grinned. "You saying you wanted me, princess?"

To take me right there on the bar? Holy yes.

But the desire had passed now, the cold winter morning putting any thought of removing clothing way down at the bottom of my wish list.

"Don't let your head get any bigger than it is, Wyatt." I started towards the car. "None of it was real."

"We'll see," he said, his tone teasing. "Once the air clears, we'll try again. Because I won't lie to you, Mooney—the way you tore that demon down? Pretty hot."

The hug of the compliment was crushed under the reminder of what had just happened and what it meant.

"Come on," I said through clenched teeth. "Let's get moving and see if Chip can track down Corrick. If we can wrap this up so I get to sleep in my own bed tonight instead of being dead, I'd like that."

The drive back to Stittsville was awkward at best, my high school nightmare at worst.

Trapped in a moving vehicle with someone I'd imagined making out with, someone who had to know I'd imagined making out with them, and who had shown no particular desire to make out with me except for a seemingly throwaway line that made me think he was mocking me?

The absolute worst in a night of worsts.

I was about ready to turn myself over to Dara right now if it meant getting away from Trace's attempt to pretend he hadn't noticed me wanting to grope him in the bar.

Not that I wanted him to mention it. That would make this moment a hundred and fifty million times more humiliating.

Before Trace pulled to a complete stop in Chip's driveway, I was out of the car. But my rushing away was not assisted by Chip, who refused to acknowledge my presence until Trace was on the porch with me, as though I hadn't walked out of the house just this morning.

The security system beeped, the heavy locks did their thing, and soon we were stamping snow off our boots in the entranceway.

The place smelled of coffee, which was so much better than the sweat, sex, and alcohol of the club, and as soon as my boots were off and I'd hung up Trace's coat, wishing I could keep it on but not wanting to drip snow all over the carpet, I breezed into the kitchen and poured myself a very large cup.

"Went well, then?" Chip called from the living room. I heard his fingers flying over his keyboard and assumed that was why he preferred to shout at us from a distance.

Or maybe he would have anyway. I wasn't about to nominate the guy for Social Greeter of the Year or anything.

"Went well enough," Trace said. "Clyde Corrick."

"The business guy? On it. And, Cheers, when you have a sec."

I rolled my eyes and dragged my feet into the living room, wrapping my fingers around my mug to ward off the chill that had set in.

I stopped behind Chip, and he leaned forward into his monitor, then swung his chair around to give me a once-over. Then another one. Then a third.

"Damn."

"Yes, well, enjoy the view. I'm burning this outfit." I wondered if Jet would mind, but when I thought about what this shirt had seen tonight, I suspected she'd encourage it.

Trace grinned and waggled his eyebrows. "I'll get the

lighter."

I hid my blush under a sip of coffee, praying to the goddess that everyone in the room believed my scowling eyes and blamed my reddening face on the steam.

Chip obviously didn't as he stuck out his tongue in disgust and spun back towards his computer. "Gross. Whatever happened in that club, I do not want to know."

He grabbed something the size of a small brick off his desk and tossed it over his shoulder at me. I missed in my effort not to spill my coffee, but Trace caught it before it could hit the ground and handed it to me.

"What's this?" I asked.

"Your new phone," Chip said, and I did a double take at the object in my hand. Maybe it was supposed to be a phone in a very secure case, but I would have had a hard time fitting it in my purse, let alone a pocket. If my tight black jeans had pockets. Which they didn't. Because women's fashion sucked troll nuts.

"I've mirrored all your phone's info onto this one," he explained. "All your contacts and whatever are there, but no one can track you. Frankly, you may as well toss your old phone away, because even if you make it out of this with your head, do you really want Big Brother to know where you are all the time?"

I was too grateful to have my own communication device

to judge him for his paranoia.

"How much do I owe you?"

"I'll add it to your tab."

I swiped my pin onto the screen and grinned when all my apps and pictures swam into view. My phone! Which meant not only could I shut my brain down for a few minutes with my favourite games, but I could also call Simon, who was no doubt losing his mind wondering why I hadn't been in touch with him since he'd dropped me off. And there was the rest of my family, of course. I'd call them too. After.

"I'm just going to…" I gestured to the door to let them know I planned to step outside, but Trace shook his head.

"Use one of the rooms upstairs if you want privacy. It's light enough now that someone might see you." The corner of his mouth twitched upwards. "Besides, you only just warmed up."

I glanced at Chip to see how he felt about his house being offered to a stranger, but he was buried in some kind of inter-net search—probably for Corrick—and didn't react.

Figuring Trace knew his friend best, I shrugged and headed for the stairs. As I climbed the first steps, I glanced back into the living room and caught Trace staring at the floor with an expression I couldn't bring myself to call disappointment.

Chapter 18
Trace

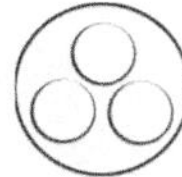

Thursday, 10:30 a.m.

I DUG MY toe into the thick beige carpet, then smoothed out the ruffled nap. Then roughed it up again. Then smoothed it out.

Only once I was sure I'd given Alyssa enough time to make it upstairs and remove my temptation to stare after her did I look up, relieved that Chip was distracted enough by his research not to notice my reaction. The last thing I needed was that stare of his navigating deeper into my soul, ready to crack it like an egg.

I shoved my hands in my pockets and turned my back on the stairs. It was time to get to work. Not to think too much about how Alyssa was probably calling her chaos demon to fill him in on her morning, or about how, no matter what she said about their relationship, there was obviously something there.

Which didn't bother me.

I meant what I'd said to Chip. I was helping her because being wrongly accused sucked, not for any other reason. She was just a bounty. One I'd already gone too far out on a limb for. First with Dara, then with that demon at the club. Why the hell had I done that? My palm throbbed with the memory of my healing wound, and I curled my hand into a fist to hide the evidence of my poor judgement. I hated dealing with demons. Compelling them, especially. Always had a nasty habit of coming back to bite me. I'd broken so many of my rules to keep this woman free and alive, and it had to stop here.

Let it be enough that I was willing to work within the lines to prove she was innocent, as we now knew for sure she was.

Unless of course she'd hired Corrick to kill Viviane and orchestrated this whole scenario as some bizarre, convoluted distraction… but I doubted it. And we were so close to having enough evidence to convince Dara to call off the job. Then I could move on to my next hunt, Alyssa could return to her pub and her demon, and everything would be as it was before.

As if that moment in the club had never happened.

I shifted on my feet to make myself more comfortable as visions of the past hour heated my blood and tightened my jeans.

My previous few visits to Club Crescent had prepared me

for what to expect, but that didn't mean the air didn't affect me. I'd stood beside Alyssa at that bar, and it had taken every last effort not to run my fingers under the straps of her shirt and snap them. Not to savour the softness of her skin, taste her berry-red lips, find out if that sweet aloe vera scent had infused every inch of her. And her reaction to me, the desire swimming in her eyes, had made my restraint that much more precarious. The way she'd turned towards me, the subtle spread of her legs, as though in her mind she'd opened herself to me.

As for what had happened on the street outside after…

I gave myself a shake. Those thoughts would only lead me down dangerous roads. I might want her, her magic might call to me with a siren's song, but I had my life and she had hers. Neither of which included the other beyond today.

I cleared my throat and focused on the tabs flying across Chip's computer screen.

"Any luck?"

"Yeah…" he said, and I didn't like his note of uncertainty. Chip didn't do uncertain. His was a black-and-white world.

"But?"

"I'm hoping that for the first time in my life I'm wrong. I knew Corrick was slimy, but this… Well, see for yourself."

I got closer and peered over his shoulder as he pulled up a tab to reveal a newspaper headline from a few years ago.

Ottawa business owner arrested on fraud, bribery charges, the headline read.

Clyde Corrick, owner of The Scorpio Lounge, Corrick's Bar & Grill, Oh My Pies, and the Doughnut Dispensary has been arrested today after an investigation by the Canadian Revenue Agency revealed…

I skimmed the rest of the article for whatever had Chip shaking in his slippers but found nothing except an impressive list of tax-dodging manoeuvres.

"So our theory was right?" I asked. "It all comes down to some egomaniac wanting to shoulder Alyssa out of her pub?"

Chip spun slowly in his chair, his eyebrow raised in a very judgemental glower. "It's 'Alyssa' now?"

I held his stare, refusing to back down under the layers of insinuation in his tone. "That is her name, yes."

"Mmhmm." He spun back to his computer without further commentary, but I sensed the radiating thrum of disapproval as he pulled up yet another screen. "Well, *Alyssa* is really up shit creek, I'd say. If you intend to stay on a first-name basis with her, I recommend investing in a solid paddle."

He moved away to give me a better view, and I leaned in to check out the photo he'd brought up. What I saw was what appeared to be a random black-and-white candid, though when I took in the context of the scene, I realized it had to be a still from some SMOAC surveillance footage. It had been taken at a swanky restaurant, probably in the heart of downtown, and the cast was some of Ottawa's heavy hitters in the local business Rolodex: restaurant owners, tech moguls, start-up CEOs. All people I'd had reason to read up on in my line of work due to underhanded connections of one type or another. Some of these people were clients who'd hired me to bring in low-ranking people on someone else's team for crimes against their bottom line. Some of them were marks that had survived their sentences or private retributions.

At the middle table was our boy Clyde, standing there laughing, enjoying his opportunity to rub elbows with his cronies. And at the sight of the other people sharing his table—a table he was clearly heading—something deep in my gut shrivelled up.

My confidence, probably. My certainty that we could get Alyssa out of this.

Because the people sitting around him were terrifying. Melanie Caplan, rage demon and general bitch; Rosie Alvarez, snake shifter; Benoit Lalonde, necromancer. And those were just the three I'd skirted in the past. All three capable of committing murder as part of their regular business dealings, and lucky you if all they did was kill you.

"I don't get it." I leaned my ass against the desk, ignoring Chip's mutter of protest. "I don't buy these people murdering random fae just to take over some pub."

"Unless there's more to the pub than liquor and money."

There was a note of smugness in his voice that made me

look at him more closely. "What do you know?"

He offered a slow shrug. "I *may* have done a bit of extra digging on *Alyssa* while you were out. Seeing as how *my friend* is showing a bit too much interest in a woman he hardly knows, and we all know how great *my friend*'s taste in women tends to be."

His pointed stare might have been intended to embarrass me, but I wasn't embarrassed. The mistakes I'd made when I was eighteen were the stupidity of youth, and I hadn't had enough to do with women since then for his comment to carry much weight.

When he saw I wasn't going to throw a tantrum at his barely veiled reference, he turned back to his screen and brought up what looked like a satellite view of Centretown.

"To be fair, I didn't find anything on the woman in question. Her life is about as exciting as this documentary on wild grasses I watched last week. The pub, though." He zoomed in over Somerset and Elgin, and I frowned at the faint haze filling the air around Mooney's.

"What the hell is that? Magic?"

"It is indeed. Couldn't tell you what kind, but it's potent enough to cover the entire property. And only the property."

"Location confined. Wards, maybe?"

"You ever see wards like that?"

I had not. Normally I didn't see wards at all. I'd never had

Alyssa's ability to see magic as colour. Or as anything, really.

"Another interesting fact—the city owns nothing about this pub. The building, the land, the airspace, the underground. Cheers could strike oil underneath this place, and she would claim one hundred per cent of the rights to it."

"What? That's impossible."

"I triple-checked. It's all under the name of Edwyn Mooney, purchased from the city fifty-seven years ago for a pittance."

None of that sounded right.

"Okay…" I said slowly, working hard to put the pieces together. "So something about the pub is more than it seems. And this something is why Corrick murdered the fae?"

"Not just any fae. *Powerful* fae. Probably among the most powerful supes in the city, short of going for the royal line itself."

"He's preparing to come after Alyssa directly. Or the pub."

"That'd be my guess. If he'd come after her in the first place, there was always the chance her family would step in, and Corrick would have stood no chance against the whole brood. They're old blood. But now… Well, if he's carrying the magic of two dead fae and who knows who else, it'll be next to impossible to stand against him."

So where did that leave us? Because between these people and Dara, I knew who I'd prefer to take my chances with. And Alyssa was caught right in the middle.

Chapter 19
Alyssa

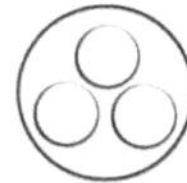

Thursday, 10:30 a.m.

A S SOON AS the door closed behind me, I pulled up Simon's number. He answered after the first ring.

"Alyssa? Thank the infernals. Where the hell are you? Are you all right?"

Warmth sprouted from my heart at his concern, and despite the chemical fire that was my life, I couldn't help but smile as I said, "I'm okay. I'm holed up in Stittsville at the house of some wacky computer genius. Did you know they actually exist? He's like something out of one of those crime shows you love to make fun of so much."

I was babbling. Great.

"Did you know someone stole your car?" he asked, ignoring

my ramblings, thank goodness. "I went back to the pub this morning to grab it like I said I would, and it was gone."

I sighed and dropped onto the edge of the bed, the weight of my night dragging my shoulders down. "I know. Someone used it when they killed a second fae. Even more evidence to throw against me."

"What the fuck?" In the silence that followed on the other end of the line, I heard Simon scrambling to parse through everything I'd dumped on him, and I closed my eyes to find some grounding. Since I'd found myself in Trace's car, all I'd wanted was to talk to my friend, but now that I had him on the phone, I had no idea where to begin.

"The person who hired Trace?" I said. "It was Dara Josef-Levesque, the fae duchess."

"Trace?" he asked, and I rolled my eyes that he'd homed in on that irrelevant detail.

"Wyatt," I clarified. "You know, the charming bounty hunter who trashed our pub?"

"We're calling him Trace now? What kind of dad-joke name is that for a bounty hunter to have, anyway?"

"It's not his real name. Even better? His computer buddy's name is Chip. I'm guessing they were drunk the night they figured out their code names."

"You're with that guy now?"

Any other time, his incredulity might have made me laugh

or feel all warm and fuzzy at the hint of protectiveness, but today I wasn't feeling it.

"Yeah. He got me away from Dara. Believed me when I said I didn't kill Vivi."

"How the hell did you wind up in front of her in the first place?"

"He, uh…" I wet my lips. "He kind of grabbed me from behind the house when I took out the garbage."

"I'll kill him, I swear to the infernals."

I waved my hand, as though he were here to see it. "It's fine. No harm done. Kind of. If he hadn't kidnapped me, I'd still have no idea who was after me, but we've been working together, and I have a few answers." I grimaced. "None of them good."

"Tell me."

"Remember Delvin?"

"Son of a demon whore."

"That's the one." I took him through everything: Delvin hiring the facestealer to take my shape to pin Vivi's murder on me, the fact that Delvin had been tasked by someone else to set me up, the fact that with every new thing we learned, the problem got that much bigger. And once I got started, the more easily the story came, if no more pleasantly. Finally, I brought us back here, to the name of Clyde Corrick and the possibility that we were closing in on the person who wanted me dead by

Dara's hand.

"Corrick?" Simon repeated, confused.

I frowned. "Yeah. You know him?"

"So do you, Lys. His people have come by the pub a few times. Left his card telling us to call if ever we wanted to sell. Remember? The woman who scared the crap out of you a few months back when she cornered you in the alley while you were taking out the trash?"

What was it with people taking advantage of my vulnerability while I held garbage? That was it. Going forward, I would use magic to clean. No more trash runs for me.

But at Simon's description, the night came back to me. A woman as large as Delvin had backed me against the wall and told me to consider leaving the business behind. That had been six months ago. I'd put it out of my mind when I'd never seen her again.

"You're sure that was Corrick?" It wasn't so much that I doubted Simon as that I wanted him to be wrong. That woman had been terrifying. If she worked for Corrick, then it meant if I wanted to confront him, I would have to go through her. "I thought Trace was phoning it in when he suggested someone might be after the bar. Who the hell would go as far as murder to get their hands on some property?"

"Take it as a compliment that you've made such a name for yourself."

I slowly patted myself on the back. "Well done, me. Earning so much success, I've gained an enemy. Just what every business owner wants." My stomach twisted. "I don't know what to do, Simon. Chip is downstairs right now doing research on this guy. I guess we know what he'll find. Do I go talk to Corrick?"

"Only if you want to wind up in a shallow grave somewhere."

"I appreciate your optimism."

"And I question your sanity. You really think knocking on his door and asking him to stop is going to make a difference? He murdered two fae."

"And stole their magic," I reminded him, as if that made the situation better. My frown deepened as my words sank in. "He stole their magic. I get the murder, sure. I mean, I guess? But the magic theft…"

"To make you look worse?"

"Hard to argue with that. It pushes me from regular criminal to SMOAC's Most Wanted."

Was that really all it was? Somehow the logic didn't make the leap for me, but maybe it was simply a crime of opportunity. Someone had been hired to commit murder, so they'd opted to up their power at the same time? What was the risk if someone else got blamed for it?

Then they'd tipped me off to Dara, hoping she would kill me before SMOAC caught wind of the murder and picked me up, because surely someone in the security office would notice I wasn't carting around any fae magic, right?

A chill ran through me at the possibility that no one would bother to check, but I shoved my fears under a rock and tried to ignore them. I had Jet and Madison on my team. Even if security got their hands on me, my friends wouldn't let SMOAC throw me in a dark prison for the rest of my life when there was so much evidence to prove my innocence.

I considered the wisdom of turning myself in before they tracked me down, but despite my confidence in my friends, my worries that Dara's influence was too strong remained. I might not be killed, but I might waste away in Moongrave Prison before they let me plead my case.

"What do I do?" I hated how small my voice sounded. "If I can't reason with this man and Dara won't listen to me unless I prove who the actual murderer is, how do I get out of this?"

I felt like I was standing on a very thin ledge over a very deep chasm and the wall behind me was inching forward.

"You don't think Dara will accept what you learned from Delvin?"

"Not unless I drag Delvin to her door, and I don't think he's up for it. Still holding a bit of a grudge."

Were my teeth chattering? I nearly dropped the phone with the force of my tremors.

"It's all right, Lys," Simon said softly, and I appreciated how well he knew me to recognize the signs of my encroaching panic attack. "We'll figure this out. Where are you? I'll come get you, and we can go somewhere safe to talk and put together a plan."

I thought about how Chip would react if I gave out his address. I certainly wouldn't be invited for a backyard barbecue any time soon. Then again, did I honestly intend to have anything more to do with these two after I cleared my name? Or if I didn't?

But boy, did I want to see Simon. Without his sweater to offer me comfort, I'd been bereft. He'd been my rock for so many years, I was lost without him.

"Chip probably has armed missiles aimed at his driveway for anyone who pulls up without an invitation," I said, "but I'm sure we'll be leaving again soon. Trace has to have a plan of attack, and as soon as I have an idea what it is, I'll call you so you can come meet us. I'd feel a lot better with you around."

"Hey," he said, and I imagined staring into his steady amber gaze. "We'll get through this."

My throat tightened, and I nodded, unable to speak until I mustered a choked, "Thanks."

When he said it, I almost believed him.

I hung up and debated calling my family to let them know where I was but opted against it. I didn't have four hours to calm my mother down, and I doubted my father would have any ideas on how to talk my way out of a murder charge. Gramps would call a family meeting and they'd debate calling in the Ontario Witches' Council, but that raised the same risks as turning myself in to SMOAC.

But at least I'd touched base with Simon. It was the contact with my normal life that I'd needed. The reminder that I had something beyond this nightmarish, shitty situation waiting for me.

And now we had knowledge, which could only move us forward. Right? I squared my shoulders and headed downstairs. Whatever our next step might be, I had to be ready to face it.

Chapter 20
Alyssa

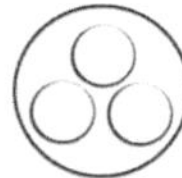

Thursday, 10:45 a.m.

TRACE LOOKED UP at me when I reached the living room, and by his expression, I guessed I had missed something serious. And very not good. So it was great that I had my own revelation to share with him about Corrick's identity. It wasn't fair that he always got to be the bearer of bad news.

"You make your phone call?" he asked, and I knew he was putting off whatever he really wanted to say.

"Yeah. It was enlightening. Turns out Corrick made himself known to me about six months ago. He sicced his…" I trailed off as my gaze landed on Chip's computer screen. "Her. He sicced her on me. The woman who looks like she could crush rocks with her fists."

"That would be Rosie Alvarez," Trace said. "She very likely could."

I turned to him and found him staring at me, silver and violet warring in his eyes. "So you know."

"Oh yeah," Chip said without turning around. "I don't suppose you're aware of any secrets about your pub you haven't shared with us? Like it was built on some crazy powerful magical field or something?"

"No, why?"

He brought up a satellite view of Somerset, and I balked at the haze around the pub. "What the hell is that?"

"Déjà vu," Chip said. "Doesn't mean anything to you?"

"Nothing."

"What about the fact that one Edwyn Mooney owns the property?"

"That's my grandfather. He bought the pub, and I know he got a really good deal and landed the property it's on too. But it's also in my name now. His, mine, and Simon's."

"Not just the property. Mooney's is basically its own principality. You pay property taxes to fool the mundanes and get the perks like snow removal, but your business is essentially its own country."

I snorted a laugh, too stunned to respond appropriately. "How about that, Trace? I guess I'm a princess after all."

Trace was still staring at me with an unreadable expression, and my heart fluttered for reasons I couldn't identify.

"Whatever the reason," Chip continued, and it took me a moment to realize he wasn't talking about my heart, "these are some bad-as-shit people coming after you. You pretty much won the asshole lottery. Keeping you alive…" He clinched his opinion with a whistle, and I ground my teeth.

"Simon thinks I would be insane to try talking to Corrick and asking him to stop." For the life of me, I didn't know why I said it. I knew he was right, and I'd already set the idea aside. All it did was call attention to my ignorance of how to handle the problem life had thrown at me—which was confirmed by Chip's snort of derision.

"You think?" he said. "If these guys didn't tear you apart before you got close, they would do something worse. Make your death look like you'd killed yourself out of guilt for these murders, or that you were killed trying to commit another one. Or that you used your new fae magic and overpowered yourself into an early grave."

"Thanks for that, Chip."

He shrugged. "Just laying out your odds."

While he'd blathered on with apparent enjoyment over the various scenarios of my demise, I'd caught the flash in Trace's gaze when I'd mentioned Simon's name, and my stomach turned sloshy.

"Chip's right," he said, and his voice was bland. "Going

head-to-head with them will only get you killed. We need to find proof we can bring to Dara. The word of two demons won't cut it."

Relief tore a hole through my growing fear, and I clung to it. Trace had a plan. Of course he did. The man seemed to be made of them.

"So where do we go from here?"

He frowned. "Your buddy Delvin might have helped us more than he meant to. By confessing that he was asked to frame you, he opened the door for me to search the Common Ledger. No one makes a deal with a demon without writing the terms in the Ledger unless they want their soul ripped out of their body the moment their guard drops. It could be proof enough to satisfy Dara."

This was the first I was hearing about any Ledger, but I took Trace at his word. I wondered how many times his name appeared in the book.

"Unfortunately, I'm not a demon, so to access the Ledger, I need the code, and the code is in my office, which is too public for you to come with me. You should stay here with Chip while I go."

I crossed my arms. "I don't think so. If you believe this is what we need to clear my name, then I'm going."

Trace's jaw flexed. "I'll be coming right back. You aren't safe outside the house."

"I can take care of myself. Besides, Simon wants to see me, make sure I'm all right. He can meet us at your office, and we can watch my back together while you do your thing."

Again that glint in his eyes, though this time I suspected it was annoyance more than anything.

"Fine. You want to stick your neck in the noose? Be my guest. I'm just doing what I can to keep you breathing."

I dropped my arms, the fight draining out of me. "I know you are, and I thank you. But I can't stand to be left behind on this. It's my life. I can't let other people take all the risk. Or not be involved in trying to save it."

He hesitated another moment before nodding. "Then let's go."

Chip looked between the two of us and rolled his eyes to the heavens. "Gag."

Trace's office was located above a dispensary on Bank Street, where parking was minimal in the summer, let alone when snowbanks crowded the street. He finally found a spot around the corner, and we rushed into the building and up the narrow staircase that led to the offices over the shop.

"I won't be long." He jerked his head to the chair in front of his desk. "May as well take a seat."

"So what is this Ledger, exactly? Is it an actual book?"

"It is and it isn't," he said as he sat down. "It exists in the infernal dimensions, and only a demon can summon the physical book into this world. Everyone else has to jump through a bunch of hoops to access a digital copy."

"A demon. You mean like Simon?"

Trace looked up from his computer. "Yes, I guess he could have done it for us. Since we're here, though, we may as well see the entry for ourselves."

The same flash crossed his expression as before, along with a glimpse of stubbornness against involving my business partner. Exhilarated confusion swirled in my chest as I wondered why that might be.

"And it contains the details of every demon deal?" I asked, hoping to drown my surge of irrational attraction under a crashing wave of curiosity.

"If the person making the deal is smart enough to add it, yeah. Dates, terms, consequences. Everything in black and white. A group of witches came up with the idea centuries ago, and thankfully, it stuck. A lot of lives have been saved because of it."

For all I knew about this world, it amazed me how much I still had to learn.

Trace booted up his computer, and I sank into the comfortable black conference room chair.

"Do you live in Ottawa?" When I realized how "do you come here often?" that sounded, I cleared my throat. "I just mean since you have office space here."

He followed my gaze and shrugged. "No, but I'm here often enough that I like to have somewhere to get my paperwork done. It's not always in this building, but I have the lease for another few months."

The office was simple but warm, with light-grey walls, a row of windows overlooking Bank Street, and a few potted plants dotting the mostly colourless space. I was surprised to see the greenery flourishing without a single brown leaf, suggesting a great deal of care went into their upkeep, until I sensed the subtle threads of magic woven into the stalks.

That made much more sense.

The carpet was a worn navy blue, the only thing about the place that appeared dated, but it was devoid of dirt or threadbare patches, so I gave him credit for the occasional vacuum. On the wall, where I might have expected to see photos of Trace with famous clients or newspaper articles of his illustrious career, there were framed movie posters, and I found myself smiling at Uma Thurman where she lay stretched out on the cover of *Pulp Fiction*.

Very much not what I'd expected of Trace Wyatt, but now that I saw it, I appreciated how fitting it was.

And how much I liked it.

An uncomfortable sensation slithered through my belly as my memories returned to Club Crescent. Not so much what had happened in the club as what had taken place outside it. The way he'd drawn his fingers along my jaw after I'd healed his hand. The warmth of his breath on my skin and the way the soft blue in his eyes had darkened with want.

How long had it been since anyone had looked at me like that?

Well, Simon sometimes, but his expression was always laced with regret. Like someone eyeing a box of doughnuts but having the willpower to stay away.

The way Trace had looked at me… I'd definitely been the box of doughnuts, but the willpower had been questionable. As though, if I'd said to hell with the pheromones, he would have dragged me back into the club's stairwell and taken me up against the wall.

Electric shocks shot out from my core as the visual flickered behind my eyelids, and I must have made a noise as I shifted in my seat, because he glanced up from his computer screen.

"Almost in," he said, and the proximity of those words to my fantasy nearly drew a moan from me.

"That's fine." I prayed he didn't notice my flushed cheeks. "Is there a bathroom in here I could use?"

"Down the hall, to your left. The lock catches a bit, so don't panic if it doesn't open right away once you've finished."

I left him to wrap up and went down the hallway to splash water on my face and scrub my head clear of inappropriate daydreams. Those pheromones had to be potent if the effects were still kicking around. I refused to consider the pulsing desire between my legs as anything other than fabricated.

We were almost finished here, and then my life could go back to normal.

Although, as I stared myself down in the mirror, I had to wonder what my new normal would look like. Would I be able to put the events of the past nine hours behind me? Would I be able to move on as though they'd never happened?

Would I be able to walk away from Trace as though I'd never met him?

Chapter 21
Trace

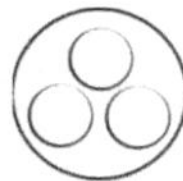

Thursday, 11:30 a.m.

I PLUGGED A few more codes into my computer, each password bringing me closer to the Ledger.

Not for the first time, I wondered why there wasn't an easy spell to conjure the thing if it was supposed to be public access, but as always, I sucked up the necessity of the barriers.

The Common Ledger was an important document for both signer and signee, but it was also filled with information that could be lethal in untrained or mundane hands. The list of demon names, for starters. The last thing the world needed was a bunch of power-seeking humans gaining that kind of knowledge. We would be overrun by poorly worked or flawed summonings. Not to mention the death, disaster, and media cover-ups we'd have to deal with. Mostly problems for the government, but if they affected my client base, then it was in my best interests to support the status quo.

Which meant tolerating all the hoops I was currently jumping through and once again asking myself why I was going so far to help a practical stranger.

There. Finally.

The screen flickered as the pages of the Ledger appeared, the digital tome not playing nicely with my remaining hard drive space.

The book appeared as a scanned document, opening on the most recent page. Maybe I should have been surprised by how many recent additions there had been over the past twenty-four hours, but I really wasn't.

I scrolled up until I found Delvinorath's name—a squiggle that came off as angry as he did. Beside his name was Clyde Corrick's, and there, in black and white, was… nothing. Nothing useful, anyway.

The terms are as follows: that Delvinorath shall ensure the presence of a chosen individual to be at the agreed-upon location at the agreed-upon time on the agreed-upon day in exchange for future reward.

Nothing about framing Alyssa, nothing about helping to cover up the murder.

Was Corrick as ignorant as that? Keeping the details vague was asking to be screwed over. Demons were never to be trusted. Not the friendly ones like Alyssa's partner, and most certainly not assholes like Delvin.

Yet for some reason Delvin had also failed to cover his ass. In exchange for future reward? They obviously had an off-the-books agreement about something, and if it was worth Delvin taking the risk of doing the job without the details being in print, it had to be something big.

And something big meant something bad for Alyssa because it meant everyone involved would be ready to fight for it.

Before I could delve too deeply into what that something bad might be, a surge of magic caught my attention.

A supernatural passing through my ward around the front door.

I dashed to the window to peer down, and my heart stopped when I spotted the black Cadillac double parked in front of the building.

Dara.

If she found Alyssa here, there was no way she'd let her walk out a free woman. Or give me time to tell her what we'd learned.

What little we'd learned.

Without hesitating, I darted into the hallway and slammed a magical barricade over the bathroom door, soundproofing and barring the exit. Alyssa could scream at me all she wanted later, but it was the only way I could think to keep her safe, and there was no time for explanations. Already footsteps were climbing the stairs towards the second floor, and in the window of space remaining to me, I stepped into my office as though I were just coming out as the door at the end of the hallway opened.

Dara and Peter looked pissed.

"Mr. Wyatt."

"Your Grace." I bowed my head, as though the last time we met I hadn't used my magic against her.

"Office," she seethed. "Now."

I stood aside and invited them in, the epitome of politeness. Not that it would speed things along, but anything I could do to salvage my bruised reputation.

Dara rounded my desk and sat in my chair, a pointed reminder of the power dynamic, but I let it slide. I didn't feel the need to have a pissing contest, but if she did, she was welcome to claim the win.

I remained standing across from her and did my best to keep my expression impassive, to let her lead the conversation and offer nothing until I knew where I stood.

Except she said nothing. Her severe haircut added to the dangerous glint in her star-filled eyes, the cheekbones under her umber skin just as sharp. Everything about this woman was lethal, and I had potentially made an enemy of her. For a woman I barely knew.

The silence stretched out, and my thoughts drifted to Alyssa trapped in the bathroom. By now she had to have noticed she was locked in. How long before her magic overpowered mine and she came charging right into Dara's arms? Even if it meant revealing my hand, I had to move things along.

"I trust you're well?" I asked.

Her eyes narrowed, but I didn't quail under her stare.

"I've been hard at work since this morning," I said. "Turns out Miss Mooney was telling the truth. We've already gotten two admissions from demons who were hired to set her up."

"You trust the word of demons?" Her rich voice dripped with scorn.

"Under the circumstances? Yes, I do." I nodded at my computer. "I was in the process of digging up some proof. You see the deal between Delvinorath and Clyde Corrick."

She pressed her lips into a fine line and spared the smallest glance at my screen before pinning me once more under her glower. "Tell me."

"Corrick, a local low-powered witch-slash-business owner has been trying to take over Mooney's Pub. He arranged to have Alyssa set up for the murders to get her out of the way."

Something I said—or maybe all of it—made Dara raise a perfectly shaped eyebrow, and, if it was possible, her disdain increased. "You expect me to believe two fae have been murdered and their magic stolen in some sort of business take-over?"

"We have reason to think it's more than that. That there might be something special about—"

"I've formed many opinions about you since this began, Mr. Wyatt," she interrupted. "I even respected your decision to defend the woman when you believed her to be innocent, but your judgement is obviously to be questioned in the presence of a pretty face. If you jump to sleeping with marks, I don't see your career taking any substantial leaps past where it already is."

I ground my teeth and didn't bother to correct her. There was no point. Denial would only confirm her suspicions. And the worst part was, sex aside, she wasn't wrong. I had broken so many house rules for Alyssa, and even if it was her magic that drew me instead of her beauty—though, goddess, she was beautiful—my judgement was clouded.

Because, while I knew Alyssa hadn't committed the crimes she was accused of, the fact I'd thought a few demons' confessions would make a difference was proof I was deluded.

"Let's not waste any more time, Mr. Wyatt." Dara crossed her arms on my desk in the most regal, stiff imitation of casualness I'd ever seen. "I came here to make a deal. You have until eight o'clock this evening to turn Miss Mooney—or her corpse—over to me, or I add you to my bounty under the assumption that you have become her accomplice in the death of my second fae commander. If you manage to survive, you will never work again, spending the rest of your life on the run. Hunted. Do you understand?"

I was amazed my molars hadn't cracked under the strength of my clenching. She knew about my history. Of course she did. She would have dug up all my dirty laundry before she hired me. Which meant she knew about Hazel and the work we'd done, the souls I'd consumed, the magic I'd absorbed. She knew about the three years I'd spent dodging SMOAC's security officers until I'd finally convinced them I could help them bring down Hazel.

She knew I couldn't live like that again, feeling more animal than human.

The duchess smirked, and for the first time since I'd met her, she was less than attractive. More beast than goddess. "I'll leave you to weigh your options. Consider your twenty-four-hour deadline extended. Meet me in my hotel room with the girl once you've decided. If you show up earlier, I might even be lenient. To both of you."

Her confidence in my choice made my stomach turn. She'd backed me into the corner I'd hoped to avoid until we had more evidence to back us up. I was penned in, something I'd been fighting against for almost a decade. It was why I'd become a bounty hunter. Travel, flexible hours, the ability to wield my magic as I wished within the bounds of the law—or at least within the bounds of my own tested morals.

Staying with Alyssa, continuing this mission, would mean giving up all the progress I'd made putting the past behind me.

Although I refused to say it aloud and stroke her ego, Dara knew she would get her way.

I would do everything possible to keep Alyssa alive, make any deal with Dara I could to ensure Alyssa's safety until I found the proof that would satisfy the duchess, but I knew it wouldn't be enough to make Alyssa forgive me.

And somehow I would have to forgive myself for letting her down.

Chapter 22
Alyssa

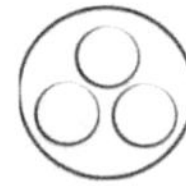

Thursday, 11:45 a.m.

I SLAMMED THE side of my fist on the bathroom door, then resumed jiggling the handle until the aged metal snapped off in my hands.

"Trace?" I shouted, banging my palms against the door. "Trace!"

His magic held the door bound, and although I'd tried to slide my power underneath the spell to tear it apart, it hadn't budged. What the fuck was he doing? Sticky lock, my ass. If this was his idea of a prank, then the second he let me out, I would grab him by the neck and dunk his head in the toilet.

Had he double-crossed me? Caged me in the narrow, dated bathroom to give Dara time to come and pick me up? Corrick?

I wished now I'd called Simon when we'd gotten here so he could turn the bathroom door into a flock of pigeons or something, but my phone was in Trace's coat pocket in his office, which meant I was on my own.

I tried to figure out why he would bail on me now, after everything, but fear rose up and choked me, adding panic to my fury. I had to get out of here, even if it meant knocking a hole through the side of the building and throwing myself out, hoping for a soft, snowy landing.

I called Trace's name again as I switched back to hitting the door as hard as I could, wrapping my hands in magic to add echo and weight to the assault. One more attempt, and then I would try another spell, and if that's what I had to resort to, he would be lucky to see the inside of the toilet. I was more likely to grab him and hurl him through his office window.

"Let me the fuck out of here!"

A moment later, the spell evaporated, and the lock quietly clicked over. The door opened, and I stood, fuming, glaring at where he stood in the hallway.

"Please don't try to tell me that was an accident," I said through clenched teeth.

"No."

At the look on his face, devoid of any amusement at my expense, my anger fizzled into unease. "What happened?"

I'd been in the bathroom for all of what? Three minutes

before he'd locked me in? What the hell could have happened in three minutes?

"Dara was here." His voice was dead, and alarms screamed in my skull. Whatever they'd talked about, it had thrown him for a loop. "She gave me… a friendly ultimatum."

The volume of the alarms increased until my ears buzzed with them, and only by luck did the deep tenor of his voice slip beneath the blaring.

"Oh?" I asked, though I could damn well guess. My chest felt tight, and I held back from grabbing on to my magic. The moment I did, he would sense it, and I needed to be able to get away as soon as the opportunity arose.

Besides, maybe I was wrong. I had to consider the possibility that being hunted, threatened, and herded had left me with a few trust issues. So far Trace had been nothing but supportive and encouraging in my attempt to escape my current predicament alive. What reason did I have to think he'd changed his mind?

"She wants me to bring you to her by eight o'clock, or she's going to hire someone to bring us both in."

That reason. That reason right there.

"Ah."

"Yeah."

He shoved his fingers in his jeans pockets and cocked his head, his gaze dropping to his boots. I crossed my arms and wished I were wearing something a little less revealing. He didn't deserve to see so much of my girls right now if he was heading in the direction I suspected he was.

"I'm not saying I'm going to hand you over," he said, though he didn't lift his eyes, which didn't do much to reassure me.

"Okay."

"But I think we need to assess our options."

"Right."

Because we had so many of those, and I was sure Trace intended to take each one step by step. Maybe make a spreadsheet. Colour code it with all the ways I was royally screwed. I was sure we could sit down and find some kind of compromise. *I'll hand you over to be murdered, but I'll buy you dinner first.*

I curled my hands into fists and dug my nails into my palms. I wouldn't summon my magic. Not until my way was clear. I couldn't afford to waste whatever slim chance I got. I also wouldn't cry, even if the corners of my eyes had begun to sting. Somehow we were back at square one. Quietly this time. Less structural damage. But there we were.

Finally, he looked up to meet my eye, and I saw the pain swirling through the violet. The despair. The remorse.

None of it made me feel better.

"Let's go to my office and sit down," he said. "We have time to come up with a plan."

I didn't move. "I can think of a plan." Where I was, I could slam the bathroom door in his face and bind it with magic of my own. In the hallway, I would be vulnerable, and until I had a better grasp on where he stood with this ultimatum, I intended to watch my back. I'd learned a lot over the past few hours. "The plan is you let me walk out of here and tell Dara you lost me and don't know where I am. Then you can pretend to hunt me down while I stay the hell away from you."

He flinched as though I'd slapped him and rubbed the back of his neck. "I do that, and neither of us will get a chance to walk away from her again. We have to work together on this if we both want to make it out."

"If *you* want to make it out, you mean. Because I thought that's what we were doing—working together, trying to find evidence to clear my name." I jerked my chin towards his office. "What about the Ledger? Did you find what you were looking for?"

"They didn't write down any details. The deal reads like a bad vaudeville sketch."

"But we have what they told us. If we put that together with what's on paper…"

He was already shaking his head. "She's made it clear she won't take the word of demons." He paused, appeared to chew on his words. "She also didn't buy the story that Corrick is coming after the pub. And to be fair, unless we find out what he's really after, it's a weak motive."

Nausea bubbled in my guts. What was he doing? Pulling away from me? Turning his back? Leaving me all alone on this cracking branch dangling over a pit of alligators waiting to snap me up?

"Sure, but we already knew that, didn't we?" I asked, though I didn't really care what excuses he was telling himself. "I thought we were working on the assumption that there's more to the bar. Something we don't know about."

"Even so, why go to such lengths to get rid of you? He's put a lot of effort into this. Murder. Delvin. Shiny. He has connections. Why not make an offer to your grandfather that Edwyn can't refuse?"

My voice was tight as I replied, "Because it's Mooney property down to its foundations, and we're not letting go of it because some mobbed-up bully wants to add it to his collection."

A light sparked in his eyes, and I hoped my confidence would be enough to keep him with me, but too soon the spark went out, and he shrugged. "Even so, he has other options. There has to be more to the story, and according to Dara, we're out of time to figure it out."

"No, you're out of time. I have all the time in the world to keep digging if you let me leave."

"Will you please come back to my office so we can talk?" he asked again, stepping backwards to give me space.

"No, I think I prefer it right here in this reeking bathroom, thank you."

"Come on, Alyssa." He spread his hands in supplication. "I'm not going to throw you to her and walk away. Do you honestly believe I would do that?"

I swallowed hard, thinking about Club Crescent and the street outside, thinking about the way he'd looked at me right before I'd gone to the bathroom and we'd found ourselves here at the beginning. I didn't want to believe it. I found myself wishing he and I had met under different circumstances. But if wishes were empties, I'd have enough bottle returns to support every cat rescue in the city.

"I don't know," I said. "I don't know you, and I don't know what you would consider part of the job. You're a bounty hunter, Wyatt. The country's best. You have no reason to give that up for someone you just met, and that doesn't allow me to put a lot of faith in you when Dara is breathing down our necks."

Again that hurt expression, and my heart twinged. How nice it would be to think our time together had made him care for me enough that he would hate to see me dead. That he would put his job, his freedom, maybe his life on the line to protect me. But I was a grown woman and had set hopes for a fairy-tale ending aside a long time ago.

Around the time I'd fallen for a chaos demon who could

never drop his magical guard around me.

I had the worst luck with men.

But, as though my words finally got through to Trace, his face hardened, and when he spoke, his voice was even and cold. "Then we need to buy ourselves time to find evidence Dara will accept. It's noon now, so we have eight hours until she expects me to bring you to her. We could backtrack, see if we missed anything. If Corrick is after something specific, maybe we can find out what it is."

Something in the way he said it kept me on edge, but goddess, I wanted to believe him.

"You really think we can still get ahead of this?"

"I do."

He sounded so certain, so confident.

Despite my better judgement, I dropped my hands and inched out of the bathroom. "I'm not going to Dara. Not unless we have something solid to present to her."

He didn't break eye contact as he nodded, and something in my chest relaxed, even as I noted that he hadn't actually agreed.

"I'll grab my coat, and we'll head out." He backed away from me towards his office. "Nothing on my computer can help us now, and we'll leave Chip to continue his research. I say we head back to your buddy Delvin and see what else we can drag out of him. There's a note that Corrick promised him something in exchange for his help. I want to know what it is."

"Great," I deadpanned, "just the demon I wanted to spend more time with."

In the face of going back into that bastard's office, Dara suddenly didn't seem like my worst option.

Chapter 23

Alyssa

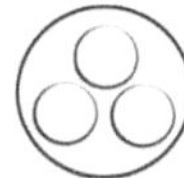

Thursday, 12:00 p.m.

THE TENSION BETWEEN Trace and me remained high after we left his office and trudged through the snow to his SUV. He said nothing as he started the engine and turned up the heat. Said nothing as he pulled away from the curb and headed towards Sparks Street.

We should have walked.

It would have taken us fifteen minutes, even through the snow, and at least then I could have blamed the silence on my face being frozen.

As it was, the awkwardness grew, stalked, loomed over us, and the longer we went without speaking, the more impossible it seemed that we would ever speak to each other again. I found myself missing the easiness that had formed between us over the course of the morning. The sense of partnership.

My heart was racing, my palms were clammy, and my stomach had twisted into knots so tight I was sure I'd snap a mental fingernail if I tried to loosen them. Trace had given me his coat again as we'd left the building, and I hunkered under its familiar weight, wishing it would give me the same comfort it had earlier.

When Trace turned left on Queen instead of pulling over near Sparks, my stomach knots squeezed, but I took a breath, wiped my palms on my borrowed jeans, and tried to relax. Parking was tricky with all this snow, and Club Crescent was closer to the Kent Street intersection anyway. It was smart to find somewhere more convenient to stop. Less walking around in the daylight where we might be seen.

Though the time of day in and of itself left me scratching my head.

"Is there any point in going back to the club right now?" I asked, popping the quiet like a very loud, obnoxious balloon. "Do you think he'll still be there? It's basically the middle of the night for him."

Trace didn't take his eyes off the road. "From what I understand, he spends a lot of time at the club. Especially considering how we left things, I doubt he'd be in a rush to leave."

"Yeah, I guess that desk isn't going to pry itself out of the wall."

Another twist of my guts as I remembered the way Delvin had come after me, his wings unfurled, his eyes burning. I didn't particularly want to see his full demon side again, having witnessed it more than enough for one lifetime. Maybe this time I would let Trace do the talking. I could hang out in the bar and have a drink or six.

Or maybe I wouldn't go in at all. I didn't know if my hormones could endure another hit of that air. I could wait in the car. In the driver's seat. Ready to speed off if I needed to.

"Do you think you can get him to tell us the terms of his deal? Do you think he knows the real reason Corrick wants to ruin my life?" The possibility that we might not actually be at the dead end of a cursed and ghoul-infested alley lit an ember of hope within me.

"It's possible. Delvin's a powerful demon. He wouldn't make deals with someone like Corrick unless he got more out of it than revenge. A promise for future contracts, maybe. And if that's the case, he'd want guarantees, details about what he was signing up for, even if they didn't put them in the public Ledger."

My ember dimmed. "But you said Dara wouldn't accept demon confessions, so what will it matter if he told us everything?"

"All we need is an edge. Something we can follow that gives us a tangible clue. The reason they're going after the pub would be our best bet."

He still hadn't looked at me, nor had he scouted for a parking spot along the side of the road. More than that, he hadn't fidgeted once in the past few minutes. No adjusting his leg or tapping his fingers on the steering wheel. No touching his face or brushing a speck of lint off his jeans. All the normal little movements a human being makes when they're at ease.

Instead, he was stiff.

Statue stiff.

His fingers were steel traps around the steering wheel, his nostrils slightly flared, his pupils tiny pinpricks where they bored through the windshield.

My palms tingled, and I pressed them against my legs to avoid balling them into fists.

"So we talk to Delvin, get whatever information we can, and then what? Go back to Chip?"

"Depends on what we learn. If we have enough weight to throw around, we could go straight to Corrick."

I shifted in my seat, closer to the door, and narrowed my eyes at him. "You said it would be stupid to go to Corrick directly."

"And I still think it would be, but if we have proof he's making off-the-books deals with demons, we could use that to get him to talk. SMOAC doesn't take kindly to arrangements they can't track in the Ledger."

The one-eighty in his thinking left me reeling and sounded as weak as our theory that Corrick simply wanted to add to his real estate. I wished Trace would have looked at me as he said it so I'd know how much he actually believed it would work.

"So we convince Corrick to confess—somehow—and take him to Dara?"

"That's my thinking. She made it clear she won't accept anything less than a full confession from the person who committed the murder, and we'll deliver. If we don't, she'll put all the resources she has into hunting us, and the farther we run and the deeper we try to hide, the harder she'll come down on us when she finds us. She's not a fae to be reckoned with, and I won't take that chance."

The intensity in his voice cut through me, and I didn't miss the way his hands tightened around the steering wheel, the knuckles on his long fingers bleeding white.

"Trace?"

"Mm?"

I clung to my seatbelt. "Why aren't we at the club yet? We passed it three blocks ago."

His throat bobbed with a swallow as he turned left onto Lyon Street. "Because I think you're right. Delvin would have made himself scarce the minute we left. He probably gave Corrick the heads up we're on to him and went underground."

"Where are we going instead?" When he didn't answer, I unsnapped my seatbelt and reached for the door handle, but silver magic shocked my fingertips. Once again, I was trapped.

Chapter 24
Alyssa

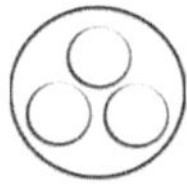

Thursday, 12:15 p.m.

"L ET ME OUT of the car."

"I can't, Alyssa. I'm sorry." He sounded desperate and pained to say it but showed no sign of backing down.

"Let me out of this car, Trace."

Panic dripped off my tongue, and I swallowed it. I had to keep my cool. I wasn't defenceless here. Yes, this man had turned on me, but I wouldn't let him get the better of me.

"Will you just listen?" he said. "We have time to come up with a strategy."

"A strategy where you turn me over to the woman who wants to kill me? Is that what you mean?"

"She won't." Despite the certainty of his words, his doubt

shone through as brightly as his magic, torn with a wild terror. "There's too much proof you didn't commit these crimes. She has to listen to reason."

"Right, because she's been so quick to do that up till now. Let me out of the fucking car."

I braved the shock of his spell to reach for the handle. The burns on my fingertips made me jump back in my seat, and I shoved my fingers into my mouth to soothe the pain.

"I'm sorry, Alyssa, I really am, but I can't go on the run again. I can't go back to looking over my shoulder, not trusting anyone I pass on the street. My sanity can't take it. I'll find a way to help you, I will, but I can't—"

He cut himself off, but I wasn't sure he knew what he was saying. A faint sheen of sweat covered his brow, and his hands slipped on the wheel. His chest rose and fell with rapid, shallow breaths, and I was amazed he could still see.

I recognized the signs of a panic attack from more than enough personal experience. If we didn't want to wind up in a ditch on these snowy, slippery roads, he had to calm down.

"You said it yourself," I said in my most reassuring voice that may have been tinged with a very unreassuring layer of my own fear, "we have eight hours. Why can't we track Delvin down and see what he'll tell us? Or why can't we go to Corrick now with what we have? We could bluff. Make him think we know more than we do."

"Because the way I see it, Corrick is the concrete wall and Dara is the wrecking ball, and we're stuck in the middle about to take the hit. Nothing we have against Corrick will hold as far as Dara is concerned, and he knows it. He planned it this way. He's way too protected not to have covered every inch of his ass. And Dara is so furious that someone has dared to attack her people that she's ready to lash out at anyone who pisses her off. You might not have killed Viviane or the other fae, but you have definitely pissed her off."

"No, *you* pissed her off. If it were only on me, I'd already be dead."

"Fine," he snapped, and turned onto Bronson Avenue with enough speed that my shoulder hit the dash. "Fine, I'll admit it. I fucked up. I thought it would be an easy thing to prove you had nothing to do with these crimes. I had no idea when I forced our way out of that hotel that you were the target of some serious heavy."

"What are you saying? If you'd known, you wouldn't have helped me?"

"If I'd known Corrick's people had even breathed on you, I wouldn't have accepted the job in the first place."

I needed him to look at me. To pull the car over and say these things to my face. The way he was staring wild-eyed out the window, I couldn't tell what was true and what he was spewing out in his fear-ridden fury.

At the same time, I didn't care. He was throwing me off the boat into the turbulent waters of the fae duchess's wrath, and I had to get out of here.

I summoned my magic into my palms and threw it against the spell he'd wrapped around my door, but it bounced off the ward. How had I not noticed him casting it? When had he done it? When he'd helped me into the SUV? Had he already made up his mind to betray me before we left his office?

My heart fractured under the pressure. He'd lied to my face, and I'd believed him. This man had abducted me and thrown me in the trunk of his car, and somehow I'd come to see him as an ally? As someone I could trust with my life? I was such a fool.

Tears pricked the corners of my eyes, but I wouldn't let them fall. First I would get out of his car, and then I would scream to the heavens about the unfairness of the universe.

"You say you want to come up with a plan," I said, trying to distract him from the magic I pulled into my hands. "Do you mean that?"

"Of course I do, Alyssa. I don't want you to die. I don't want to turn you over to her. But right now I don't see any other way forward. Maybe I can leave you with her and ask for a day to find more proof that Corrick is behind this."

"And leave me standing there with a noose around my neck? What if she gets impatient? What if you don't find what you're looking for?"

"There has to be something Dara wants more than you. Something we can use to negotiate for your safety until I get back. I won't abandon you. I will keep fighting until you're free. I promise."

Such a promise might have made me feel better if I didn't think he was deluding himself.

"We could run," I said.

"They'd track us."

"Only until we had something to give them."

"We'd never get close enough. Dara knows what we're trying to do, and we have to assume Corrick does too. We'll have people lying in wait for us to make a move. I'd give it to the end of the night before we were trussed up and thrown at Dara's feet as a sacrifice. The only chance I see for us is to bring you to her and beg for leniency. At least for a time."

"I don't have the same faith in her mercy as you do. I saw the look in her eyes in that hotel room. She would have struck me down right there. And if she was angry then, I can't imagine how quickly she'll act now. You probably won't get the chance to beg for an extra five minutes."

"We can make it happen."

We couldn't. We both knew we couldn't, and his desperation to believe it was possible made me equally desperate to understand why he'd lost faith in his ability to help me.

"You said 'again.'"

"What?" Impatient, irritable. Still in a panic.

"You said you couldn't go on the run *again*. When were you on the run before?"

Finally, his gaze shot my way, his expression so pained, so vulnerable, I almost felt bad for him. A moment later, his eyes were back on the road. His neck grew taut, his words tight when he said, "I was eighteen and got mixed up with an older woman. Hazel. A witch. Stronger by far than I was and always looking to learn more. Dig deeper into whatever power she could find. I was a curious kid. Of course I followed her lead." His voice was so bitter, I tasted it at the back of my throat. "She taught me everything."

I could guess what he meant by that and prayed he didn't go into detail. Fortunately, he stayed focused on the magic.

"Before long, she was looking into spirit magic. Illegal. Dangerous. Fascinating. We played with souls of people who'd died ages ago. Souls no one else cared about. She had a theory that my telekinetic magic would help me contain the spirits in a sort of energy cage. Safeguard me from any ill effects."

A shudder ran through his wide shoulders, and his fingers shook as he pushed his hair out of his face.

"I didn't want to do it. I told her so many times I thought it was a bad idea. But she threatened to leave me, and I couldn't let her walk away when I still had so much to learn."

My magic slid along the door, inch by painful inch, and as we turned onto Riverside. I knew where we were headed: back to the hotel off Prince of Wales. But I had time. Rushing would only risk shrinking my window.

"What did you do?"

His throat bobbed. "I went along with her. And she was right. My power was able to contain the souls we experimented with. But then she started talking about *using* them, and I couldn't let her do it. That was magic theft, even if they were already dead. I told her I'd report her to the witches' council or even SMOAC if she kept going down that path."

Goosebumps rose along my arms.

"And?"

"She got to SMOAC first. Told them I had cast the spell. Harvested the souls. Planned to take more. I'd already let them go, but that didn't matter. The feds came after me hard. I ran. For three years."

"Three years?"

He jerked his head in a nod. "Never stayed in one place longer than a day. Left the country for a while, but their reach is long, and magic theft… Well, no country fucks around with magic theft. Three. Fucking. *Years*, Alyssa. Never showing my face, only travelling at night. Giving up so much—*so much*—just to keep breathing for one more day."

I couldn't imagine. Not only on the run but betrayed by

someone he'd trusted? Loved? To a point, I was standing in front of a pretty big mirror.

"What changed?" I asked. My magic had finally slipped under his ward and was slowly prying it away from the door. He didn't seem to have noticed.

"I finally found someone in SMOAC willing to hear me out. Someone who recognized that Hazel was the bigger threat and wanted to bring her down for a dozen other reasons. They told me if I wanted my freedom, I'd have to work with them. So I did. The bitch has been rotting in Moongrave for nine years."

At least there was that, though I suspected the thought didn't bring him as much satisfaction as he wanted it to.

A lot of things suddenly made sense. Why he'd helped me. Why he would stop helping me.

Why he looked as though he'd swallowed a handful of glass.

We turned onto Prince of Wales. From here it was only a short jaunt to the inn. If I was going to make a move, it would have to be soon.

Would Dara already be in her room, waiting for me to be dropped off like a Thanksgiving turkey? Probably. She likely suspected Trace had made up his mind while she was in his office and would want to get me off his hands as quickly as possible.

Threatening him by using his past against him had been

clever. Almost a guarantee to get him to follow orders. But if that were the case, why hadn't he handed me over right then? He could have gotten rid of me without all this fuss.

The fact he hadn't gave me hope he was telling the truth when he said he didn't want this. If so, I still had a chance to get him to change his mind. Find another solution.

"Okay, so we can't run, but we could fight. Our united magic could stand against anything Corrick threw at us."

He rubbed a hand down his face. "And get us killed in the process."

"We could win."

"We could. We could also bring the heat of the entire supernatural business community down on our heads."

"That's a big assumption. My family would stand with us, and their involvement would bring in others. We wouldn't fight alone."

"I can't—I'm not you. That's a big risk for me to take."

And why should I take it for you?

The question went unsaid, but I heard it anyway.

It was the question I'd asked on his behalf since this started. I'd been waiting for the other shoe to drop, and it had. He'd come to his senses, realized the witch behind the bar wasn't worth his life, and decided to call it a day.

How could I hold that against him? I was a mark. Nothing more. He'd said as much to Chip when he didn't know I was listening.

But he would have to forgive me because I wasn't about to give up.

I picked away at his magic, and finally the spell around the door dispersed. I bit down on my cheer of victory, hoping in all his panic, he'd missed our shift in power. The traffic on this patch of Prince of Wales was too busy to try to break free just yet, but I set my hand beside my leg, ready to grab the handle at the first opportunity.

"I'll do everything I can to get you out of there. I swear I will." His fervor soothed my ego even if it did nothing to change my intentions. "I won't leave you to them."

He crossed an intersection, and as his speed picked up, I was pulled back to last night. Nine hours ago, I'd been in the trunk of his car working at the spell around the latch. I'd escaped, and he'd come after me. I couldn't let him get that close again. He would bind me, something he should have done the moment he'd made up his mind to turn me over to Dara. But he hadn't. Sympathy for me—or empathy, or desire, or whatever it was he felt towards me—had stayed his hand in blocking my magic, and unfortunately for him, that act of kindness would kick him in the ass.

"I believe you," I said, and I meant it. Regardless of what he'd decided to do with me, he didn't want to throw me to the wolves without any defence. I believed that after his panic died down, he would wrack his brain to come up with a way to get me out of their hands.

I just didn't believe it would be enough.

This was best for both of us. He wouldn't have to lie to Dara about what had become of me, and he could go back to being the hunter instead of the hunted. I would have to move quickly, but I would find a way to save myself.

He must have heard something in my voice because he tore his gaze from the road and looked at me. I saw the pain in his violet eyes, the questions, the hope, and I offered an apologetic smile in response.

His expression turned to one of confusion, but as the car jerked towards the ditch, his attention returned to the road. He grasped the steering wheel, but I already held it firm under a twist of purple magic, and I wrenched it to the right, further setting him off balance.

"Alyssa—What the fuck—What are you—"

The traffic to our left opened, and I spun the steering wheel again. The SUV careened off the road, slipped on a patch of ice, and soared into the ditch on the opposite side. As soon as we lurched to a stop, I grabbed the door handle, leapt out of the car, and threw a spell behind me to lock the doors before I sprinted down the street, leaving Trace trapped in the wreckage.

Chapter 25
Alyssa

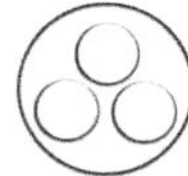

Thursday, 12:30 p.m.

MY SHOULDER ACHED beneath Trace's coat, the side of my head throbbed, but I ran up Prince of Wales towards Hunt Club Road with my focus solely on getting somewhere safe. I looked back every few steps for the first while to make sure Trace hadn't found a way out of the car, and I only started to breathe a bit easier when the gas station on the corner came into view with no sign of him.

I hoped he was all right.

While I needed to stay ahead of him, I didn't want him injured.

Not seriously, anyway.

I wouldn't mind if he had some aches and pains that

inconvenienced him for the next few weeks—he deserved it for trying to screw me over—but nothing more than that. He'd prioritized his freedom over mine, and if I wished him harm for something so natural, I would be no better than Dara wanting me dead for someone else's crime.

Bitch.

Now that I was away from Trace's fear, with some temporary freedom ahead of me, I had time to mull over the fact that he'd told her our evidence, every last scrap we'd gathered over the past nine hours, and she'd discounted it. The woman was so hyperfocused on blaming me that she was willing to overlook the person who had actually killed her people, and I had no idea why. Did she not care about her people? Was she just looking for an easy donkey to pin the tail on?

Did she already know who had murdered Viviane?

The thought nearly stopped my heart, but finding out the truth was a later problem. First I had to get somewhere public where I could both hide and be around enough people that if Trace found me, he couldn't wrestle me away too easily, and then I had to call Simon. He would pick me up, we would go somewhere to lie low until we figured out what the hell my next step was, and then I would act.

It occurred to me my family might be the better point of contact, but somehow I couldn't bring myself to reach out to them. There would be too much to explain, too many worries to soothe, and I didn't have time for that. Not until I had a plan to present to them.

I rushed into the Tim Hortons and sank against the door to catch my breath. My head swam as my blood caught up with my heart rate, and I sank my chin to my chest until the stars in my vision disappeared. At least I'd made it this far.

To a coffee shop.

Where I had no purse with me.

Goddammit.

I stuffed my hands into the pockets of Trace's coat, only feeling a smidgen of guilt that I'd run off with it, and almost crowed in victory as my fingers found a lone bill tucked into the corner on the right side.

Thank you, goddess.

I pulled it out, happy enough to see a blue fiver, and got in line. Now that I'd stepped into the warmth of the familiar coffee shop, my priorities had shifted. First warmth, then call Simon.

I ordered my drink, waited the thirty seconds until the peppermint tea steeping in boiling water was placed in front of me, and made my way to the farthest corner where I could see the street and have early warning if Trace tracked me down.

Part of me hoped to see his face cutting through the snow that had started again, and I told that part of me to shush. If everything went how I needed it to, I wouldn't see him until I had irrefutable proof of my innocence in my hands, and then I could throw the resolution in his and Dara's faces.

And I could repay his five dollars.

If things did not go my way, it was possible I would never see him again and my last view of his handsome face would be the terror in his eyes as his SUV had veered off the side of the road.

My chest squeezed, but I breathed through the pain. I'd done what I had to do. Either he understood that, or he was an asshole. I really hoped he wasn't an asshole.

I pulled my brick phone out of the left pocket and opened it to my contact list. Simon's name was at the top, making it the work of a moment to pull up his number. But before I could hit dial, an incoming call came in.

My heart jumped into my throat that it was Trace, but a moment later, Madison's name showed up, and my stomach sank into the soles of my snow-filled boots. Somehow I knew that whatever news awaited me on the other end of the line would not make my day better.

"Hey, Madi, what's up?"

"Alyssa, thank goodness."

At her greeting, I pulled the phone away from my ear to check the call log and found three missed calls from her in the past fifteen minutes. My stomach sank a little deeper. Definitely not good news.

"What's wrong?" I asked, though I really didn't want to know.

"Word just came through that our security team has pegged you for the fae murders. I pulled my weight as much as I could with the minister, but he's leaving our officers to sort out the details, and from how it looks right now, it's not good. Whoever is setting you up, they've done a great job paving the way for it."

I groaned and bowed my head into my hand. "I don't suppose you know anything about Clyde Corrick that I can hold over his head?"

"*He's* behind this?"

"Turns out, yeah."

A low groan of frustration buzzed in my ear. "I don't. The only person better at covering his tracks in this city is the leader of the Death's Head Syndicate, and as pieces of ogre excrement they're two of a kind."

I shuddered at the mention of Canada's most notorious crime gang. "Hey, could be worse. Could be O'Malley himself I'm up against."

"Be careful, Alyssa. Corrick doesn't have a lot of magic, but he got where he is because he knows how to work the right crowds and win the favours of the right people. Keep your distance."

I didn't reply, not wanting to make promises I fully intended to break.

Though a question did pop into my head. "Hey, Madi, do you know anything about Mooney's Pub? About the deal Gramps made when he bought it from the city?"

"No," she said, and her tone gave away her surprise. "And believe me, I looked into it years ago. I didn't believe it when you told me your family owns it straight out, figured there had to be more to the story. But no, you absolutely do, and the details of the deal make zero sense to me. I have no idea why the city approved it, and not just because of the low offer. Why?"

"Just wondering. We—I—think it might have something to do with why Corrick is after me."

"I wish I could help you more, but I can't offer anything else in case it looks like I'm moving against the department. I love you, but I can't go that far."

"I get it, don't worry. You've done more than enough."

"Keep your head down. Hopefully Trace's resources won't fail you."

"Yeah. Here's hoping. Thanks, Madi."

"Good luck. I'll keep doing what I can on my end, all right? You're not alone in this."

I wished she could see my poor attempt at a smile, but maybe it was for the best she couldn't. I doubted it would have done much to reassure her.

I hung up, sipped my tea to steady myself, and picked up my phone again to call Simon.

"Where are you?" he greeted, and by his tone, I guessed I'd just stepped into another pile of demon shit. At this rate, I'd be swimming in it up to my neck before the night was out.

"The corner of Prince of Wales and Hunt Club. Can you come get me?" I asked. "There's been… a change. A few of them, actually."

"No need to tell me. SMOAC just left, and they had a million questions. They searched the pub, and I think they've already searched your house. Whatever Corrick is up to, he's fooled them as well as Dara."

"I know." I pinched the bridge of my nose. "He's got me backed into a corner."

"Not for long, Lys. I'll be there in twenty."

Chapter 26
Trace

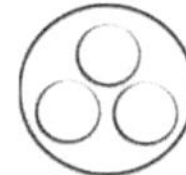

I GROANED AND squeezed my eyes shut against the pain lancing through my skull. Warmth dripped onto my nose, and I wiped my hand across it only to find my fingers smeared with red.

Outside the driver's side window, the snow-and-mud-covered ground was too close, and the windshield showed the world tilted at an awkward angle that made my head spin.

Shouts reached my ears from the road, and I groaned again on seeing a few civic-minded people barrelling towards me. Others stood by their stopped cars, phones pressed to their ears, no doubt calling for help.

Everything to slow me down and waste my time. Alyssa

couldn't have waited until there were no witnesses before she tried to kill me?

Alyssa.

I looked to the passenger side and found the seat empty, the door closed. No sign that she had ever been here. Lucky witch.

I rolled my neck to stretch out the stiffness and fumbled for my seatbelt. As soon as the catch unlocked, I sagged against my door, but when I grabbed the door handle, I was jolted with the same sort of ward I'd used to keep Alyssa in.

Fuck me.

I'd messed up. Bad.

When we'd left my office, I'd fully intended on seeking out Delvin, just as I'd said. But as I'd driven up Bank Street and listened to Alyssa run through all our horrible options, my own fear had run wild. She didn't trust me—she had no reason to trust me—which meant, at the first opportunity, she would bolt and I would be left empty-handed with no choice but to go to Dara and beg for an extension or hightail it out of the city and try to get a head start on whoever she sent after me.

Neither of which would gain me more than a few hours before everything I'd worked for was lost.

Terror had drowned out every other voice in my head, including everything telling me to talk to Alyssa to find a solution. We could have come up with a solid plan. We still had seven hours for fuck's sake. And yet my fear of being chased—caught—penned had let me see no way forward but to submit to Dara's demands.

And now Alyssa was out there by herself thinking I was nothing but a scumbag who'd betrayed her.

Or did she?

That look in her eyes before her magic had taken hold of the wheel had carried no anger. Just desperation and understanding. Almost like she was doing me a favour by crashing the car, doing what I couldn't in letting her disappear.

She might have ruined my future, but I couldn't hold it against her. We were both out to protect ourselves.

I hoped for her sake she had an idea of what to do next, because Dara wouldn't be kind if she had to hunt her down.

I passed my hand over my eyes and wiped the blood off my forehead where I must have slammed it against the window. My head throbbed, my stomach squeezed, and I rolled the window down to get some air. At least Alyssa's spell hadn't blocked that from me.

"Hey! Are you all right? Are you conscious? Can you move?"

The voices from outside pummelled my brain, and I almost reversed the direction of the window to block them out. No one would be able to get the door open unless someone tore it off or another witch without a head injury showed up to unravel the ward, so I slid my arms through the open window and pulled myself through.

"Whoa, guy, maybe don't do that? You should wait. Here, let me help. Paramedics are on their way. You're going to fall."

All their fussing melded into one messy jumble in my scattered mind, and I ignored it as I crawled through the window and collapsed into the muddy snow. The cold air on my face was a sweet relief, but even that was quickly chased away by the realization that I had seven hours to enjoy this freedom before Dara stole it away.

I had to find Alyssa. Had to explain things to her and convince her to come with me.

Not going to happen.

Shouldn't happen.

The thoughts warred in my head, both of them more correct than I wanted them to be, but one at a time, they lined up in an arrow that cut through my lingering panic and directed me down one obvious path.

Alyssa was innocent of the crimes she'd been accused of.

Dara would not listen to logic. For whatever reason, she was determined to kill Alyssa on sight for what she believed to have happened.

Corrick would win, and no one would be able to stop him before he entered the final stage of his plan, whatever that might be.

I closed my eyes and breathed against the snowflakes falling on my cheeks.

The hit to my head had done one thing for me, at least. It helped me see I only had one way forward, and it was the road I should have taken the moment Dara and Peter reached my office. I had to find the evidence that would set both me and Alyssa free. I had to use my seven hours to try to gain the rest of my life. Otherwise, I could kiss it goodbye forever.

Which meant I had to trust Alyssa to find her own answers, no doubt with her chaos demon, while I did what I'd told Alyssa we would: I had to backtrack and see what else Delvin could tell me.

Chapter 27
Alyssa

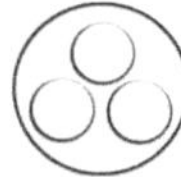

Thursday, 2:00 p.m.

SITTING IN THE passenger seat of Simon's Jeep, I watched the city fly by away from Prince of Wales, and I hated that part of me regretted not going past the crash site. Was Trace still there? Was he conscious? Was he alive?

All these questions, but I was too much of a coward to ask Simon to go check.

Soon enough, we hopped east on the 417. I had no idea where we were going, but at the moment, I didn't care. Anywhere that took me away from at least one of my problems.

"My sister's out of town for the winter," Simon said as he drove. "Way out in Orleans, but whatever. Somehow I doubt Dara Josef-Levesque is in a rush to hit the 'burbs."

"Agreed. She really doesn't seem the type."

He shot me a look. "You all right?"

"Oh, you know, my life is falling apart one fragment at a time, and the person I'd started to trust to get me out of it freaked out and decided to throw me into the deep end with a chain around my ankle so I drove him into a ditch, ran for fifteen minutes, had a tea that burned my mouth, and found out the government is officially on my ass, so yeah? I guess so? All things considered?"

Simon snorted a laugh and reached out to wrap his fingers around mine. My magic sparked, his responded, but I tamped my power down before it set him off. We were driving. The icing on my cake today would be the Jeep morphing into a flying horse, or a three-headed dog, or an open tractor.

"I need to figure this out," I said, pulling my hand away and tucking it in my lap. "Up until now, I've let Trace take the lead, believing he knew what to do, but now I see he was fumbling as much as I was. Now it's up to me."

"Do you want to talk about what happened there?" Simon asked.

I shifted in my seat to stare out the window. "Not especially. It's fine. He's fine." *I hope.* "We just veered at the crossroads."

"Uh huh." The questions hung heavy in his response, but he didn't voice them, for which I was grateful. If I told him what Trace had tried to do, I suspected he'd spin the Jeep around, drive back to the crash site, and finish what I'd started, but I didn't want that. For Simon's sake and for Trace's. I didn't even know Trace's real name, for goodness' sake. I couldn't kill a man whose name I didn't know.

What the hell was I thinking? I couldn't kill a man period. That was the whole point. That was why this entire day was a joke.

A very not-funny-for-anyone-involved kind of joke.

"The point is," I said, turning the conversation back to the more important issue. "I need to do something. Sitting around at your sister's place is all well and good, but as soon as eight o'clock hits, I'll have SMOAC, Dara, and Corrick after me, whereas right now I only have two of the three. If we can sort this out before it becomes a full trifecta, our odds are thirty-three per cent better, wouldn't you say?"

"One could argue that, yes."

"So what do we do?" I realized what I was doing, putting the responsibility onto Simon's shoulders now that Trace's were gone, and pulled back with a shake of my head. "No. Never mind. I don't care what you think. I want to talk to Corrick."

"That is most certainly not what I think."

"As I said, I don't care. This man has a boner for my death, and I want to know why. Trace is right—it can't just be for the business. Do *you* know the secret? Are we bringing in more income than I know about, and you've been stashing it away and altering the books?"

"Darn. You caught me." He flashed me a sideways look. "What secret?"

"Chip—Trace's computer guy with the on-the-nose name—brought up a satellite image of the pub, and Simon, I'm telling you, the whole place is choked with magic. It looks like the Toronto skyline."

"Impressive?"

"Smoggy. But only over our property, like whatever it is stops at the wards. The magic was sort of…yellowish? Nothing I recognized. So what's the deal with the pub? Was it built on some kind of powerhouse? Were those wards always there? Are they new?"

"I have no idea. If it's magic, it hasn't interacted with mine, which means it's neutral."

"For now. But if it's related to why Corrick wants me out of the picture, will it stay that way?"

"Have you asked Gramps?"

I blinked.

And blinked again.

And nearly bashed my head through the window as I processed my stupidity.

I'd been so focused on getting myself out of the crosshairs, it had never occurred to me to reach out to Gramps to ask if he had any idea why I'd been targeted. One of my greatest priorities had been not contacting my family so I didn't need to spend hours talking them down from their million and ten questions. My sister, especially, would have no idea how to cope with the fact that I was wanted for murder. The woman had trained throughout high school to be The Drama Queen. And while my mother would do her best to keep her cool, my father would double-check every minor detail and form his hypotheses in a self-soothing analysis that would help him but only make me focus on everything that was going wrong. My brothers would probably laugh.

My grandfather, though…

I pulled the brick out of my pocket and called his cell phone, thanking all the gods that my mother had pushed him to get one in case of emergencies, allowing me to bypass everyone else to reach him directly.

He answered right before it switched to voicemail, and at the sound of his familiar voice, my heart nearly cracked. What I wouldn't give to be calling him for some everyday issue at the pub. An invitation to a beer tasting or some thoughts on investments. The man was my entrepreneurial and magical mentor, and now I needed to dump this crap on him.

"Hey, Gramps."

"No, I don't want my air ducts cleaned, I don't care how many times you ask me. Stop calling!" he said, and hung up.

I stared at the empty screen but didn't bother putting the

phone away or calling again, holding out for a minute until it rang.

"Sorry, Pip," he said when I answered. "I was in the living room with the rest of the family, having a meeting about what we're going to do with the news that you've murdered two people. I figured you didn't want them to know you were calling."

At his blasé tone, a few pounds fell off my shoulders. At least for the time being, I could pretend this wasn't a huge fucking deal and just talk with my grandpa.

"Thanks, Gramps. You know me best." I switched the call to speaker so Simon could hear.

"Have time to give me a rundown on what's happening?" Gramps asked. "Mental breakdown? Latent homicidal urges we should have addressed in your childhood?"

"Not an issue yet, but it's always good to cover the bases. Coles' Notes—Clyde Corrick has been hiring people to frame me for murder. Reason I'm calling is to ask if you know of any deep, dark secrets around the pub that might have given him cause to want me dead? Or what the hazy yellow magic is hovering around the building?"

As though it were nothing, as banal as balancing the end-of-the-month books or organizing inventory. I hoped Gramps read the room and answered in kind, but as the seconds passed without him saying anything, my heart lurched.

"Magic?" he asked.

"Yeah. Looks like it might be a ward. Nothing I've seen in person, though. It was caught on satellite. Like a giant lemon bubble around the property."

"And you're saying it's Corrick that's after you?"

"According to Delvin. You remember him, right? Reason I needed a career change?" More silence on the phone that stretched long enough that I needed to break it or lose my mind. "Gramps?"

"Yeah, Pip, I'm here." He sounded as though he'd aged a decade in the past thirty seconds. "I suppose it was too good to hope the truth stayed buried."

Chapter 28
Alyssa

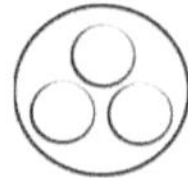

I FROWNED. "WHAT are you talking about?"

"The land. You know we own it."

"I do. You bought it straight out at a price that has Madi tearing out her hair trying to figure out how you pulled it off. But getting the property from us isn't reason enough for Corrick to work this hard, is it? I know property taxes are wild, but it's not like he can't afford them."

"It's not the cost. Not the financial cost, anyway. It's what's hidden under the office." His voice was leaden, as though speaking those words had taken their toll on a man who had always struck me as untouchable.

I stared at Simon, who shrugged and shook his head.

"Under the office?"

"Are you good to talk? No one should hear this who doesn't have to."

"Yeah, it's just me and Simon in the car."

He knew I trusted Simon with everything. If he felt this went beyond even that friendship, then whatever was coming was astronomically bad, but fortunately he said, "Then what I'm about to say stays in that car. Forever. Got it?"

"Got it."

Why did a tiny voice in my mind wish Trace were in this car to hear it as well?

"The floor of the safe is a false bottom. Underneath it, under the floorboards, is a locked box, buried as far down as I was able to get it. The box cannot be removed. It's magically anchored to the earth beneath the pub. The key is somewhere at the bottom of the Ottawa River. Inside the box is an amulet."

I stared at my phone as though my grandfather had started speaking in tongues. Did he think I was a child asking for a bedtime story? Amulets and locked boxes?

"All right, I'll play along. What is this amulet? Some kind of curse?"

The way my life had gone lately, I almost believed it.

Gramps snorted. "If it were a curse, you don't think I'd give the information to Corrick with pleasure? Let him take it off our hands? No, we're dealing with something much more serious. Much more deadly. Something I thought I'd hidden without anyone knowing, but I obviously failed. Or, by the sounds of it, the protections I put over it have finally given up the ghost. So to speak."

"I don't understand what you're saying. If something is buried under the pub, why didn't you tell me when I took over? Especially if that something is now ruining my life?"

"I know, Pip, and you're right. I should have. But I honestly thought no one would ever find out. It's something I've spent the last forty years trying to get rid of."

"You're freaking me out, big guy. What is this thing?"

"What do you know of spirit magic?"

My brain stuttered to a halt. I'd never really been one to believe in fate or destiny, but how could I hear that question and chalk it up to coincidence?

"Before today, not much more than that it's super illegal. No better than after-the-fact magic theft."

"Sums it up." Another deep sigh. "All right, my girl, I need you to brace yourself for the blinders to come off about our family, all right? Because you're not going to like where this is going."

"I'm already there."

"It all goes back to the early 1800s and the building of the Rideau Canal. You know much about that?"

A scream of frustration clawed at my throat at what seemed

like a sharp detour in our conversation, but I swallowed it. "I know a lot of people died building it. I know it was built as a defensible supply route for the military. I know it's the largest skating rink in the world. What I don't know is how any of that is relevant."

"It was built as a military aid, but not only for the mundanes. It also marked a divide in territory between the fae and the shifters. These days it doesn't matter. They've made their peace and their people have happily co-mingled, but before that, tensions ran high and some of our kind under Colonel By worked together to make sure their hatred for each other didn't devolve into war. Our time on this side of the unseen wall was still new and the thought that Queen Meril might change her mind and absorb us back into the supernatural realm was still too real, so they took precautions. Some of our family were among the builders."

"Okay..."

I knew part of this, vaguely, but as it had never been an especially exciting history lesson, many of the details had travelled from ear to ear and back out again. It had been hundreds of years since Meril, queen of supernaturals behind the unseen wall, had granted her blessing to those of our kind wanting to live among the mundanes. I didn't have much reason to think of her, never having experienced the instability of those early days, so hearing her mentioned in this part of the story was interesting.

"One of the tragedies to hit the build was a rock fall that killed hundreds. After all the poor working conditions, low pay, and harsh bosses, the builders rioted, too caught up in their anger to remember their purpose. Understandably, perhaps, but the odds were too great that the rioters would destroy all the progress they'd made, the canal would never be built, and everyone—mundane and supernatural—would be at risk of a greater threat than most people realized. So your great-great-grandfather, one of the supervisors on the build, did what he had to. He summoned the souls of those who died in the rock fall and stored them in an amulet."

Goosebumps bubbled on the back of my neck. "You're saying our ancestor is a criminal?"

"No. Well, yes, but not for the reasons you think. The souls agreed to be bound."

"Mmhmm." My skepticism filled the car.

"Those who died in the accident understood the necessity of finishing the build. If it wasn't completed, not only would they have died in vain, but their families would be in danger. So they agreed to enter the amulet provided the binding was broken as soon as the canal was finished."

"Which it obviously was. This is a different amulet currently buried under our pub, in a locked box, under a safe."

"Yes, well, that's where the deal fell apart, isn't it?" Gramps said. "Spirit magic touches on some dangerous ground with regard to power. Not only does it amplify whatever magic the user already has, but in some hands it can… sway people."

I covered my eyes. "It can control people."

"To a point," he said, though the way he said it made me think I was closer to the truth than he wanted to admit. "Make them biddable, anyway. Easier to persuade. My grandfather wielded it nobly enough. He convinced the builders to return, quelled the riots, urged the bosses to make compromises on the working conditions, and progress continued. But every time he let things take their course, the discontent rose until he was forced to keep the amulet with him at all times to ensure everything ran smoothly."

I guessed where this tale was headed. "And when the canal was finished…"

"You got it. We all know the story of the magical item that corrupts the bearer. He couldn't get rid of it. He'd tasted the power of compelling others to his will, and the thought of losing it was too much. So he kept it. He started his own general store, watched it thrive. Passed the amulet down to my mother, who saw what it did to her father and refused to use it. Then it passed to me."

"Who also refused to use it, right, Gramps?"

I thought of my grandfather with his bright green eyes lined with deep crow's feet, his full white beard, his once muscular frame carrying a bit too much weight from his pub days. The man who'd taught me everything I knew about using my magic and running a business, all completely by the book. No magic involved.

"Ah, Pip." His voice dripped with regret and shame. "We all believe we're stronger than our forebears. I believed my mother could have used it without issue. Even that she should have. That if she had, she wouldn't have wound up in a lousy marriage with a husband who didn't have the time of day for her, working sixty hours a week to put food on the table while Pop sat on the couch and drank away the money my grandfather had earned. When she told me what the amulet was, I saw it as our chance to reclaim what we were. So I used it. I got through college, I had the idea for the pub, and I convinced the city it was a great idea to sell me the land in its entirety."

I groaned and bowed my head into my hand. Fantastic. The business in which I had placed all my family pride had been built on lies, compulsion, and the souls of hundreds of dead workers.

"It was after I had your mother and her sisters that I realized the power was going to my head. I was persuading their teachers to give them passing grades. They were the best-behaved kids on the block. My mother didn't put up a fuss when I gave my father a pauper's grave, even though I knew she thought he deserved more." A low grunt slipped out of him, and I swore the car dropped on its tires under the weight of it. "This is the first time I've told anyone this story since your grandmother. She saw what was happening and finally figured it out. Told me she was ready to leave with the kids before I destroyed them. The temptation to use the amulet on her to stop her... I had the damned thing in my hand. The look in her eyes made me stop. I understood that if I took that step, I would be damning everything that mattered to me. So I tried to do what my grandfather couldn't and get rid of it. I put it under my heel and damn near broke my foot. I wedged it under a car tire and backed up—punctured the tire. Your grandmother and I worked together on it for years. Spells, curses, magical attacks, physical ones—nothing worked. Whatever plan my grandfather had to release the souls disappeared along with his conscience, and all I could do was hide it as deep as I could and keep looking for an answer."

He fell silent, and the air in the car stretched taut. Simon had pulled over to the side of the road, too caught up in the story to navigate the highway during early rush hour, and the two of us sat there, stunned.

This was a lot to learn in three minutes. It put my whole situation into perspective.

"Corrick knows about the amulet," I said.

"I would certainly guess that's the case," said Gramps. "I can't begin to think how, though if you're saying you *saw* the magic… well, I guess it's possible that after all this time, its power is spreading. If my wards around the safe are fading and the magic from the amulet is leaking out, then for anyone paying attention, it would be on full display. And Corrick— his ancestor was there right alongside ours, wasn't he? Not so unbelievable that rumour of the amulet reached him."

Of course it had. And of course the amulet had given itself away at a time when I stood between it and the person who wanted the power it offered.

I squeezed my eyes shut. "You said the amulet amplifies the power of the user?"

"It does."

"So the stronger the user…"

"The stronger the effect of the spirit magic," he replied, as though he knew where I was going. "My grandfather was a powerful witch—stronger than I ever was. I think that's why he was able to get thousands of people to follow him, whereas I could only sway one person at a time. Which was enough, don't get me wrong."

"So if someone murdered two fae and stole their magic?"

"Then we could be looking at a very serious problem if they got their hands on this amulet."

"Good. Excellent. Fan-fucking-tastic."

That was that sorted.

It didn't matter how Corrick had found out about the

amulet. A drunken conversation. The magic around the pub. A demon who'd watched my grandfather's progress, understood what it meant, and sold the information for a soul and a quickie. Whatever the case, he knew what it was, what it did, and where it was hiding, and I wouldn't put it past him to tear my bar down to its foundations to find it.

"The wards around the safe—you bound them to our family's magic?" I asked.

"I did. No one without Mooney blood can break them. Not quickly, anyway."

I rubbed my brow. "He needs me out of the way so he can take his time breaking down the wards. And to hide what he's doing from anyone else who might know about the amulet. Which means it's not about me, I'm just the first step. Once he—or Dara—has dealt with me, he'll turn to Simon, you, anyone else who could stop him from getting his hands on the pub."

"And at the speed the bodies are piling up, he's not going to be patient," Simon said.

My magic swirled deep in my chest at the thought of anyone going after my friend, let alone my family business, and I struggled to keep it at bay, knowing all it would take was a freak surge to draw Simon's power out to meet it. I had to keep my cool, stay focused.

"I won't let him get that far, and since I don't think my

asking nicely will be enough to make him give up his plan, maybe what he needs is a little persuasion."

"Pip, I hope you're not thinking of doing anything stupid."

Simon met my eye, and I recognized his deep look of resignation. "Sorry, Gramps. I think she is. I think she really, really is."

Chapter 29
Alyssa

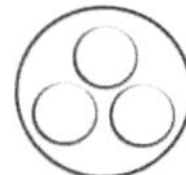

Thursday, 2:30 p.m.

IT TOOK SIMON a few minutes to reach an exit, turn the car around, and get back on the highway going west, though it felt longer considering every second that passed came with a fresh argument from him about why my idea was horrible.

"I don't see you coming up with anything better," I said after he'd started his third loop.

"That's because I don't have anything. Yet. But I could with enough time."

"We don't have time. Look at this traffic. It'll take us another hour to get back downtown, and that'll leave us with four and a half before Dara comes for me. I already don't know if I can fit through that tight of a window."

"Fine. Walk me through your idea again. Maybe this time it won't sound so suicidal. You're going to go to the pub, break the amulet out of its forty-year-old hiding place, take it to Corrick, and use this incredibly illegal magic before he can?"

"Why not? These souls don't want to be used for evil, right? They wanted the canal built to protect their families. Now the amulet can't be destroyed. I'm not looking to use them to get anything for myself, just to prevent a monster from using them in a way they wouldn't want."

"And to save your life."

"If that's a friendly side effect, then yes, sure, my motives may not be entirely altruistic. But these guys have been stuck in a necklace for over two hundred years. That's gotta suck. After I get Corrick off our backs, I'll see if I can figure out how to free them."

"You think you'll succeed where your grandparents failed?"

"I think it's worth a try, don't you? I might think of something they missed. And they didn't have you." I gave him my best "I love you, bestie" smile, and he rolled his eyes.

"Nice of you to include me in your madness."

"So what are you going to do? Will you come with me, or will you stay at the pub and make sure Davis doesn't break in and drink us dry?"

Simon squeezed the steering wheel, then slumped into his seat as a pickup truck swerved to cut us off. "I think the cost of an empty bar is worth less than your life. You don't think your family would be better for this?"

I gritted my teeth. "Usually, there would be no better reinforcements. But I don't think I can round everyone up in time, and Gramps—as strong as he is, I don't think he'd be enough."

"Then you have me. You're not going in by yourself."

I waited for the warm flutter to stir in my stomach, and although the warmth did come, it lacked its regular pals, desire and regret. The reasons for which I didn't want to consider too closely.

I rested my hand over his where it lay on the gear shift. "You know you're my favourite person, right?"

"I know."

Simon parked the car a few blocks away from the pub, and as soon as I was out in the open, I conjured my cloaking spell and pulled it over me. In the middle of the day, it wouldn't hold up well if anyone looked too closely, but I hoped it would be good enough to hide me if any SMOAC officers happened to glance my way.

Simon kept his distance from my spell to avoid turning the snowbanks into dinosaurs or whatever, but now that we weren't trapped in the car, there was less danger of our powers interacting, something we'd learned the hard way on more than one occasion during the too-brief hot-and-interested stage of our relationship. That hopeful few days of steamy touches, longing gazes, and wild trial-and-error as we struggled to figure out how to be together without our magics combusting.

The final verdict: impossible, but many important lessons had been learned along the way.

Not least of which being, again, my doomed taste in men.

With me stepping in Simon's footsteps to avoid leaving tracks of my own, we reached Mooney's without any major disasters, and Simon let us in through the back door. The alarm beeped at us, but he disarmed it while I headed for the safe in the back corner of the office.

All my life I'd wondered at the big, black behemoth. It looked like a prop out of a *Murdoch Mysteries* episode. A cool antique in a modern building.

Now I understood why. The size meant it had to sit on the floor instead of being installed in the wall and couldn't be lifted without heavy machinery.

Clever, Gramps.

I pulled off Trace's coat, threw it on the desk, and shook out my hands to psych myself up for whatever I was about to find buried who knew how deep under the pub. This was a treasure hunt I had no wish to be a part of.

Another tick on the "I have the worst luck" whiteboard of

fate.

I swivelled the lock to the latest combination, heaved the door open, and set to work emptying all the contents along the bottom. The floor creaked as Simon moved into the doorway, and I heard a faint catch in his breath.

"What in the infernals are you wearing?"

I glanced down at the dove-grey straps and rolled my eyes. "Simon, my dearest friend, don't fucking start."

A low snicker echoed behind me, but he didn't push it. "I'll stay here and watch the windows," he said. "Anyone looks like they're coming close, I'll warn you."

I nodded my agreement as I stacked our extra cash, contracts, and odds and ends in a pile on the floor, then, on hands and knees, half-crawled into the safe to find the lever Gramps said was tucked away in the back. He hadn't liked any part of my plan, but when I'd filled him in on the details, he'd agreed to go along with it so far as to tell me how to access the box. It took quite a few minutes and more than one bump on the head before I found the lever, and I never would have known what it was if he hadn't told me. It was one inch long and felt more like a crooked nail than a handle, but when I pried it up, a wisp of familiar purple atmospheric magic swept over the bottom of the safe.

With a deep ker-thunk, the base of the safe rose an inch, then folded in on itself to reveal a dark recess underneath.

"Son of a bitch," I whispered.

Half of me had believed Gramps had made up the story. Or maybe half of me just hadn't wanted to believe members of my family were guilty of the crimes I was now being accused of, or that my own grandfather had benefited from their actions, but there it was: the proof that my great-great-grandfather had turned against his own kind. That my family's success was as false as the bottom of the safe.

Not the time, I told myself. After I dealt with Corrick, I could deal with the massive ancestral guilt and what it meant for my future with the pub.

I backed out of the safe to grab the flashlight in the bottom drawer of my desk. Once it was tucked between my teeth, I grabbed the hand trowel we used for the flower pots in the summer and crawled back in to peer into the hole. It took some digging with trowel and magic, more than one cracked nail, and a gradual descent as dirt piled up along the floor of the safe, but about five feet down there was the box with a thick padlock sitting on top.

This close, I sensed the magic coming out of the box, strong enough that it made the hair on the backs of my arms stand on end. The yellow haze was faint, growing dimmer as it reached the surface, and I realized Gramps was right: the wards around the box had failed and this thing was leaking magic like radioactive waste. Calling to Corrick with an airhorn if he'd known what to look for.

Simon might think my idea was stupid, but as I fended off the waves of power smacking me in the face, I realized it didn't matter. Whether I used the spirit magic or not, the amulet was no longer protected here.

Now I had to find a way to remove it.

There was no key, of course.

All well and good, but I doubted Corrick would be put aside by something as simple as a padlock, and if he was going all out, I had no choice but to do the same.

A tiny voice in my head pointed out that Trace's telekinetic magic would have been useful here, but I stomped that voice under the much louder voice of reason. I didn't need him.

With a spell I'd practiced when I was a kid—at the age when I used to lock myself out of rooms just to see if I could break into them—I sent my magic into the lock. The yellow haze reacted to it, and I watched in awe as my simple purple spell became more vibrant, creating a bright purple glow that nearly blinded me.

I blinked the afterimages out of my eyes as the light dimmed a smidge and focused on pushing the spell farther into the lock. Gramps's magic lingered deep in the mechanism, another defence, but our signatures recognized each other. That, combined with my amplified power, didn't so much open the padlock as blast it into a thousand metal shards. I ducked and covered my head to protect my eyes.

"Lys? Are you all right?" Simon called from the office.

"I think so?" I answered, though I waited a moment to make sure the shards had fallen before I raised my head.

The box sat in the dirt, an innocent metal case, and with oodles of caution, I reached down to flip open the lid.

My breath caught when my gaze landed on the coiled necklace sitting on its own at the bottom.

A teardrop tourmaline, yellow and the size of a big honking canary stuffed with souls, was stuck in a silver setting and hung from a thick silver chain.

I swallowed hard as I reached in and picked it up, settling the amulet across my hand, where it stretched from the base of my fingers to the heel of my palm. Its magic sang to me, begging me for something, and while it sparked a deep desire to use it for what it had been created for, I suspected the call was more for release. It wanted to be broken.

I curled my fingers around it and clutched it to my chest. Corrick couldn't get his hands on it. With this gem in his possession, he could own the city, and what was to say he would stop there? He could have the entire business community eating out of his palm before he went on to dominate the province. The entire country.

A shiver ran down my spine as I hooked the chain around my neck. I would have preferred to keep the amulet out of sight, but wearing it seemed the safest place for now, even if it did dangle obviously above the draped neckline of my incredibly revealing top.

Speaking of which...

First I climbed out of the hole and shovelled all the dirt back into it, closed the false bottom, and arranged everything so it wasn't a dead giveaway that I'd spent over half an hour inside it. Then I went to the closet in the corner and pulled out a Mooney's Pub T-shirt, with its top-down view of three pint glasses on a round serving tray—a subtle protection spell offered to everyone who walked into our establishment. A moment later, I was wearing more clothing than I had in hours.

Not much warmer, but at least the amulet was hidden.

Armed with gem and magic, I slipped Trace's coat back on and nodded to Simon, who leaned towards the windows to scope around outside. He raised his hand and twitched his fingers to give the all clear, and I wrapped my cloaking spell over me as I followed him out.

So far everything was going great, but we'd only reached the edge of the parking lot when a familiar voice called out, "Hey, Fletcher! Not locking up already, are you?"

I winced and glanced over my shoulder to find Davis slinking towards the door. The man had earned his epithet of Daily Davis honestly—he'd never missed a night in all the years we'd been open—and never before had I resented it so much.

Simon drew to a halt and slowly turned, pasting an apologetic smile on his face. "'Fraid so, Davis. Taps are down, won't be fixed till tomorrow morning. Lys and I figured it was a good opportunity to take an early night."

"Fuck tap. You got cans, don'tcha?"

I closed my eyes and refrained from sighing, but I must have made some kind of noise, because the sloth demon's red-tinged eyes slid my way. His gaze skipped over me, thank goodness, but got close enough that my blood froze. Although he made most of his money peddling drugs of various kinds—never in the pub—Davis's true income source was passing along information. He was one of the busiest pipelines in the city. If he thought he could skim a few bucks by ratting me out, I'd lose whatever hair's-breadth of wiggle room I had to squeeze out of my cage.

"Not tonight, Davis," Simon said, his smile still in place but his tone firm. Bronze magic prickled on the tips of his fingers, and I sent him a silent wish to keep it tamped down. Who knew how mine would react if his let loose. Cloaking spell gone, amulet floating mid-air, hair an unflattering shade of green.

Davis grunted but didn't walk away. "You seen that partner of yours around anywhere? Contacts say the feds are looking for her."

The glint of bronze magic grew more intense, and I swallowed hard and wished I could back away to create more space between us. But if I did, the sudden footprints in the snow would point right to me.

As his magic spread, so did the fire in Simon's amber eyes. "I haven't seen her since last night. When a bunch of witches tore in and roughed the place up. Probably what busted our taps. I don't suppose you had anything to do with them showing up?"

Davis snarled, the tips of his pointed canines flashing in the weak evening light. "Hey, I don't piss where I live, yeah? Only reason I ask is to give you a heads up, let you know all resources are being put to work to track her down. You see her, you tell her to keep her head low."

After a beat, Simon's magic eased and his shoulders dropped out of their defensive posture. "Thank you."

I understood his surprise. I hadn't thought Davis had developed such an affection for me.

The demon snorted. "Yeah, well, more hassle than it's worth to stake out a new place that'd let me work up such a tab. Easier to get her back behind the bar."

There it was. Nice, familiar territory.

"Come back tomorrow night," Simon said. "First drink's on us."

Davis grunted, touched his fingers to his black ball cap, and slouched off. I wondered where he'd spend tonight if not on his regular stool. Did he have a place to live or just linger in the ether somewhere? I doubted I'd ever know.

Simon released a breath and continued on to the Jeep. I fell into step beside him, and we both kept an eye on the side streets as we wandered up Elgin to where we'd parked.

Not far from here, just a few blocks over, was Trace's office. Would he go back there once he got himself clear of his car? What would his priority be? Getting out of town or tracking me? If it was the former, I wished him all the best. If it was the latter… well, the thought that we might pick up where we left off—as bounty hunter and mark, of course—put some extra kick in my step. I had to stay ahead of him as much as I did Dara, which meant getting to Corrick before Trace guessed my next move.

And he would.

The man was already good at his job, but now we'd spent hours in each other's company. I'd be a fool if I thought he hadn't tucked away pieces of information about me, my life, my thought process during that time. He probably had a better understanding of who I was than I did.

My only advantage: years of working behind a bar had helped me develop a similar set of skills. People dumped their problems on me all the time, and it was second nature to assess every face as they walked into the pub. Who would I be dealing with? What sort of persona should I adopt to interact with them?

It was how I knew deep in my bones that Trace wouldn't let me go without another attempt to catch me—and not because he wanted me dead like everyone else, but because in his mind it was the only way I stood a chance of surviving.

I didn't share his optimism.

Instead, I was walking right into the monster's lair.

Clearly one of us had the better grasp on reality, and only time would tell which one of us it was.

Chapter 30
Alyssa

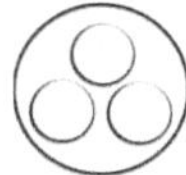

Thursday, 3:00 p.m.

Simon navigated his Jeep through the streets of the Byward Market where Corrick held court at The Scorpio Lounge, a high-end nightclub that catered to the rich and infamous. Mostly mundane, though I suspected there was some overlap with Club Crescent. Scorpio was where the demons started their night; Crescent was where they ended it.

I'd been a few times in my early twenties—the occasional girls' night when we wanted to dress up and play sophisticated. The ambiance was sleek, the cocktails were expensive, and security was impressive. A man had groped me once, and within seconds, a bouncer three times as large as me had grabbed the guy by the neck and "escorted" him out the door. Both men had disappeared and only one had returned. As far as I knew, the groper had spent his last few minutes on earth being thoroughly trounced for his misdemeanour, but at the very least, I'd never seen him there on any other visit.

It was the one thing I could say for Corrick: he understood the importance of keeping his public face well scrubbed.

The club hadn't opened for the night yet, so for a minute we sat outside in the Jeep, motor running so the heat stayed on. From here, it didn't look like anyone was inside. The windows were dark, the heavy grey commercial blinds lowered. Everything was silent and still, a contrast to the bustle of the street outside.

The Market was a hub of activity year-round in Ottawa, even in the winter when people had to climb over snowbanks to pass around each other on the narrowed sidewalks.

Not one of them gave a passing glance to The Scorpio, which I found curious. Places like The Afterlife, the club in Centretown, catered solely to supernaturals, which meant any mundane that walked by only saw an empty building, the truth hidden behind the perception filter. The Scorpio Lounge was fair game, so if people were walking by as though it didn't exist, it meant someone had warded the place.

Goosebumps bubbled on my skin, and I rubbed my arms to warm myself up.

"Something's off," I said.

"I feel it too. My magic is sparking like a microwave on the fritz."

As though to confirm Simon's statement, the radio popped on and a soft German voice poured through the speakers.

I flicked the radio off—which did nothing given it wasn't actually on—and got out of the car. Simon followed a few steps behind me.

"What are you thinking?" he asked.

"That someone's inside. That, at this very moment, Corrick could be planning his next murder or laying out his plans for how to frame me for it."

"That's not a good reason to barge in on him. In fact, it's a great reason to turn around and go the other way."

"Are you done?"

His wide shoulders slumped. "Yeah."

I tried the front door, expecting to have to make my way to the side door, and swallowed the ball in my throat when it opened.

"This is such a stupid idea," I muttered to myself as I stepped into the darkness of the empty club.

Simon was so close behind me I was surprised he hadn't stepped on my heels. His magic buzzed like static against my back, and I clenched my fists at my sides to keep mine restrained. As soon as we were inside, I'd need to create distance between us to use the amulet without our magics exploding, but until then, I appreciated his steadying nearness.

And only partly wished it were someone other than Simon standing with me. Someone whose magic worked with mine in a way that strengthened both. As it was, Simon and I would both be on our own.

Beyond the blinds was a nightclub at rest: high-backed stools overturned and propped on the standing tables in the centre of the room, empty booths along the walls, house lights on, music off.

Corrick sitting at the bar with his back to us.

"As soon as Delvin told me you'd been to see him, I figured you would make your way to me," he said without turning around.

A shadow moved in my periphery, and I wheeled towards the door to find our exit blocked by a familiar behemoth of a woman, her bulging arms crossed over her chest, her face screwed up in an unflattering smirk. Rosie Alvarez, the snake shifter. Smugness did not become her. The last time I'd seen her in person was behind the pub when she'd tried to scare me into giving up the deed. She didn't look any friendlier today.

Stepping away from Simon to give us some space, I summoned my magic into my palms and faced Corrick, who had half turned away from the bar but made no move to leave the comfort of his stool. Of course not. Why would he get his hands dirty when he had others to fight his battles for him?

Which he did. A whole gang of them. They crept out of the corners of the room, closing us in. My magic surged in response to the number—five that I could see—and Simon's bronze power rose to meet mine. We widened the gap between us to prevent our magics from intertwining before we were ready.

"I didn't come here to fight," I said.

Corrick threw back his head with a laugh that grated my nerves like nails scraping on a pint glass. "You're attempting diplomacy? Trust a healer to try to keep the peace. I love it. So endearing. But it won't do. You have something I want, and before the end of the night, I'll have it. One way or another."

The amulet buzzed against my chest, and I pressed my hand against my leg to stop myself from grabbing it. Corrick didn't need to know how close his prize was. I sent my thoughts towards the soul-infused tourmaline to tap into its power, but the souls within barely nudged me back before Corrick made his first move.

And a big move it was as all five of his lackeys came at us at once. Not as they were, but transformed. The behemoth behind me was gone, but I caught sight of green-and-gold scales as the giant snake wrapped around the tables, silently blocking our escape routes, caging us in the centre of the room. I spun in a quick circle, but her head remained out of sight. Not good.

Simon's back pressed against mine, and at the contact, our

magics surged, melded, and the table to our left vanished with a loud pop. In its place was a glowing cinnamon roll. Instinct screamed at me to flee, and I grabbed Simon's arm and threw us away from it just as the roll exploded in a burst of flame and magic and a wonderful aroma. Shrieks pierced my ears, and I peered up from under my arm to see a black-cloaked witch rolling around on the ground to put out the flames. Someone had obviously watched his fire safety videos growing up. Pity.

Still, at least that was one down. For now.

The three others hesitated, caught off guard by the unpredictability of the magic spewing out from between Simon and me, but the damned snake was still a question mark.

Until she wasn't.

With a hiss that froze my blood and rattled my bones, the hooded cobra snapped out of the shadows, jabbing the air between me and Simon and sending us flying in opposite directions. The bond between our magics snapped, and I rushed to pump more atmospheric power into my hands. It spread around me in a quick protective barrier, and I whirled around to track the snake. Somehow she was gone again. I caught the flick of a tail out of the corner of my eye as she rounded another table, but there was no more time to track it before a ball of black-hued magic slammed me in the chest and sent me soaring into the wall. My head snapped against the wood panelling behind the booth, and I slumped into the upholstered seat with only a second to dodge before another black ball flew my way, this one promising death now that my ward had been fractured.

I rolled off the bench under the table, crept to the edge, and launched myself out of a crouch into the necromancer trying to end my life with the energy suck of oily black magic. He snarled as we slammed to the floor, his clawed fingers slashing at my neck, drawing blood that rose into the air and swept around him, fuelling his strength.

Magic shot from my palms into his chest, and the pulse rolled across his body, giving his insides a good rattle. His limbs jerked, his back arched, and I grabbed my opportunity to roll off him… immediately into the path of that fucking cobra.

The snake snapped at me, fangs dripping venom, but I rolled again and escaped with only a tear to the shoulder of Trace's coat.

New sweater for Simon, new coat for Trace. My expenses were climbing, and I had no idea if I'd survive to pay them.

The snake coiled and snapped again, but she caught a mouthful of metal chair instead of me as she clamped her jaws down. A magic chaser bound her into a stiff rod, and she collapsed to the side with a jarring thud. I prayed the binding would hold her long enough for me to get a grip on my current position.

I'd come here prepared to fight. None of this was

unexpected. Even so, I hadn't been raised to go on the offensive. My family had taught me enough for survival and how to fight with the rest of my coven, but I was out of my league here, facing down a group of professionally nasty magic users. I'd already doled out my best and had barely made a dent.

The amulet called to me, reminding me it was there and ready for me to use it, but I couldn't bring myself to do it. My plan had been to compel Corrick to stand down, but he'd acted too quickly. Using the soul magic to amplify mine was too tempting, suspiciously tempting, and I feared that if I gave into it, I wouldn't be able to give it up, no matter how this battle ended.

I was also afraid to tip my hand. If Corrick had the stolen power of two fae generals mixing with his own magic, I couldn't risk him overpowering me to take it.

Across the room, Simon was up against a hulking man caught mid-shift—some kind of golem, if I had to guess—his pasty skin dark grey and thick in patches around his mouth and neck. As Simon launched his magic at him, stone crumbled down the side of his face, and he raised a boulder-sized fist to clobber Simon across the head.

I screamed as Simon soared into the wall and slumped to the ground. Ignoring every other threat in the room, I bounded around and over tables to reach his side before the half-golem could get another swing in. My heart raced and my lungs ached as

I stood over my friend in a protective stance. I pressed through my fear, summoned a spell, and lashed out at the golem, using atmospheric energy to create a vacuum around him. His eyes widened as he choked for breath between his now-blue lips, and he dropped to his knees, clawing at his throat.

Before I had time to celebrate, a spell hurtled towards us, a mix of the necromancer's black power and the elemental green of another cloaked witch. I threw up a barrier, but it only slowed the magic down, lessening the impact as it wrapped around me. At once burning and freezing, the magic squeezed the air from my lungs. I wrestled with it, worked to push it away before it burrowed too deeply into my blood, afraid of what it would do if it reached its target, which I assumed was my internal organs. My heart sped up in response to the power surge, and I was sure that in another moment, it would burst out of my chest along with the rest of my squishy insides.

I gritted my teeth against a bitter laugh as I fought against the growing agony. It'd serve Corrick right if I burst. Let his people spend the rest of the night scrubbing my viscera off the walls and floor. Not to mention picking up the fragments of the amulet he was working so hard to find.

If the gem was destroyed along with me. From what my grandfather had said, we wouldn't be that lucky.

Not that I needed any extra motivation to push this spell back beyond saving my life.

I dug deep to gather my strength, heaved my magic out from under the weight of the combined spells, and shoved. My defensive spell met their offensive one, redirecting it back at the necromancer and witch. Their screams twisted my gut as their faces tore with bone-deep lacerations. Blood sprayed across me and Simon and everything in between, and they both collapsed, writhing in an attempt to escape the pain.

Sucking in breaths to calm my nausea, my nerves, my heart rate, I scanned the scene in front of me. Three of the five were down, two more bound and incapacitated, leaving Corrick standing on his own.

He should have looked shocked. Concerned. Instead, the arrogant gleam in his eyes, burning and taunting, turned my stomach until acid climbed the back of my throat. A moment later, I saw just how spot-on my instincts were as another ten lackeys stepped into the room. I had to squint to make out the cascade of power pulsing in the air from the new arrivals. I noted the demon, witch, and shifter energies, a few of each. All of them strong, all of them rested. Corrick had started with some of his best, but he'd been holding back. We hadn't been.

Simon groaned at my side, but though his eyelids fluttered, they remained closed. If I was going to fight, I was doing this alone.

I squeezed my hands tight at my sides, straightened my spine, and pumped as much magic as I had left between us and them. It was a weak ward, but if I could hold it until Simon came to, until Corrick's army tired themselves out, maybe we stood a chance.

My chest heaved as I fought back tears of exhaustion, terror, frustration. My throat felt gritty with the effort, and heat swept through my veins to sizzle under my skin, making me feel the need to tear off my clothes or rend my flesh to cool down.

How the hell had I gotten here? I'd made a point in my life to do no harm, to help where I could, whether that was offering some healing spells or pouring a refreshing pint of craft beer. Somehow my predictable, quiet life had led me to this point, and I didn't know if I could hold on long enough to get past it.

Magic swirled throughout the room, the combination of so many colours creating a pukey green-brown haze. Or maybe that was my vision going spotty as I hurled spell after spell through the barrier, aiming at whoever appeared to be working hardest against us.

Lightning fizzled against my ward, shaking the fillings in my teeth. Fire licked at the weaknesses, devouring patches of my magic and leaving room for Melanie Caplan in her rage demon form to blast through it with her energy-sucking spell. I blocked, parried, redirected everything that came at us, but each time with a bit less force. My strength was waning, fatigue weighing down my limbs until all I wanted to do was curl up and let them win.

I couldn't. I'd come here for a reason: to prevent this murderer from getting what he wanted and hurting other people in the process. If I gave in, everything up until now would have been a waste. He would find the amulet on my burned-out corpse and use it to unleash whatever mind control plans he had to gain dominance in this country.

The reminder of what was at stake renewed my determination, and I focused a repulsion spell against a shifter on my left. She barrelled backwards into a witch whose magic had been slowly tearing through my ward. They both collapsed into a table, breaking Melanie's concentration.

In the corner of my eye, a green-and-gold tail slithered along the bar, and in a smooth motion, swept through the air towards me. Rosie had escaped her binding spell. I dropped to the floor as the tail sailed over my head and wove a spell around it as it passed back, creating a magical net that snapped across the room on the tail's return and took three more lackeys to the ground.

The amulet warmed at my neck, its power seeping out, begging me to use it. Again I tamped down the desire to draw from it, though this time, refusing was a much greater challenge.

I caught the slight narrowing of Corrick's eyes as his gaze

roved over me, and I drew my magic closer, thinning my ward further.

It couldn't be helped. If I couldn't save myself, I had to save the rest of the city.

Sending out a silent apology to Simon and a thought to my family, my friends—*Trace*—I released the hold on my ward and focused my magic on the amulet. I wrapped purple around tourmaline, tucking it close to the links in the chain, the facets of the gem. With each pinch and pull, I strengthened the cloaking spell, hiding its form and its power beneath the shroud. The effort of hiding the necklace left me a sweating, panting mess, but beneath the bone-deep exhaustion was satisfaction that I'd succeeded.

Melanie let out a shriek of victory as she absorbed the remains of my ward, and in a smooth manoeuvre, Corrick's people swarmed us. I threw out whatever spells I could scrape together, knowing with every defence I attempted, I was leaving us more vulnerable. Digging for my magic felt like sucking the last of a milkshake through a too-thin straw, but I couldn't give up. Not willingly.

Though willingness was soon a non-issue. The enemies were too many, their spells too strong. Pain struck from every direction, within and without. Blisters ruptured over my arms. Blood dripped from my nose. Simon's back arched as he cried out, but he remained unconscious, his magic flaring in involuntary protection, doing nothing but holding them off—barely.

My knees buckled, and I collapsed to the floor, too tired to lift my arms, in too much pain to draw more than quick, shallow breaths.

I'd come here to prevent Corrick from getting his way. As the horde closed in and Corrick's order rang out to leave us alive, all I could do was pray I'd done that much.

Chapter 31
Trace

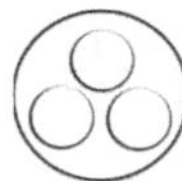

Thursday, 5:00 p.m.

IT TOOK OVER four hours to get myself away from the cops and paramedics who showed up at the scene of the accident. My car was driveable once they towed it out of the ditch, if mangled at the front end, and aside from the gash on my forehead, I was unhurt.

I'd rushed through the paperwork and liability forms, removing any and all responsibility from the EMTs for my refusal of medical care, and after gathering the heaps of information I would need to hand over to my insurance provider, I was finally back on the road and speeding towards Sparks Street.

I had three hours to help Alyssa before Dara came looking

for us.

Barely enough time for *me* to find Alyssa.

Throughout the past four hours, I couldn't keep my thoughts away from the woman who'd upended my life, wondering if she'd reached safety without trouble catching up to her, trying to guess what she might do next.

She'd mentioned going to see Corrick, and while I believed it was the most dangerous move she could make, as long as she brought the chaos demon with her, maybe they stood a chance of surviving the encounter.

But I swore to myself I would track her down. Ideally before she got herself killed.

First, though, I needed to talk to Delvin. If I had to break my rule a second time and compel every last detail out of the bastard's mouth, I'd do it, damn the consequences.

My head throbbed as I strained to focus on the grey-hued streets, the heavy snow clouds darkening the day even more than the setting sun. By the time I found a parking spot close to the club, a migraine had me squinting, but I breathed through it and imagined the muscles in my neck releasing some of the tension hugging my spine. I didn't have time to be slowed down by the inconvenience of a headache.

The door to Club Crescent loomed up ahead, but when I tried the handle, I found it locked.

"Goddammit."

I tried again in case the accident had made me forget the difference between push and pull, and when the lock held, I pressed against it with my magic. Not only did the mechanism not budge, but a magical pulse sent me recoiling a few steps into a melting snow puddle.

Sock and pant leg wet and with nothing to show for it, I stomped away from the club and rounded the corner, hoping to find another entrance. They had to have some way to deliver their alcohol and whatever other inventory they kept downstairs, and I couldn't see people wheeling carts up and down those steep steps.

Even if Delvin was gone for the day, there could be something in his office to give me what I needed. Hell, my life would be easier if he wasn't there.

With or without his help, going in would be worthwhile.

I had to trudge all the way to Wellington to find access to the back of the building, and under other circumstances, I might have found it funny to discover how mundane the rear access to the club looked. A standard service door and reeking trash bins, just like every other business.

I tried the handle, and this one responded to my efforts. Still locked, but not the quadruple-reinforced show from the front. I summoned my magic into my hands—sparing a thought for Alyssa, wondering what this spell would look like to her—and channelled it into the lock.

The mechanism clicked, the handle turned, but just as I prepared to open it, a familiar sweet scent on the air caught my attention. Reverie.

As her lust-filled aura swept over me, my cheeks flushed with a primal heat and my pants grew tight. I squeezed my eyes shut to fight the artificial surge of desire, wanting to be in full control of my faculties before I turned around.

Reverie leaned close to my ear, her breath tickling the back of my neck and making my pulse race. My mouth went dry, and it took all my strength not to turn around and crush my mouth against hers. Not to slide my hand up her thigh and between her—

Illusion. Magic. Run.

My brain, which was much smarter than the rest of me and retained a passing grip on reality, screamed its warnings, and they worked to wedge a gap between her desires and mine. I drew in a deep breath, steeled myself, and turned around.

Her crimson lips were upturned in a seductive smile, though her star-filled eyes were hard with irritation and anger.

"Mr. Wyatt," she purred, pressing her body flush against mine and pinning me against the grungy wall of the alley. "You're the last person I expected to find digging around back here with the rats."

I grinned, aiming for a show of indifference to the power surging against my defences. "The last person? Really? You obviously don't know me all that well. I've spent half my career in trash bins."

Her nose wrinkled with a subtle sniff. "Explains the smell."

It was a challenge to hold my smile in place. We'd obviously ended the charming part of the evening.

"Well, lovely as always to see you, Reverie, but I'm here to see the Big Cheese. He still in?"

I turned back to the door, but again had only gripped the handle when her smooth voice wrapped around me. "He's still inside. Still raging. If you step one foot in the club, he'll kill you on sight."

I glanced at her over my shoulder. "I hardly think breaking and entering is a murder-worthy offence."

She crossed her arms. "Not only did you show up here with a woman he loathes more than possibly anyone else on the planet, but you're trying to deprive him of his revenge. He won't stand for it, and if he thinks he can prevent it by getting rid of you, he won't hesitate."

"What about his reputation? He won't want to risk that by killing me at his club."

She shrugged, and even the casual gesture oozed sex in a way that left me wanting to run my lips over the slip of shoulder visible above her sleeve. She was really playing up her succubus half today. "You're in a challenging business, Mr. Wyatt. You travel the country chasing dangerous supernatural criminals.

Do you think anyone would notice if you disappeared for a while? Would anyone bat an eyelash if your body floated up on the shores of the St. Lawrence?"

I appreciated the vivid picture she painted, though it wasn't close to the most graphic threat I'd received in my career. "Ah, I see. You're a big-picture type of person. Always looking at every angle."

"I have to in this business, or else it'd be my body floating in a river." She feigned a pout. "And that would do nothing for my hair."

Although her description of my imminent demise failed to carry the impact she might have hoped for, I had to accept she was right. Unless I moved faster than Delvin could—which would be a miracle given his demonic strength and my raging migraine—he would destroy me without hesitation.

I would have realized it and saved myself the trip if I weren't so hyperfocused on Alyssa. This was why letting women into my life was a bad idea.

So where did that leave me?

Fighting a sense of defeat, clinging to my determination to find another way forward, I started back up the alley, skirting Reverie to avoid any further mind-addling contact. "Glad we had this talk. Guess I'll see you the next time a mark wanders into the club. Or, you know, you become a bounty yourself. See ya, Rev."

She stood aside, but I felt her stare trailing my backside as I walked away. Before I had time to feel flattered, she called after me. "Perhaps I could help you."

I stopped, hesitated, turned around. It would be rude to ignore her but equally foolish to trust her.

She smirked, as though my thoughts were available for everyone to hear, and added, "For a price."

With an exaggerated exhale, I let my shoulders sag. "Thank goodness. Far more comfortable ground. But I don't make deals with demons. Especially not half-fae demons."

"Not even to save your friend?"

I clenched my teeth.

Everything in me demanded I say no. Not even for her. Putting my name in the Ledger would be asking for trouble. I'd made promises about following rules that would be dangerous to my health to break.

But the thought of turning down this opportunity to help Alyssa after my cowardly betrayal made me feel like the worst kind of scum. I had to make it up to her, even if it meant damning myself.

"What are you proposing?"

For the first time, uncertainty flickered in Reverie's glittering eyes, and her shoulders closed in, a subtle shift but one that piqued my curiosity.

"I tell you what I know and help you fight the inevitable

battle in exchange for the use of your skills."

I frowned. "What category of skills are we talking about?"

My official reputation in this country covered a lot of ground, but I knew there were rumours about my unofficial reputation—that dark history of my past with Hazel that I didn't dare cross. Not even for Alyssa.

"Your professional skills," Reverie said, and I swallowed a breath of relief. Though by her disdainful expression, I wondered what skills she thought I'd referred to. "I need something found. A contract. With your resources, it shouldn't be too much of a challenge."

"I'm a bounty hunter, not a PI. I find people."

She huffed. "Is it really so different? Or is all the talk of you being a think-outside-the-box, relentless hunter all bullshit?"

I opened my mouth to retort, then closed it again. She was right. All things considered, it was an easy price to pay to save Alyssa.

"Give me something first," I said as I shoved my hands in my jeans pockets. "You're Delvin's pet. Have been for years. I'm not putting anything in the book until I have a damn good reason to believe you're not going to screw me over."

Her eyes narrowed, and I could see the arguments forming in her head, which were soon replaced by a flash of desperation followed by acceptance. Whatever this contract was, she wanted it badly.

"I overheard what Delvin and Corrick agreed to," she said. "They didn't know I was still here, or they wouldn't have been so loud. Corrick is after some amulet. He plans to use it to take control of the businesses in the city. To be more specific, the business *owners*. Become powerful enough to push O'Malley out of the way and take over, create a new syndicate. And I don't get the impression he plans to stop there. Delvin agreed to help in exchange for a place at the table once the dust settles."

My stomach dropped and, somehow, my mouth grew drier, my throat closing until I felt like I was about to choke.

The Death's Head Syndicate was a big enough problem in this country, but it was a consistent, understood problem. This sort of change would mean the overturning of every balance in place. And for a demon to join a witch at the head of that change?

SMOAC would be in a bind to keep crime out of view of the mundanes. There would be a power struggle among groups. Already the demons and the fae kept a fine balance between war and peace, and the vampire queen was always looking for ways to spread her rule. Meril, the queen beyond the unseen wall, might be forced to step in if things got too bad, which had the potential to start a war between the supernatural and mundane. Even if Corrick played it smart and kept his head down, the shifts that happened throughout this city—throughout the country—would have an echoing effect on life as we knew it.

"You know the lieutenants Corrick keeps around him," Reverie continued. "I'll help you fight them to get to him, help you save your girl, and in return"—she crossed her arms and jutted her hip, but I read her insecurity through the show of confidence—"I want my freedom."

She could have knocked me over with a prod of her perfectly shaped gel-tipped nail. "Your freedom," I repeated. "I thought you said you wanted a contract. Freedom from what? From this earth? From the high fashion world? From those heels?"

"From Delvin." There was no mirth in her voice and all uncertainty was gone. "From the club."

Still stunned, but this time too much so to even crack a joke, I stared at her and waited for an explanation.

She propped her hands on her hips, then crossed her arms again. "For the past few years, I've been working off a debt. A loan of sorts." When I only stared harder, asking more silent questions, she threw her arms in the air. "I killed the wrong person, okay? I was young, assigned to a fancy dinner as a fledgling fae emissary. End of the night, I was talking to some politician with connections, but he got all handsy with me, so I turned him into dinner. SMOAC got close, and Corrick got them off my back. He sold my contract to Delvin, who's kept me off their radar."

"In return for you working his club."

Reverie nodded. "It was supposed to be a term of five years, but he likes what I've done with the place and is threatening to turn me in unless I keep doing what he tells me. I can't stay here. The patrons are sleazebags, and Delvin's been digging deeper and deeper into deals and connections I want nothing to do with. If I help you, I need *your* help to find that contract so we can destroy it and get me out from under his thumb. Do we have a deal?"

She snapped her fingers, and a glowing red light sprang up between us, solidifying into a thick, ragged tome. The Ledger.

Making a deal under fae rules would have come with its own risks, but putting my name in that book would throw away certain protections I had, put certain people on my trail if they found out. But if it helped me save Alyssa, what else could I do?

I picked up the pen sitting in the centre of the fold and wrote in the details, being very careful and specific with my wording, then signed my name. Reverie took the pen after me and signed hers.

"All right, then," she said. "Let's go."

The Ledger disappeared. No trumpets or ominous music, just a professional contract between two acquaintances before they headed into battle.

How anticlimactic.

With a shaking hand, I pulled my phone out of my pocket and pulled up my contacts. I'd already put my head on the block. Now it was time to call in the sword.

"Who are you—" Reverie started to ask, but I held up my hand to silence her when the line clicked.

"Mr. Wyatt?" drawled the voice on the other end. "I hope you've had time to think about my offer. Should I be expecting you?"

I drew in a deep breath and held it. We were ending this tonight.

"No, Dara," I said, "but I'll be expecting you."

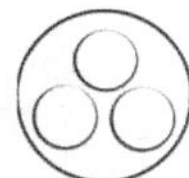

Chapter 32
Trace

Thursday, 6:00 p.m.

REVERIE AND I arrived at The Scorpio a little less than an hour later. The sky was already midnight dark except for the orange glow of streetlights reflecting off the low-hanging snow clouds. We were in for another storm, I could feel it in my bones, and I wondered if there was a way we could use the weather to our advantage. Drag Corrick into a squall and bury him under a snowbank.

The image gave me a pleasant thrill, and my magic responded, flooding into my hands and dancing around me.

Reverie shot me a dark look. "If you're going to be so obvious, we won't waste our time trying to sneak through the back. They'll sense you from here."

Gritting my teeth, I shoved my magic down and followed her to the front door. Where a familiar tingle of power buzzed along the back of my neck.

"What is it?"

"Alyssa was here. Not that long ago, either, by the feel of it."

Reverie frowned. "I didn't know you witches could recognize each other like that."

It was only when she made the observation that I realized how strange it was that I'd had no trouble identifying Alyssa's signature. Usually all magic felt the same to me: a pressure in the air, like the tension before someone breaks bad news or the thickness of a dry house filled with static. I differentiated power level by the intensity of the sensation, oncoming spells by how the air moved, but rarely could I tell one person's magic from another's.

I grunted. "I guess spending so many hours with someone under high-pressure circumstances changes the dynamic."

"Mmhmm. I'm sure that's the reason. Also the reason we're about to challenge a murderous witch, his demon pets, some shifters, and half a coven. Because of a 'changed dynamic.'"

I evaded her bland stare, refusing to consider the weight of her implication. First we'd get Corrick off Alyssa's back, then I'd take the time to sort out just what it was about Alyssa's magic that made me feel as though some missing part of me had been restored whenever I was with her.

"Can you use your newfound talent to tell if there's anyone inside?" she asked.

I closed my eyes and stretched a tendril of magic under the door but sensed no interactions with anyone else's power. And since no one reacted to the invasion, I had to guess there was no one around to see us walk in.

"They might be inside, but the way seems clear."

"Or they're ready to ambush us and you're a fool."

"Or that."

I set my hand on the door, then paused and turned around. "You don't have to come with me, you know. Whatever we face inside, is it really less horrible than working the club?"

Reverie's throat tightened as her mouth flattened into a thin line, but after a moment, she jerked her head in a nod. "Let's trade places one day. We'll see how long you last seducing desperate humans and following the commands of a spiteful, power-hungry demon. Open the door."

With a final deep breath, not wanting to admit to anyone, myself included, how badly I did not want to go inside, I turned the handle and pushed. The heaviness of recently released magic created resistance, as though a carpet had curled under the bottom of the door, and I had to force myself to take the first step into the darkness of the nightclub within.

The empty room told of a fight: Four tables destroyed,

metal chairs bent and twisted, more than one hole in the wall. Broken glass littered the floor by the bar. It was like Mooney's Pub after my and Alyssa's fateful introduction, without the hominess and with three times more swank. I knew which venue I preferred.

As I'd expected, no one was here to greet us, and even from the middle of the room, no sound reached my ears. I wished I had the ability to see what had happened here, some gift that let me read the memories of a place. Then I'd know what had happened to Alyssa. I'd know what I was walking into.

My boot slid on something slick, and as I wheeled my arms to catch my balance, I dropped my gaze to find a pool of blood beneath my feet. My heart leapt into my throat and my vision turned black around the edges. I knelt down and held my hand over the blood, trying to get a read on the magic. Alyssa would have seen colours, no doubt, but all I could tell was that the vibration wasn't familiar. It wasn't hers.

My shoulders sagged with relief, and I squeezed my eyes shut as I forced myself to take a few deep breaths.

"Do you hear that?" Reverie whispered.

I looked over my shoulder and found her close behind me, head tilted as though to pick up some distant sound. I copied her pose but heard nothing except the raggedness of my breathing. Why were my lungs acting up? Stress? Apprehension?

Fear.

The truth hit me like a punch to the solar plexus, and my next breath caught on its way in. Not fear for myself, but for Alyssa. She had come here on her own and met with trouble. Even if the blood on the floor wasn't hers, I recognized the feel of her magic throughout the room. Threads of it. Nets. Enough that she must have expended an entire power reserve to fight off whatever had been thrown at her.

So where was she?

"Over this way," Reverie said. "It sounds like banging. Someone calling. It's weak, though. Be careful. It could be a trap."

She didn't have to keep saying that. Until I was out of this building, I would assume enemies lurked in every shadow waiting to catch me off guard.

Magic at the ready to watch Reverie's back, I followed her to the staff-only door on the far side of the room. She stopped, and I used the same trick I'd used at the front door, stretching a tendril of power through the gap to test for a reaction. When no noise followed, I squared my shoulders, twisted the handle, and shoved the door open, making sure to stand to the side, out of range of any sudden attack. The hallway was empty.

"Too empty," I grumbled aloud, and ignored Reverie's stare.

None of this felt right. Every step threatened to spring the snare shut, a giant maw ready to devour us, yet I sensed no magic other than—

No, up ahead. Warmth spread under my skin like the sense of coming home.

Leaving Reverie to follow or stay as she chose, I followed the trail of Alyssa's power to a locked room in the middle of the hallway. Between my magic and a good shoulder-butt by the handle, the lock gave and the door swung open to reveal a small storage space, no more than eight feet by ten. Wooden shelving units lined the walls, crammed with boxes labelled with various kitchen necessities. Barrels sat on the floor. Lots of goods, no people. No bodies.

Relief battled with confusion. I'd expected to find a bled-out, magic-drained Alyssa, so to not see her sucked the air out of my lungs. But her magic lingered, prickling my tongue like sugar.

"Is this where you heard—" I started, but a soft thump made the question unnecessary. I spun in a slow circle to find the source, but the room was too full, and the sound echoed off every crate. "Can you tell where it's coming from?"

Reverie's flawless face scrunched in a scowl. "I'm fae, not a blood hound."

I pinched the bridge of my nose, gave myself a shake, and flexed my hands at my sides. "We're not going to get very far if we're at each other's throats the whole time. Let's assume for the next hour that nothing I say is intended to be offensive.

Deal?"

"Should I get the Ledger back out?" she asked, but when I stared at her without replying, she sniffed and dropped her chin in a subtle nod. I took that as the most agreement I would get.

"Okay. So what do we have?" I spun in another circle, checking the walls for hidden doors.

Reverie shook her head as though I were the stupidest man on the planet and shoved one of the shelving units into the middle of the room as easily as if it weighed the same as an empty box. Show off.

The thud came again, this time accompanied by a weak cry.

I opened my mouth to call back, but a pointy elbow to the ribs shut me up. I deserved that one. We'd been lucky so far, but how long would that luck hold? Especially if I went shouting out our presence. I pressed my lips together and knelt down to find the handle to whatever trap door Reverie had uncovered. Although the cracks in the floor were clear, revealing a door roughly two by two metres, there was no obvious point of entry.

"Do you see anything?" I asked after I caught the fae standing in the corner with her hands on her hips.

"I promised to help, not do everything for you."

I ignored her and crawled forward inch by inch, searching every crack for some kind of release or handle or magical trigger. Finally, my fingers dipped into a groove between floorboards camouflaged as a knot. "Got it." I heaved the door open as Reverie moved behind me, half facing the door to the storage room but turned enough to peer over my shoulder into the cubby.

My brain short-circuited, my heart slammed against my ribs, and I cursed as I released the door to get a clearer view.

The storage space under the floor must have stretched a little more than half the length of the room, though it was only a three-foot drop to the concrete floor. Lying on her back, her hands and face smeared with blood, was a barely conscious Alyssa. She must have been kicking at the trap door to get enough force for us to have heard it from the lounge. The strappy shirt she'd worn to Club Crescent was gone, replaced by the tatters of a black Mooney's Pub tee, half hidden under my coat. It wasn't possible to say how much of the blood was hers or how severe her injuries were, but by the way her eyelashes fluttered, as though she didn't have the strength to do anything more than that, I guessed she wasn't in good shape.

I spared a quick glance for her demon bartender, who lay unconscious on his side, but my attention was all for Alyssa.

Everything moved underwater slow, my muscles refusing to cooperate with their usual dexterity as I slid into the cubby to crouch beside her. She rolled her head towards me, and I brushed the loose hair out of her eyes. My fingertips tingled at the contact, a rush of energy that burrowed into my heart. I couldn't bring myself to take my hand away, instead running my fingers over her cheek, her jaw, her neck as I told myself I was checking for wounds before I risked moving her.

Aside from a few bruises, blisters, and minor lacerations, she didn't appear injured, which told me most of her trouble wasn't physical. Hit by too many spells and wiped out by using too much magic, most likely, but the only way to know would be to get her out of this cramped space.

"Do you plan to stay down there all evening, or do you think we can get moving before the masses return?" Reverie asked from above.

Shifting as carefully as possible so I didn't jostle Alyssa, I scooped her into my arms and lifted her out of the hole. She stirred, turned her face into the crook of my neck, and I swallowed the heartbeat that throbbed in my throat, the vibrations travelling down my chest to tighten my lower stomach. Beneath the metallic reek of blood was the scent of aloe vera, sweet and simple—the scent I'd come to associate with her—and my mouth watered.

"What about this one?" Reverie asked, pulling my thoughts away from Alyssa towards Simon. "Do we lock him back up? Leave him?" Her lip curled back to expose a hint of elongating fang. "Kill him?"

"We take him with us," I said. "Gently."

Whatever I felt about demons in general and this one in particular, I owed him. He'd been there for Alyssa when she'd needed him, which was more than I'd given her.

Reverie shrugged her disappointment, leapt into the hole, and slowed her approach as her head tilted to the side. Her eyes widened, her nostrils flared, and she turned to look at me. "A chaos demon? You and your *dynamic* keep strange company, Mr. Wyatt."

I snorted and gave her a pointed once-over. "Tell me about it."

Reverie hooked her arms under Simon's armpits and tugged him with apparent ease to the lip of the trapdoor and over the side until he rested on the ground at my feet.

While the fae set about closing the door, I nudged Alyssa's jaw with my thumb to bring her awareness back to the room. We needed to get moving, but I had to make sure she was all right.

It took a few tries, but finally she shifted her bleary gaze to meet mine. Her eyes widened as panic set in, but after a moment, the fear softened into relief and—dare I say—a hint of happiness before the panic returned in a wave and she tensed in my arms.

Her reaction nearly broke me, and I set her on the ground so I could back away and give her space. I deserved her distrust, but it pummelled my heart in a way I hadn't expected.

"Are you okay?" I asked when it became clear she wasn't up to asking questions of her own.

Slowly, she nodded. "I think so." Her voice was rough but steady. "Nothing time and a hot bath won't cure. Not that we have the luxury of either of those right now."

"May I?" I held out my hand, and although her stare was filled with wariness, she rested her palm on mine. "Your healing experience likely outpaces mine by a few dozen spells, but I know enough to at least get you back on your feet."

"Anything's better than nothing," she said. "Not like I'm capable of casting much myself right now."

She closed her eyes as warmth passed through my hand into hers. I sensed the surge of her magic as her strength returned, if not to full capacity, at least so far as to not leave her defenceless.

"Thank you," she said, pulling her hand free.

I hated letting her go. The weight of her palm in mine strengthened me in ways I'd forgotten, and I didn't want to lose that. "Alyssa, I am so sorry. I fucked up. I know I did. I really did plan on making a deal with Dara, I never would have left you with her to die—but that's not the point. I lost faith in myself and left you in a shit position, and I—"

"If we could finish this beautiful display of self-flagellation on our way out, I'd be eternally grateful," Reverie said as she pulled the unconscious Simon over her shoulder. He had to outweigh her by eighty pounds and have a foot on her, but she showed no discomfort in bearing his weight. I envied demonic strength.

I cast a longing look at Alyssa, hoping to see that my apology had cracked any part of the granite wall she'd put up between us, but her gaze was focused on the door. Resigned to having to wait—willing to wait as long as I had to if it meant I could have hope—I opened the door and checked the corridor. Once I was sure it was empty, I led us out of the storage room towards the back entrance. We were parked closer to the front, but I didn't want to draw anyone's attention with Simon in his current condition, and he didn't look ready to wake up.

As we made our way to the door, Alyssa kept shooting looks between me and Reverie, her expression flitting through concern, confusion, jealousy, hostility, and curiosity. She jerked her head towards Reverie. "You were just out for an evening stroll with the assistant of a demon who wants me dead?"

I considered how it must look to her, me being here with the half-succubus, half-fae who had attempted to seduce her at the club before witnessing the horror of Alyssa's past rising up to wave hello.

"Turns out Lady Rev has as much reason to hate Delvin as you do," I said. "After I escaped the EMTs at the crash site"—a flinch from Alyssa—"I went back to the club thinking I'd take another stab at getting Delvin to talk. Reverie directed us here. More than willing to get her hands dirty if it means Delvin's brutal demise, right, Rev?"

The fae snorted, making even that unladylike noise sound alluring.

"Right…" Alyssa said.

I didn't blame her for her disbelief. It sounded bizarre enough to my own ears, and I'd been there. I did wish I could read her thoughts about my showing up and that she could read mine so she'd know how sorry I was for letting her down and how badly I wanted to repair the trust I'd broken.

"What about you?" I asked. "What the hell are you doing here?"

Nice work, Wyatt.

Alyssa scowled. "I already told you. I wanted to talk to Corrick to see if I could get him to back off."

"How'd that work out for you?"

"I learned he doesn't intend to back off." Her anger faded, and her shoulders slumped as she sighed. "He was waiting for me. He had about fifteen guards on standby, all of them ready to throw a punch. I must have looked like a naive child coming here the way I did with only Simon to back me up."

Fifteen? I pictured her standing her ground against the small army, and rage sparked in my blood. Against Corrick, but more against myself. I'd let my panic get in the way of keeping my promise to this beautiful, fascinating, courageous, stubborn woman. Fear had turned me into a coward. A traitor. I'd be lucky if she spoke to me again after this.

Though my curiosity was piqued by what she'd said.

"Why did they keep you alive?" I asked.

Reverie grunted and shifted Simon on her shoulder. "And where have they gone?"

She was slowing down, and Alyssa was moving too gingerly to hurry. The door was only a few metres away, but at the pace we were going, it seemed three times as far.

"Two questions, same answer," Alyssa said. "They're looking for something. Something they won't find where they expect it to be. Corrick probably kept me around so he could torture me into giving up its location."

I frowned. "The amulet?"

Her eyes narrowed. "What do you know about the amulet?"

I realized my error when I saw that brutal distrust flicker in her eyes. "Not much. Only what Reverie told me."

My explanation didn't appear to help matters as Alyssa turned her glare on the fae.

Reverie shrugged. "Only what I overheard from outside Delvin's office. A magical artifact he plans to use to gain power in the city."

Alyssa continued to stare at me, and I clenched my hand at my side, silently begging her to believe in me. "I promise you, Alyssa, my reason for being here has nothing to do with some amulet. I came here for you, to help you."

A groan sounded behind us, and I turned to find Simon

blinking his amber eyes open. Reverie set him down, and Alyssa crouched by her friend's side. She rested her hand on his shoulder until he was able to lift his head and assure her he was okay, then she turned back to me. "Whatever Corrick is after, he's not going to get it."

I told myself I wasn't hurt that she hid the details from me, knowing I would need to do more than apologize to make things up to her, but damn if it didn't pinch.

The slam of a door opening came from up ahead, and our time for regrouping and planning ended.

"Well, shit," Alyssa said, raising her hands in front of her. "Here we go again."

I caught her eye as I drew my magic into my palms. "Come on, princess. Let's give them hell."

Chapter 33
Alyssa

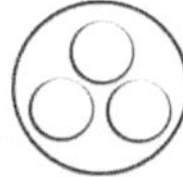

Thursday, 6:30 p.m.

THE GLOW OF lights from the back alley spilled through the open door as a group of people walked in, but I paid no attention to their faces. I wasn't ready to jump into battle again. Every part of me ached, my magic was only starting to filter back into my bloodstream, and my head was in a tizzy thanks to Trace's flustered, emotional, perfect apology. The bastard.

But Corrick wasn't about to give me half an hour to prepare myself, so I settled for creating a ward that would gain us a few minutes at least. Given what I'd seen of Corrick's army, they'd break through it quickly enough, but the extra time would let Simon shake off the knock to the head and let me get ready for round two.

Trace added his magic to mine, layering his telekinetic power on top of my atmospheric. His jaw was set as he raised his hands to smooth out the silver threads of his magical net. My purple-tinted spell pulsed under his, shifting to mingle with it until it had created a knit sweater of a ward, something I'd never seen before but wanted to pet.

My head was obviously still messed up, and not only because of the earlier fight. As I watched the flex of Trace's long fingers and felt the soft stroke of his magic moving around me, my heart fluttered. The warmth of his basic healing spell lingered, the faint buzz like a hit of alcohol, though I wasn't sure if it was all from his magic or the fact that he'd returned to fight at my side.

A big part of me knew I should stay on guard. He'd planned to take me to Dara. He'd wanted to turn me in to buy his freedom. Yes, he'd hauled me out of a hole, but who was to say Dara wasn't waiting outside to drag me away regardless of what I'd learned about Corrick's intentions.

But he was standing beside me knowing what waited for us. Knowing we might not make it. I might not have reason to trust him as soon as we left The Scorpio—if we left The Scorpio—but right now I had to have faith he would watch my back.

The succubus, on the other hand, I had no reason to trust. I shot her a nasty look and tried to ignore the way Simon's bronze magic bounced off her gold-touched, cotton-candy-pink power, the two navigating around each other instead of exploding into a confetti cannon.

"Do you think I could heal you without setting the room on fire?" Trace asked Simon once the ward was done.

Simon shook his head. "Best not to chance it. The ward is already pushing my limits. I'll be fine."

Trace nodded and turned to me. "We'll hold here until you're ready. I'll take the brunt of any attacks until you give the word."

I shifted to check how Simon was doing. His auburn hair was mussed and his amber eyes were less than clear, but he stood on his own, mouth set with determination, his bronze magic a puff of cloud around him.

My gaze narrowed in on Reverie and the way she stared at Simon as though he were a surprise gift under the Christmas tree. I was nearly overcome by the desire to wedge myself between them, but a nudge from Trace's magic reminded me of my priorities. The ward was important right now, not the way the succubus looked like she wanted to devour Simon for dessert.

The first blast of power struck the ward. Our joined spell vibrated but didn't give.

"The snake shifter has to be the first to go," I said, shaking out my arms as though that would get my magic working faster.

"Strong?" Trace asked.

"And a huge pain in my ass. But yeah, if she has room to shift, she can knock all four of us off our feet with a single swipe. Take her down and Corrick loses his second. Her and the rage demon."

"Got it."

"And the witches."

He smirked. "Take them all down. I get the picture."

Was I procrastinating? Yes, very likely. But as another spell hit the ward and the edges frayed, I accepted our time was up.

I summoned my magic into my hands. "See you guys on the other side."

Trace caught my eye, I nodded, and together we dropped the ward. As soon as it was gone, I stepped forward with a propulsion spell that threw three witches and a demon back the way they'd come.

Three more of Corrick's guards swarmed into the doorway and over them, charging towards us, trying to gain control of the tight space, but we held firm.

"We need more room," Trace said. "Back towards the front door. Let's get them into the club."

Heat blossomed behind me as Simon summoned his power, and I latched on to it with mine—purple woven with bronze—before hurling the random, chaotic tangle over my head into the witches closest to us.

The one on the left shrieked at a bloodcurdling pitch as he stumbled backwards, blood seeping between his fingers where he pressed them to his face. Panicked, he ran backwards only to bump into a witch just regaining his feet, and they crashed to the ground in a tangle of limbs. Beside them, a shifter was trapped mid-change, claws extended, fangs dripping, one eye yellow, the other brown. She snarled and swiped her unfinished paw at my face. I ducked, and Reverie barrelled into her waist to tackle her into another witch behind her.

The last lackey struck by the chaos magic was no more than a puddle of steaming goop burning a hole in the thin carpet. Trace leapt over it to take the demon to the ground, a magic-wrapped fist pummelling the surprised fiend against the floor.

Simon and I reached the staff-only door, but more voices spilled through from the other side. We were surrounded.

I looked over my shoulder to see the status of the other two in time to watch a red cloud rise from the demon beneath Trace. I launched myself forward, knocking Trace clear before the spell released. Reverie hurled the shifter into the spell's path, and based on the agony of her screams, I was glad I looked away before the effects kicked in.

Apparently not satisfied with her kill, Reverie leapt in a flash of cocktail dress and talon into one of the witches who had regained their footing. A bolt of Simon's bronze magic shot towards her, and before I could call out a warning, it struck her and sent her flying.

Literally flying.

Sheer bronze-hued wings spread out from between her shoulder blades, allowing her to lift mid-air, raising her out of the man's reach. She raked her lengthened fingernails across his neck as she soared over him. Blood sprayed across the wall, and her lips pulled back in a grin.

A shiver ran through me, and not only because of her obvious enjoyment at the gore. Simon had expended magic, and Reverie's power hadn't interfered with it. He'd had an intention, and it had come to pass.

Shock—and a touch of jealousy—coursed through me, but I shoved it aside. For now, I had to stay focused on the advantage their combined abilities gave us. Simon's power, unobstructed, was stronger than anything else we had at hand.

The amulet pulsed at my throat.

Almost the strongest. The strongest I intended to make use of.

For the moment, the hallway was clear, but the other voices were coming closer, and the vibration in the air warned of magic being summoned. Lots of it.

I dragged more into my palms, felt it surge, and looked down in surprise to find Trace's silver power still twined with mine. A glance over my shoulder showed him braced in a defensive position, the silver magic between his palms laced with my familiar purple. A million questions circled my mind about how it had happened, but for now I was grateful it had. Between his telekinetic magic and my atmospheric, we could assemble a decent offence.

Ahead to my left, with Simon's magic wrapped around her in a glowing shield, Reverie looked ready to tear open more throats. We were as ready as we were going to get to face the rest of Corrick's crew.

A lump formed in my throat that my final hours might be staring me in the face, but the only way to see the end—either way—was to go through it.

All my life I had done my best to avoid using my magic for anything other than helping people.

Now I'd been cornered.

These bastards had destroyed my safe haven. I was tired. I was sore. I wanted my couch and my tea and my TV. More than anything, I wanted this fight to be over.

Hands balled at my sides, I took the first step towards Simon and the club. Reverie fell into step beside me, and I sensed Trace close behind.

I released a pulse of magic that blasted open the staff-only door, and Reverie flicked her fingers at the room beyond. I blinked at the duplicate image of her that appeared inside, a perfect replica, down to the malicious smile. Half of Corrick's people turned to face it, freeing us to focus on the rest.

But the witch in the doorway wasn't fooled by Reverie's illusion. A swirling ball of red magic floated above his open right palm. I shoved Reverie out of the way as he released the spell, and it smacked into Simon's ward. I ducked as the spells met and fireworks exploded in the narrow hallway. Sparks landed on my coat sleeve, the wool smouldering, but the witch took the brunt, not having expected the bright flash of light in the dimness. He staggered back, and I followed up with a spell that threw him into the club, hopefully onto something pointy.

Trace allowed no time for the others in the nightclub to recover from the surprise of our entrance. As Reverie's illusion faded, he charged around me and skidded across the floor, a spell wound between his fingers. He released it at the four witches to our left, and the table behind them splintered. Wood shards flew, impaling two of the witches and sending the other two to the ground as they leapt out of the way.

Not a bad start for our final showdown, but of course luck couldn't stay on our side.

In another breath, my vision grew hazy and my head swam as Melanie Caplan in full rage demon form tapped into my emotions and feasted on them. I dropped to my knees and clapped my hands over my ears as though that would block out the buzzing created by her feeding.

Simon called my name, but I couldn't move. Not even

when a green-and-gold body slithered past me, head and tail hidden in shadows.

I had to find my strength, had to fight back against the demon's pull. I dragged my magic from my depths and created a ward that I wedged between me and her, and for one blissful moment, the energy drain eased. I used that moment to rise to my feet and throw out my hands, releasing my power in a full circle of atmospheric pulse, taking down ally and enemy alike. Simon grabbed onto Reverie before she could land on the sharp point of a snapped metal chair leg, and Trace threw his arms over his face as he rolled across the floor. Guilt that I'd given no warning to the others pierced me, but at least the spell gave me space, a moment of breathing room, before the demon's magical suckers latched once more onto my soul.

A metal chair wrapped in Trace's silver magic winged from my periphery and slammed into Melanie's head. She staggered into the wall and her connection to me snapped, giving me time to turn my attention to the two witches who had found their footing and were preparing their next onslaught. Spells zipped around the room, landing just as often on one of theirs as on us. Fire sprang up from the floor, ice frosted the tables.

Trace stumbled, hit by some kind of mental stun, and I stepped in front of him, hands raised to fend off the follow-up attack that would have turned his innards into outards. The spell fizzled off my ward. I wished Simon had been nearby to redirect it, but in my periphery, I saw he'd taken on the rage demon.

Behind him, Reverie was entangled with one of the witches. His eyes were glazed over, a dopey expression on his face as Reverie leaned in, her eyes burning with golden-pink fire and a teasing smile on her crimson lips. My blood sang and my core sizzled at the force of the sexuality wafting off her, and I turned away before I found myself cutting between them. Damned succubus.

A hand brushed my shoulder as Trace shook off whatever had stalled him, and I fled his side to get in the way of a shifted coyote attempting to take advantage of Simon's distraction.

How many more were there? And where was that damned snake?

At the centre of it all, Corrick stood still, his expression as smug as it had been earlier. What a lazy son of a bitch to put everything on his minions. As though his time and effort were worth more than everyone else's.

Out of spite, I drew my power into my palm and shot a jagged spell in his direction. It glanced off a shimmering ward, blue with his syphoning magic, which had wrapped around him unseen, but he started back and glowered in my direction before shouting "Rosie!" and storming towards the edge of the bar.

I spun on my heel at his implied order, searching for the

snake shifter. A table leg squealed against the floor, the only warning I had before the massive tail swept into my side and sent me flying. I crashed into another table and rolled onto the floor, cringing at the stickiness that greeted my palms. The cobra's head darted in, and I threw up a ward, but after two snaps with her arm-length, dripping fangs, my spell fell apart.

A scream built in my lungs, but exhaustion kept me from releasing it. My barely recovered magic was tapped, and I was caught under this table, ten seconds away from being this bitch's snack.

Desperate, I reached behind me for something—anything—I could use to defend myself, and my fingers touched on a fragment of the table I'd broken. I gripped the piece of wooden frame tight in my weakening fist and drove it upwards as the snake struck. Wood sank into flesh. She recoiled with a sharp hiss and tried to snap the shard lodged in the back of her throat, but it was too short for her to reach.

I took advantage of her distraction to run, staying in a low crouch to prevent my head from being an easy target, but I had no free route. Everywhere I looked were more enemies. Trace had fallen to one knee with a grim expression as a demon bore down on him, flames licking from its eyes and out of its blackened mouth. Beyond him, Simon's magic sputtered, the air around him sparking like fireflies. Reverie fought on, blood staining her face, her hands, her shaking legs, her black dress slashed across her torso. Although she stood with her hands curled, ready to keep fighting, the way she swayed on her heels told a different story.

And the enemies kept coming.

We were going to lose. Corrick would destroy the others and keep me alive on a barely dangling thread until he got what he wanted—which was hanging around my neck within a few metres of him.

Warming against my skin.

Responding to my need. To the threat to its power.

I'd sworn I wouldn't heed its call. That I wouldn't make the mistake my grandfather had made, or his.

But we were out of time and out of strength. If we wanted to win this—survive this—we needed an unexpected edge.

And what could be more unexpected than using the very power Corrick was searching for?

Crossing my fingers that my plan didn't backfire and kick my ass, I reached for the amulet. Its magic vibrated over my fingers, fuelling me, and despite my misgivings, I latched on to what it promised. Heat swept through my blood—not the anxious fire from earlier but a rejuvenating surge that pumped new life into my veins. I had no idea how long its effects would last and wanted to make the most of the advantage the souls gave me, so I solidified my ward and cast my thoughts to the guards closing in on us.

The unfamiliar magic seeped through my pores, mixing with mine, charging it, ramping it up. I felt more alive than I ever had, capable of more than I'd ever done.

Beyond the thrum of magic were the voices. Whispers egging me on, begging for freedom, begging for control. I felt myself slipping beneath their hushed cries and ground my teeth together as I squeezed my hands at my sides. I was in charge here. I had to remain in charge, or else I was no better than the people who had contained the souls in the first place.

My magic warred with the angry yellow power, and my desperation to overwhelm it—either before it overwhelmed me or before Corrick's people overwhelmed us—forced tears to roll down my cheeks, cooling my flushed skin.

The voices grew louder. My body trembled so badly I couldn't hold myself up, but I refused to bow to someone else's command. Even if it was amplified, my magic was *mine*, and it would do what I told it. Gramps and my parents had spent years teaching me how to control it. It would not control me.

Slowly—too slowly—I bent my power to my will, coiling it in my centre, pinning it in place to ensure it wouldn't launch free before I was ready. I held it until the throbbing magic nearly knocked me on my ass. The image of a metal spring popped into my mind. Apply enough pressure on the coils, and when you let go, it would jump forward with extra force—so much stronger than an unplanned, uncontrolled attack.

With my focus on my target, I squeezed my eyes shut and wrapped my heightened magic around me as close as I could get it, fighting against the vibrations that rattled my teeth. Screams and shouts reached me from beyond the bubble of my concentration, but I didn't let them distract me. The stakes were too high if this failed.

My magic grew unstable under my grip, and I knew in another moment it would consume me, losing us whatever advantage I'd hoped to gain. *Tick tock, Alyssa.*

With a deep breath, I opened my eyes, rose to my feet, and let go.

Arcs of glimmering purple-yellow shot through the room, still streaked with hints of Trace's silver, each bolt targeting Corrick's people. The witches and coyote shifter disappeared in puffs of dust and bone, and a lower-ranking demon melted into a puddle of brown sludge. Melanie, Rosie, and Corrick were pushed backwards, and as Corrick regained his footing, our eyes met. Awareness settled in his stare, and with a silent command to his lieutenants, the intent of the battle shifted.

I'd revealed my cards, and now had to pray I could maintain the upper hand. Fortunately, the advantage wasn't only mine. The mass attack had given Trace, Simon, and Reverie space to catch their breath, and within moments, they'd reconfigured themselves around the room. It took me a second to realize their positions were defensive—around me. As though they understood the game had changed.

And by the look in Corrick's eyes, the way his syphoned fae magic sparked across his fingers and his shadow against the far wall grew to tower over us, it most certainly had.

Chapter 34
Trace

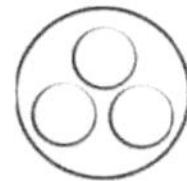

Thursday, 7:15 p.m.

Pain pulsed in my skull, my hip, my knee, my wrist. It had been a long time since a fight had pushed me so hard. If my motivations had been any weaker, I might have been angry with myself for taking it on.

But if I had any regrets, they weren't about showing up. More that I had come so close to *not* being here.

Never mind the absolute bastard I'd been to Alyssa, Corrick had ordered two murders, if not a thousand more that had gone unnoticed. He had stolen the magic of those he'd killed and blamed an innocent person so he could claim her power too. He needed to be stopped before he caused any more harm.

Taking him down was a matter of principle.

Determination firmed my resolve, strengthening my need to get back to my feet and ignore my injuries until the last blood was drawn.

I summoned my magic and hurled a bent and twisted metal stool towards the snake, who'd shaken off whatever strange power Alyssa had launched her way. The spell crashed into the side of Rosie's massive head, sending her crashing into the bar. Wood and glass smashed under the snake's weight, but too soon she shook herself off and turned those green eyes on me.

With a curse, I broke into a run, zigzagging around the remaining tables to make it more difficult for the creature to keep up. If I was lucky, she'd get herself tangled in table legs and take herself to the ground—but my hopes weren't high.

To my left, Simon let out a yell and charged Melanie—Corrick's third. Power emanated from Simon so strongly I felt it from halfway across the room, and I sent a quick, silent prayer of gratitude to the goddess that this demon had chosen a life of bartending instead of the true chaos he could have sown in this city.

Yet, for all that, it wasn't enough. Within a few metres of the other demon, he staggered. His face grew pale, his eyes wide, and he braced himself on a chair as he sagged to his knees. I veered towards him, but the snake snapped at my heels, and I lurched away to avoid a second assault.

Right. Keep the snake away from people.

I cursed again and rounded another table, realizing too late I'd caged myself in the circle of the cobra's lithe body. Having no time to think things through, I hurled myself over the thick scales, rolled across the snake's back, and landed on the other side, wishing I'd been a second slower and raised the odds that a mistimed attack would have had her biting her own tail.

My boot slipped in a puddle of blood, and I crashed onto my back, half under a table. My head cracked against the floor, and my vision swam with black dots that soon took the form of the snake's giant hooded head.

Fuck.

I rolled to the side as she struck, scrambled to my feet, and started running.

Where was Alyssa?

A scan of the room showed no sign of her, but that didn't mean much. The snake took up so much space I was amazed there was any air left for the rest of us.

Unfortunately, there was no sign of Corrick either, which set alarms screaming through my skull.

She can take care of herself.

I spun the words through my frazzled brain, trying to convince myself, but doubts assailed me with every fresh stab of pain that wedged between my ribs and into my eye sockets.

A blood-chilling hiss shook my head, and I turned on my heel to find the cobra at full height. Her green eyes bored down on me, her lips spread in a wide, fangy grin. An opalescent fluid slid down a lethal tooth and dripped onto the floor to eat into the surface.

My life flashed before me, all my greatest mistakes and unfulfilled wishes lined up, eager to feed themselves to the belly of this beast. But before I could process how I felt about facing my end, Alyssa shouted my name. I rolled onto my stomach and raised my head to find her running up the room towards me. Her hair was a flyaway mess, enough blood stained her face and clothing to make me see red, and she swayed with a notice-able limp, but she was moving.

Something had changed about her, though. Her signature was strong enough to punch me in the face as she approached, and it wasn't the warm hug I'd come to know. It was a hug laced with steel. As though, if she were to throw her arms around me, she would be just as likely to crush me as comfort me.

"Net me!" she called, reminding me that my imminent death was the priority, not her power, and without hesitation, I threw a weave of magic her way. It wasn't nearly as strong as it could have been, my power running on fumes, but as I opened myself to catch the vibrations of Alyssa's returning spell, I real-ized it didn't matter.

Whatever had changed in her, it had turned her into a behe-moth. Her spell's power was so great, I had trouble keeping my grip on it as it struggled to escape and fill the rest of the room.

It made my palms prickle and my arms shake, but I wrangled it into place and, although I couldn't see our magics fusing, I felt it, the two signatures braiding together, strengthening, sharpening. As the snake shot forward, ready to tear my head off, I rolled into a crouch and pulled the conjoined spell taut, turning it into a magical strip of razor wire.

The snake attempted to recoil at the last moment, but Alyssa had continued forward, dragging the net between us. I watched in morbid fascination as the spell sliced into the thick of the creature's neck, passing through scale and bone. Blood sprayed across the floor, coating my arm and the side of my face, and as the head slid from the cobra's body, its shape shifted, and the remains of a large, hulking woman tumbled to the polished floorboards.

My heart pounded in my ears as I dropped my shaking arms to my sides. Too stunned to consider how close I'd come to not seeing tomorrow, I switched my attention to where Reverie was facing off with Melanie. To where the rage demon was obviously working on consuming the fae's soul.

I readied myself to charge into Melanie to disrupt the connection when a delicate hand grabbed my ankle. I looked down and did a double-take on finding Reverie tucked behind a table. I looked between her and the other her, confused and wondering if the snake had gotten me after all.

But Reverie's smile was wicked. Knowing. And when I

looked back to the other her—to Melanie's confused expression as she feasted—I understood.

Simon was hidden under the glamour. But demons didn't have souls. Their life energy was a void, similar to the undead vacuum of a vampire's aura. Yet somehow the demon had missed that blatant emptiness in her pursuit of a meal. Her lethal meal.

Melanie realized her error too late. She attempted to release the magical hold on her victim before the poison could sink in, but the damage had been done. As I watched, the glamour around Simon faded, and Reverie climbed out from behind the table. Her smile was red and vicious in triumph, and she offered a finger wave to the rage demon, whose face withered—her cheeks growing gaunt, her eyes sinking, her flesh turning sallow. She clawed at her throat as though that would prevent the pangs of starvation as her body processed the death she had consumed.

Within moments, Melanie's skeletal corpse crumpled to the ground in the folds of her empty clothing, and all that remained in the room were us… and Corrick.

Chapter 35
Trace

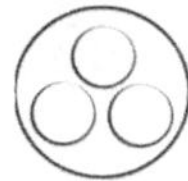

THE WITCH STOOD in front of the bar, his gaze focused on Alyssa, his eyes full of greed and desire. I looked between the two of them, wondering what the hell I'd missed. Obviously something to do with the strange magic emanating from Alyssa. The vibrations around her were wild, angry. Stronger than I'd ever known hers to be and less controlled. Now that the immediate threat to my life was over, my magic veered away from hers as though not wanting to be tainted by whatever had sullied it.

Her fingers drifted to her chest—to something hidden under her T-shirt—and it clicked. The amulet. She'd tapped into it and drawn on its power, and Corrick was coming for it.

I wouldn't let that happen, whatever the cost.

As the energy in the room changed, swirling like a stiff breeze that ruffled my hair and raised goosebumps along my arms, I wondered just how much of a cost it would be.

The shifting magic increased, turning into an electric buzz that tingled across my skin. Corrick's eyes spun with stars as he channelled the fae magic he'd stolen, and my stomach dropped at the sight, at the force of the power that crested off him and rattled the mirror behind the bar. His deep laugh echoed through the room.

Simon and Reverie must have felt the change too, because both of them backed away, creating more space between them and the man I swore had grown a foot in the past few seconds. Sparks crackled at his fingertips, and as his lips spread into a sick grin, more sparks shot from his mouth. From everything I knew about Corrick, he wasn't an elemental witch, which meant this magic wasn't his either. Was everything about this guy a fraud?

"You fight a losing battle, Miss Mooney." Corrick's grating voice radiated from every direction. "Even with your friends at your sides, few as they are. I've killed more than you know to prepare for this moment. Fae, demons, witches, humans—all gave me more power to contain the souls you've brought right to my doorstep."

My mouth went dry. Everything went dry. As though my

blood had drained through my feet into the floorboards.

Souls?

The stain in Alyssa's magic became starkly, terrifyingly clear.

What the hell was her family playing at keeping an amulet filled with stolen souls?

Alyssa must have caught the horror on my face because her gaze filled with anguish. A moment later, the pleading was gone, and she turned a feral, determined snarl towards Corrick. "You will never get your hands on this amulet. It never should have been created, and my family has kept it safe from people like you for generations. Our guardianship won't end today."

Corrick's laugh grew louder. "Kept it safe? Is that what your grandfather told you? Every single member of your family has risen to where they are thanks to the magic in that gem."

She squeezed her hands at her sides. "Well, I haven't. And if it's down to me to finish what my family was supposed to do, then so be it."

"You'll wield the magic to stop me? Hypocrite!"

She slid the amulet out from under her shirt and gripped the stone tightly in her palm as she smiled. "The souls know what they want, Corrick, and they would rather help me than serve you."

Without giving him a breath to prepare, she threw her hands forward, and bottles behind the bar exploded in a shower of glass. Shards lodged into the back of Corrick's neck and the sides of his face and rained down over the bar. He responded with a spell that hurled Alyssa off her feet. She slid on her ass through the blood on the floor until her back slammed into the wall.

I tried to step in to cover her until she shook off the hit but found myself unable to move, my feet bound to the hardwood. A growl worked up the back of my throat, but no matter how great my anger grew, I was useless to her. Across the bar, Simon struggled to throw himself out of his bindings, and Reverie looked ready to tear Corrick's face off with her fingernails given a moment's opportunity.

Instead, we were forced to watch as the witch stepped down from the bar and picked up a broken metal chair leg that had splintered into a lethal point. Alyssa staggered to her feet and unleashed another spell, this one craggy and oily as it zipped past me. Corrick dodged before it landed but never lost his footing, moving as smoothly as though time had slowed to allow him to step leisurely out of its way.

For all I knew, that was exactly what he'd done. If he'd killed as many as he said, across as many species as he claimed, who knew what abilities he'd picked up? He'd hidden behind his lieutenants, making himself appear weak and in need of guarding. All it had taken was for them to sacrifice themselves for him to show his true strength. The selfish prick.

He retaliated with another spell, and I became a bystander

of an old-school duel, magic flying back and forth, hitting walls, tables, bottles. One of Corrick's spells hit Alyssa in the shoulder, and blood spurted from the wound as she fell to her knees with a gut-deep scream. She had no time to launch a defence before the chair leg Corrick had grabbed earlier hurtled towards her at break-neck speed. I opened my mouth to shout, but it was too late. The metal point struck her in the chest, and a flash of yellow light blinded me to the room.

My heart pounded against my ribs, and in a panic, I blinked again and again to clear the reflective spots from my vision, fighting to see through them to make sure she was still alive.

My legs nearly gave out in relief when I saw her prop herself up on her hands and knees, blood spilling from her shoulder, too shaken to stand, until her confused expression turned into one of terror and chilled my last shred of hope that Corrick's final sweep had failed.

Her lips formed a silent *no*, and I felt a shock of twisted magic as it surged away from her towards Corrick.

My already cold blood turned icy as I realized what he'd done. The metal spike had shattered the gem. Shards of yellow stone lay scattered around where Alyssa knelt, and her blood-ied hand was wrapped around the end of the empty chain as though wishes would restore it.

The souls were loose and heading for a man who would use them for all their amplified power.

Even as I watched, his reign of terror began. The glow in his eyes grew brighter, leaching out in glittering veins across his face and down his neck, disappearing under his shirt before appearing again at his wrists and stretching into his hands all the way to his fingertips.

The hair on the back of my neck stood on end, the chandeliers trembled, and the floorboards under my boots quaked. Then, one by one, the fallen witches rose from their fallen heaps on the ground. Heads bent, arms stiff but moving, they shuffled into battle positions, ready to resume their fight.

With a jolt that shoved me backwards, the binding holding me snapped and my magic flooded the void Corrick's spell had left. My first instinct was to turn to the advancing witches, but Alyssa's cry stopped me.

At first glance, nothing about her seemed to have changed. She remained on all fours, still bleeding, still terrified, but the agony on her face screamed *wrong*, and it took longer than it should have to realize what was happening. As soon as it did, my horror melted into fury and my blood thawed, caught flame, spiked into an inferno as I summoned my power and threw it at Corrick.

The son of a bitch was draining her magic along with the souls he'd unleashed. Tapping into one last power source before he sat comfortably at the top of Ottawa's magical hierarchy.

I'd hoped that, in his ravenous greed, he'd miss my attack,

but at the last moment, he raised his hand and sent it back at me, throwing me off my feet. Stars burst through my vision and my ears rang as my head once more struck floor, but I dragged myself back up.

I couldn't stay down. I had to do something. Alyssa couldn't cut off the drain on her own, not in her current state. Simon's shout of rage gave away his own failed attempt to stop Corrick, and the smash of glass told me Reverie hadn't managed any better. Unable to go after him, they turned their attention to the shambling corpses.

The solution to the problem shouted at me, battered my thoughts, and I couldn't ignore it. Especially not when Alyssa raised her head, appearing to need every last effort she possessed to do so, looking so heartbroken at her failure that it directed all my attention to the one option remaining to us. The one that would end me.

A worthy end if it meant saving her life. Maybe we could have found another solution, but I'd panicked and fled. I'd pushed her to take on this last resort, and now I had to help us get out of it. For the sake of the entire city, for the first time in over a decade and despite my long-time vow to myself never to allow my heart to make decisions, I had to make this sacrifice.

The back of my throat burned with guilt and disappointment and shame, but I pushed it all aside and closed my eyes against the crime being committed in front of me.

So I could commit my own.

With deep breaths, praying I would go unnoticed until the task was done, I sank deep into my memories, into the words of invitation, of binding, that I had spent so many years trying to purge from my skull, and opened myself to the cursed magic that bubbled between Alyssa and Corrick.

A face I'd once known so well and had blocked from my mind for so long flashed behind my eyelids—dark hair, brown eyes, full lips, strong jaw—her smile ridiculing me. *Hypocrite. I knew you were weak. That you couldn't resist the pull of sweet temptation. How you screamed at me. Yet here you are.*

I closed my ears to the imagined taunting and reached further for the souls loose in the room. My magic pulsed as it danced inside me, creating an empty pool waiting to be filled. A safe space for the spirits looking to land.

Then, when I was sure my body was ready, I sent the first nudge to the closest spirit my power detected. It hesitated in its path towards Corrick, started down the route the others had taken, then stopped again when it sensed my unspoken promise.

Protection. Safety. Guidance.

I would not use these souls for whatever purpose they had originally been harvested. I would work hard to prevent the corruption from taking me the way it had taken Hazel. Corrick's intentions were as dark as his magic, and if there was any goodness, any innocence left in these spiritual entities, they would avoid him in favour of a better option.

I had to be that option.

I had to be strong, iron-willed, worthy of this undertaking.

And as though that single spirit recognized my intentions, it approached, slipping through my magic to rest in the welcoming pool. Its presence shocked my system like an ice bath, but I held firm and extended my invitation deeper into the room. More souls responded, seeking the likeness that now resided in my centre, and as more came, more turned my way, until the deluge nearly overwhelmed me. But it didn't stop, and soon more than the souls' power settled in the pool. A strain of magic more powerful than anything I'd ever tasted coated the back of my throat. Not a single flavour, but a mix of many. Corrick's. His own and all the power he'd stolen from others.

Intertwined with the souls, it was impossible for me to filter it out, and all I could hope was that it would be contained as well as the rest.

Another magic trailed after his, though. Sweet and simple, as comforting as a blanket on a cold day. Alyssa's. Her natural essence offset the slickness of Corrick's falseness and the sorrow of the trapped spirits. It wound deeper through my centre, encasing the void I'd made to hold the others, buffering their darkness with her brightness.

I forced myself to block her signature, afraid my enjoyment

of her magic would push me to slip and join Corrick in his effort to drain her.

Soon enough, the influx of souls slowed. As it did, more of Corrick's power burned my throat, and at last I cut myself off, hoping beyond hope I'd absorbed enough of the stray spirits to make a difference.

When I opened my eyes, Corrick's face told me all I needed to know. His skin was flushed a deep purple—of outrage or pain, I didn't know or care—and he held his hands in front of him as though trying to summon magic that was no longer there.

A roar spilled from his throat, shaking my eardrums, but we couldn't give him time to regroup. If I'd wanted to draw every last spirit away from Corrick, I'd failed. The air around him shimmered, as though steam were wafting off him, and behind the bar, more bottles exploded, alcohol and glass spraying in every direction. The chairs in front of him flew out of his way, smashed into walls, into the bar. A table slammed into Reverie and pinned her to the ground. Simon wheeled on his heel and threw a spell over her before a broken bottle could pierce her chest. The bottle hit his magic and transformed into a butterfly.

Alyssa kept her gaze on Corrick. Sweat dripped down her face as she struggled to stand, and just as she straightened her legs, mine gave out. Nausea twisted my guts, and I grunted against the pain of containing so much extra magic. I had to get it under control, complete the binding. Until I did, I was vulnerable, open to basic attacks. Simon was focused on the corpses, Reverie was trapped, and I was down.

That left Alyssa, weak and shaken as she was. And she knew it. I saw it written on every line of her face as she gritted her teeth and raised her trembling arms. With a scream of effort that came from the depths of her being, she unleashed her remaining magic at the same time Corrick did. The air crackled, the lights in the ceiling flickered, and the force of the two spells colliding shook the foundations of The Scorpio. Plaster crumbled from the ceiling, landing in my hair and sending dust into my eyes. Both Corrick and Alyssa threw themselves harder against each other's power, each one vying for dominance. I wished I could help, that I could lend Alyssa my strength as we'd done before, but the souls within me were too unstable. To offer her a boost would risk all the spirits I'd taken in being set loose and once more within Corrick's reach.

So I pressed my fists against the ground and prayed she would survive. I'd seen how determined she could be. I'd watched her challenge herself and surpass every obstacle that came her way. "You can do this, princess," I said, not wanting to break her concentration but needing her to know she wasn't alone. "Hold on a little longer, you've got this."

More vibrations caused the shelves behind the bar to collapse, and Alyssa took a step forward, as sluggish as if she were pushing through a snow drift. Corrick had leaned in, but although he also attempted to move forward, his snow drift was more of an ice wall.

With a final yell, Alyssa launched a ball of energy so strong the chandelier above her crashed to the floor in a shower of glass and crystal and twisted metal. Without giving myself time to question the wisdom of my actions, I launched myself at her and covered our heads under the protection of my arms as Corrick flew backwards into the mirror behind the bar. It cracked from one side of the frame to the other.

In the silence that followed, the stunned pause after the bomb blast, the voices outside the club were as loud as shots fired. They went quiet a second before a door slammed open. Footsteps on hardwood marched towards us.

I raised my head from my arms in time to watch a battalion of fae pour into the club, followed by Dara Josef-Levesque's honour guard and the duchess herself. Every muscle in my body tensed in a defensive lock around Alyssa, and a sob escaped the exhausted witch's throat.

Dara's expression, stormy and terrifying on entering, now shuttered in shock, and she stood staring, taking in the devastation that, an hour ago, had been the jewel of Ottawa's nightlife.

Shaking, queasy, sore, I rose to my feet, keeping my arms around Alyssa as I helped her stand beside me. On the other side of the club, Simon shoved the table off Reverie, drawing

Dara's attention for only a moment—her star-filled eyes flickering with contempt when they caught sight of the mixed-race fae—before it rested fully on me and Alyssa.

The silence stretched out.

I'd called the fae duchess myself, promised answers, and I had them, so if she made one move towards Alyssa, I was ready to fight. Without hesitation.

Alyssa's trembling ceased, and she pushed away from me, standing firmly, defiantly, on her own feet. Just as ready to battle her way free as I was.

Dara clasped her hands in front of her, the smooth lines of her white slacks and the crispness of her sapphire sweater so at odds with the destruction in which she stood.

"Well then," she said, her large eyes giving a barely-there glance at us before darting around the rest of the room. "Is someone going to tell me the story?"

Chapter 36
Alyssa

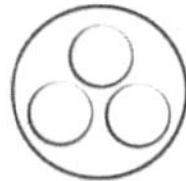

Three weeks later…
Friday, 4:30 a.m.

I SCRUBBED DOWN the freshly oiled bartop and cleared away the last of the empties.

The shelves behind me were stocked, the broken bottles replaced. All hint of the damage caused by my fight with Trace had been cleaned up, the furniture back in its proper places.

To the random person coming in, everything about Mooney's Pub would look the same as it always did. Never mind the few nights we'd been closed for the first time since we'd renovated. Never mind the bruises yellowing on my arms and torso, mostly hidden under my cardigan, or the healing cuts on my face that I blamed on a minor car accident. Never mind the way I occasionally jumped if the front door opened a touch too vigorously, or the way Simon made sure to stay close, his gaze following me around the room from his place behind the bar.

We were adjusting. Returning to the way things were before That Night.

And we would get there. I had to believe we'd get there. Otherwise, I would spend the rest of my life putting extra wards on my apartment door and going to sleep in the living room with the television on, unable to stand the silence for fear that every minor noise outside or from my tenant downstairs was someone out to get me. Not to mention that I was really, really over randomly bursting into tears when memories of The Scorpio Lounge came back to me or when I thought about how many times I'd nearly died in an eighteen-hour span.

Gritting my teeth and forcing a smile, I waved goodbye to Davis as he walked out the door, leaving Simon and me alone.

Everything back to the way it should be.

"Hey, Lys?"

I shook myself out of my thoughts and turned to Simon where he stood with a mop in his hand. Three weeks ago, the sight of him would have made me sigh with longing. Now my heart just tightened with gratitude that I had him in my life.

"Mm?"

"I thought I'd check out a few minutes early tonight, if

that's all right with you."

"Oh?" Although he'd finally stopped offering to follow me home to make sure I made it into the house, this was the first time he'd suggested leaving me on my own. "Big date?"

The sheepish smile that bloomed on his face made me raise an eyebrow in surprise.

"Maybe?" he said. "I thought I'd see if Reverie was free for breakfast."

I waited for the pinch of disappointment that never came. Disapproval, however—that was there in spades.

"You've kept in touch?"

He shrugged. "I haven't actually seen her since that night. I just… I don't know. I thought I'd swing by the club and make sure she's recovered."

"You do remember she's half-succubus, right?" I said, doing my best to keep the judgement out of my voice.

"And I'm a chaos demon," he replied, hearing it anyway.

I turned away from him to rub down another section of the bar. "Just be safe, okay? You're my favourite business partner. I'd hate to have to train a new one."

I didn't hear him move, but a heartbeat later, I was bundled against his chest in a tight Simon-squeeze. I didn't want to give in. He was putting himself at risk with that lust-provoking half-fae, and I didn't like it. But in another breath, I relented and hugged him back.

How could I resent his chance at companionship? I wouldn't go so far as to say happiness because, well, half-succubus, but at least the ability to spend time with someone whose magic wouldn't risk everything in the immediate vicinity exploding at any heightened emotional contact.

"All right, get out of here." I patted him on the back, then playfully shoved him away. "Some people still have work to do to make up for the slackers."

He grinned, his amber eyes sparkling, and kissed the top of my head before he disappeared into the office to grab his coat. At the door, though, he hesitated, and his expression was serious as he faced me. "Straight home, okay? If you sense anything weird, message me. I'll come right back."

My heart warmed at his concern, and I waved him off. "I promise, no wandering dark alleys or chatting with strange garden gnomes."

With an uncertain pause, he left, closing the door behind him.

As soon as I was alone, I took a moment to sit with the silence. This was the first time I'd been by myself in my own pub in three weeks, and I'd forgotten how much I loved it. The lack of magic, the smell of hops and food and lemon-scented wood polish. I could almost pretend that day of terror hadn't happened. Jet and Madison certainly pretended it hadn't—after I'd given them a few stern looks and threatened to ban them from the pub for their veiled references to it.

Gramps and I had reworked the wards on the windows and doors and confirmed the leaked magic from the amulet wouldn't be a problem. Some power remained in the earth under the safe, but as long as it stayed where it was, Simon was at no risk of spontaneously sprouting flowers from his ears or turning our cash into dung beetles.

All my regulars had asked after the closure, but most of them believed our story of a busted tap. My reputation remained intact, even if more than a few witches gave me a second glance as though wondering if the rumours that had slipped out about the fight with Corrick were true.

Really, the greatest change that had come from that day was my acceptance of spending night after night alone in my quiet apartment.

Though I didn't let myself consider too often who I'd rather be spending time with.

As I turned my back to stow the rag and cleaner out of sight, the now-squeaky hinge of the front door creaked at someone's entrance.

"We're closed," I said, the word half out of mouth as I turned to find Trace crossing the floor, his hands in his jeans pockets.

He wore an open grey button-down over a white T-shirt, the colour bringing out the violet in his eyes and the golds in his strawberry-blond hair, which was tied back out of his face as he usually kept it. He hadn't shaved in a while, the stubble longer than five o'clock shadow but not quite beard status.

At the sight of him, my heart lurched, and I wagged an imaginary finger at my chest until the unsettled thumps settled in my ribcage, though with a few extra beats per second. "Well, well, look what the imps dragged in."

A small smile twitched at the corner of his mouth as he sank heavily onto a bar stool. He jutted his chin towards the Ottawa landcape on the wall to my left. "I like the artwork."

"It's new." I grabbed a glass and raised an eyebrow in question. When he nodded, I poured him a pint and slid it across the polished bartop before pouring one for myself. "Thanks for the cheque, by the way. I suppose it makes up for you trashing my pub in the first place."

"Cheers," he said, and I raised my glass and watched him over the rim as he took a sip.

I hadn't seen him since the night we'd fought Corrick. Three weeks and not a word.

Not that I was hurt by his silence. Nope. Not at all. It wasn't like I'd wanted him around while I coped with the fall-out of our epic battle.

After Dara had shown up and demanded answers, SMOAC security officers had arrived, and everything that happened had been dealt with in the expected, official way.

Sort of.

Dara's guards had carted an unconscious Corrick off with them before SMOAC had seen him, leaving the investigation open-ended, and I had happily made the decision never to think about what she'd done to him out of revenge for her fallen generals. Especially since she'd done me a favour and left one of her people behind to weave a false story for the security officers. According to them, Corrick's lieutenants had gone rogue and attempted a coup. Rosie the snake shifter had killed the fae and many others in her bid for power, and when I went to warn Corrick, I'd found him gone and his people waiting for me. The fight ensued, I'd won, and we all lived happily ever after.

By the expressions on the security officers' faces, they didn't put much stock in the tale, but they also hadn't pressed, content to close a dozen pending cases and leave one unwanted CEO missing. And of course they wanted to keep their favourite after-work pub open for business. My freedom meant Mooney's remained unchanged. Each of the officers present in The Scorpio that night had come to the pub a few times since then, and I had served them with a grateful smile.

Trace had disappeared before the security officers finished with me. I'd called and texted him more than once to make sure he was all right, and when his voicemail had filled up and my messages went unanswered, I'd done my best to put him out of my mind. Dara had cancelled the bounty on my head. He had no more reason to come after me. I'd assumed the end of the contract had been his reason for cutting me out, but seeing the state of him now, I had to wonder if it was something else.

Up close, under the bar lights, the circles under his eyes looked like someone had punched him, his cheeks were sunken, his stubble uneven. His shoulders were stooped as he hunched over the bar, and the sight of him in only the button-down shirt made me rush to the backroom and come back with his peacoat.

"It's a little worse for wear, but I had it dry-cleaned, and I stitched up the tear in the shoulder myself."

He accepted the coat with a nod and set it on the stool beside him. "I had no doubt I left it in good hands. How are you holding up?"

I tried not to feel disappointed by his lack of reaction. He was obviously dealing with a lot. "Living the dream. A weird dream where I keep having to look down to make sure I'm wearing pants and stressing that I didn't finish my homework, but all things considered, better than the alternative. You know. Dead."

He sniffed a laugh and took another swig of beer.

"What about you?" I spun my pint glass slowly between my fingers. "You ran off so quickly, and I haven't heard from you. And you look… Well, frankly, you look like you've been shacked up with a pack of wolves since that night. Have you even seen a bed?"

"Oh yeah. Hardly dragged myself out of it for the better part of three weeks. That fight took a lot out of me. I'm surprised you're so steady on your feet considering how hard you fought. It was impressive."

My cheeks warmed with the compliment, but I wasn't distracted by it.

Whatever was wrong with him, it was because of more than a tough battle. If even a quarter of the stories about Trace Wyatt were true, he'd faced worse. Unless he always looked ready to collapse after a bounty and the stories left that part out.

But no, if I had to guess, whatever it was had something to do with the turn of events in that final showdown with Corrick. With that moment the souls poured out of the amulet and spilled through the room in a yellow wave towards Corrick until the current had shifted. I remembered how Trace had stood there, magic stilled, eyes closed, taking in the power of those trapped spirits in a way that made his expression contort with grief and despair. So different from Corrick's exultation.

Everything had changed as my magic had been pulled out of me, first fuelling Corrick's insatiable greed, then following the spirits towards Trace until he'd realized it and shut me out.

I didn't know if he knew that I knew exactly what he'd

done. My ability to see the colours of each magical signature had given me insight I doubted anyone else in the room held.

It was how I knew Simon and Reverie's magic didn't mingle and interact the way his and mine did but remained separate entities. How I knew Corrick absolutely would have drained me dry if he'd had the chance.

And how I knew that Trace had absorbed the power of the amulet into himself. I suspected the evidence I saw before me was only a fraction of what the effort had cost him.

"Will you be all right?" I asked in response to his comment, hoping he understood my deeper meaning.

His gaze bored into mine, the expression in their violet hue shifting from concern to shame, and I knew he had.

"Yeah. Eventually."

"What exactly did you—I mean, how did you—" No matter how I tried to phrase the question, there was no way to make it not sound judgy AF. "Whatever you did, however you did it, you saved my life. You saved a lot of lives. Somehow Corrick was strong enough to shatter an unbreakable gem. Or maybe my using the amulet weakened it? I don't know. It doesn't really matter. What does matter is that if he'd absorbed those souls… I don't even want to think about what he would've done with them."

Trace dropped his gaze into his beer and nodded. "That's what I keep telling myself. No matter how anyone else sees what I did, I can't regret it." He lifted his eyes once more to meet mine. "I don't regret it."

My insides fluttered and my cheeks flushed under the weight of his intensity. My disappointment from earlier faded under the certainty that whatever my feelings had become for this man over the events of those eighteen hours, they weren't entirely one sided. What that meant for us, I had no idea, but it was a relief to find out I wasn't alone in my emotional confusion.

I swallowed my sudden self-consciousness and rubbed my thumb over a non-existent blemish on the bar.

"Are you stuck with them?" I asked in an attempt to derail my thoughts from heading in directions I wasn't quite ready to handle. "The spirits, I mean. I know there was no way to safely purge the amulet, but the situation's changed now."

He flexed his jaw and chugged the rest of his pint. "I'm looking into it. Somewhere out there is an answer, and I'll find a way to set them free."

And set himself free along with them. My heart ached for him—with gratitude, with compassion, and with a butt-load of guilt. "Will you get in trouble? I know the whole taking souls into yourself thing isn't exactly smiled upon by the powers that be."

"Under the circumstances, I doubt a trip to Moongrave is in my future, but I don't intend to advertise my condition. As long as I don't wave the souls in anyone's face, what happened should go unnoticed until I get rid of them."

That was a lot of hedging, so I could only think he would be in a crap heap with SMOAC and the witches' council if they found out. Well, they wouldn't. Not from me, anyway, and as I didn't think anyone other than the two of us knew the whole truth of what happened in The Scorpio, hopefully that meant his secret was safe.

"Whatever help you need, I'm here."

He smiled again, this one reaching his eyes and bringing life into his haunted face. With a bit more pep in his movements, he raised his glass. "For now, you can pour me another drink and keep me company while I finish it." He quirked an eyebrow. "Unless you have somewhere else you need to be?"

I thought of Simon out on his maybe-date, of my empty apartment with its creaking windows and waiting television, and grabbed Trace's glass, refilling it and topping up my own before I set both down on the bar.

"Nowhere I want to be but here," I said, and hoped he didn't notice my face flush red at the unintended honesty. I cleared my throat and lifted my glass. "To unusual meetings, unexpected allies, and whatever comes next."

His smile widened. "To whatever comes next."

Thank You for Reading

Thank you so much for taking a chance on an independent author. We're living in a wonderful age where it's easy to upload a book to the internet, but that doesn't reflect the blood, sweat, and tears that go into making a book the best version it can be. It takes time, patience, perseverance, and to have the final result end up in a new reader's hands is the best reward. You are the reason we keep writing, so thank you.

If you enjoyed the read, please help support the author by leaving a review at the retailer where you purchased the book. Reviews make a world of difference for an author, helping us reach new audiences and bringing more people into the worlds you've spent time in.

For exclusive character content, announcements, promotions, and special offers, sign up for Krista's mailing list at https://www.kristawalshauthor.com/pages/about-the-author

Acknowledgements

We're embarking on series seven, and you'd think it would be rote by now, releasing new characters into the world. Not so much. There's still a certain nervousness at how the characters and story will be received, and excitement to be trying something new. Alyssa and Trace stepped onto the page together and swept me away with their chemistry, their story so far writing itself as I hang on and try to keep up.

But even the most fun ideas need people to corral them and make them worth reading.

To that end, I have people to thank for making this book what it is.

My earliest readers: Lynn Morrison, Lisa McBride, and Stephanie Mirro. Your eyes helped me transform this book into a stronger version of its starting point, and your encouragement pushed me to keep going with the series.

Kate Sparkes, for being the amazing, wonderful powerhouse that is you.

Emily Stewart, my editor, for catching all my inconsistencies and foibles and raising the level of my writing to something that shines.

My beta readers: Traci, Noelle — thank you for all your support and encouragement!

My writers groups, because where would I be without my community? Sobbing in a corner, that's where.

My reader group, street team, and Patrons. Holy smokes.

I adore you. You make me laugh, you keep me going, you are the best readers an author could ask for.

Husband, Child. A nod to you for putting up with all my chaos as I gear up to launch another new release. Your patience with me at my worst makes it all the sweeter when I'm able to give you my best (few and far as those moments may be).

Alyssa and Trace's story is far from finished. I can't wait for you to see what's coming!

About the Author

Known for witty, vivid characters, Krista Walsh never has more fun than getting them into trouble and taking her time getting them out.

When not writing, she can be found reading, gaming, or watching a film – anything to get lost in a good story.

She currently lives in Ottawa, Ontario with her husband, toddler, and epileptic blue heeler.

You can find her at www.kristawalshauthor.com or at the local Second Cup coffee shop... but only if you come bearing a Vanilla Bean Latte, half-sweet.

Other Works by Krista Walsh

Epic Fantasy

The Meratis Trilogy
The Cadis Trilogy
The Nayis Trilogy

Urban Fantasy

The Dark Descendants Series
The Ghostmaker Trilogy
The Immortal Sorceress Series
The Hour of Witches Series